I0642062

Alan St. Aubyn

In the Face of the World

Vol. II

Alan St. Aubyn

In the Face of the World
Vol. II

ISBN/EAN: 9783337050955

Printed in Europe, USA, Canada, Australia, Japan

Cover: Foto ©Andreas Hilbeck / pixelio.de

More available books at **www.hansebooks.com**

A Novel

BY

ALAN ST. AUBYN

AUTHOR OF 'A FELLOW OF TRINITY,' 'THE JUNIOR DEAN, ETC

IN TWO VOLUMES

VOL. II.

London

CHATTO & WINDUS, PICCADILLY

1894

CONTENTS OF VOL. II.

IN THE FACE OF THE WORLD

CHAPTER XVI.

'SOMETHING LIKE CHARITY!'

'Thou canst not move me from thy side,
Nor human frailty do me wrong.'

'You are late, Mr. Lushington—you are half an hour late; the meeting has been over more than an hour!' the little Sister said reproachfully, when Tristram came in to tea after that interview.

He often dropped in to tea at the small corner house with the grape-vine in front. There were so many things he wanted to talk over with the Sisters, and he talked them over while he drank his tea.

The tea was cold to-day when he came in, and the little Sister was cross; she did not like being

kept waiting; her time was so full, and she had lost
half an hour dawdling at that tea-table. Sister
Katherine was there, resting in the one easy-chair
that the little establishment boasted. She had
been out visiting all day in the close courts in the
hot August sun, and she was tired and worn out,
and glad to rest in the big chair, in the cool, shaded
room. Sister Winiver had come in a few minutes
before Tristram, and she had dropped into a chair
by the open window. She was looking hot and
tired—very tired; she had been up all the night
before with a trying case, and she had only just
come away for a few hours' rest. She was going
back again presently, after an hour or two's sleep.

She did not look fit to go back as she sat by the
window, with her tired face, with all the beautiful
colour gone out of it, leaning on her hand. She
had taken off her bonnet and pushed back her hair,
and the pins that fastened it had come undone, and
it fell in a rich, dark, luxuriant mass about her face.
She was too tired to fasten it up; she was only

waiting to drink a cup of tea before she went to bed, and while she was waiting Tristram came in.

'I have been detained,' he said. 'I have had the most wonderful offer. I could not get away a minute earlier.'

'Who has detained you, and what is the wonderful offer?' the little Sister asked crossly. She was not easily mollified.

'I have been offered ten thousand pounds.'

'Ten thousand pounds!' the three Sisters repeated in a breath. 'Who is going to give you ten thousand pounds?'

Then, before she would give him a single cup of tea, the little Sister made him tell her all about the interview with the strange lady and her munificent offer.

'Oh, this is something like charity!' she said, when he had told her all there was to be told. 'But you have not said who the lady is,' she added sharply.

She had some doubts about the story; she

thought someone had been taking him in.   He was so easily taken in.

'The lady wrote down her address,' he said, fumbling in his pocket for the scrap of paper, 'and she said I could have the money whenever I liked to write for it.'

The little Sister took up the bit of paper and read it eagerly: 'Mrs. Lomax, Kensington Park Gardens.'

'I don't know her,' she said suspiciously; 'I never heard of such a person.   I hope it is all right.'

'What name did you say?' Sister Winiver asked, with a faint show of interest.   She was so utterly tired that she could not be moved by ten thousand pounds.

'Lomax—Mrs. Lomax.'

Sister Winiver repeated the name softly: 'Mrs. Lomax—it cannot be Mrs. Lowry Lomax, surely!'

'Do you know the name?' the little Sister asked.

'No—o; I don't know anyone called Lomax,' Sister Winiver answered wearily.

She was dreadfully tired, but she sat at the open window snipping off the fragrant tops of the mignonette growing in the box outside long after she had finished that cup of tea, when she ought to have been in bed.

'Oh dear, what are you doing?' the little Sister said sharply, when she saw the havoc that Winiver had wrought. 'You have spoilt all my darling mignonette!'

Sister Winiver smiled wearily.

'I was thinking,' she said. 'I did not know what I was doing. I am so sorry.' And she got up with her bonnet hanging on her arm to go to bed; and then, for the first time, she discovered that her hair was unbound, and that it was falling in a disgracefully untidy state—like a Magdalene's—about her shoulders. She flushed scarlet in her sudden way, and put her hand up to gather it into a hasty knot, but the little Sister stopped her.

'You will do nothing of the kind,' she said, coming over to her and smoothing down the beautiful dark hair. 'You will not wait to put it up; you will not wait for anything; you will go straight to bed, and you will sleep till I call you.'

'You will be sure to call me?'

'I will be quite sure to call you.'

'Remember, I have promised to be back by nine. The doctor is coming again at nine; I would not miss him for the world!'

'I will remember; I will call you in good time. Sleep soundly till I call.'

The little Sister laughed softly to herself as she closed the door.

'She looks very tired,' Tristram said, when the Sister had gone out. 'She does not look fit to sit up again to-night.'

'She will not sit up to-night; she has been up two nights already. It is a dreadful case; it requires continual watching. She cannot take a minute's rest night or day.'

'What will you do?'

'I will go myself. I had a lot of rest last night.

My patient died at daybreak, and I came away early, when—when it was all done.'

'You have been running about all day in the sun ; you must be tired already. Do you never give yourself any rest ?' he asked.

' We shall have plenty of time to rest by-and-by,' the Sister answered brightly.

Tristram sighed.

'I wish you would let me help you,' he said. ' I am strong, and can sit up as long as you like without feeling it. Let me take your place to-night.'

'You ! What do you know about nursing ?'

'I can learn,' he said humbly. 'I will do what you tell me.'

' No ; I don't think we can trust the patient in your hands. It is a woman. Her little child has just died with diphtheria, and she has it in a malignant form. It is a very critical case ; besides, there is the risk of infection. Her husband is with her now ; he has just recovered from it. He is as weak as a cat ; he cannot sit up more than a few hours at a time ; he wants all sorts of nourishing things—port wine and beef-tea; and, oh, what would I give for some grapes to take her to-night to cool her poor parched throat !'

Tristram flushed rosy red.

'There will be that ten thousand pounds,' he said. 'I—I think we might anticipate it; it is for just such cases. I do not see why we should hesitate to take it.'

'Hesitate !' The little Sister threw up her hands in astonishment. 'Bless the man! you didn't for a moment think of refusing it ?'

'I didn't know, with the condition attached, whether we were justified in accepting it at present,' he said awkwardly.

'Condition ? Oh, I know, about the order. Of course you will found an order. I would found a dozen orders for ten thousand pounds !'

'I must consult Jayne and the rest.'

'I shouldn't wait to consult anybody. You have consulted us, and our verdict is unanimous. Accept it, accept it, accept it! What more do you want? The offer was made to you. Oh, I am sure you ought to sit down at once and write that letter. While you are delaying the people are dying. You don't know what suffering to-night that ten thousand pounds, if we had got it, would—well, make bearable. You should stand beside sick-beds and see what things are needed, are indispensable, and you would not hesitate a moment.'

Still Tristram hung his head.

' If she had only selected any other man !' he said, with something like a groan ; ' they want a stronger man than I.'

' She has selected exactly the right man. Don't you know that God chooses the weak things of the world, and the foolish things? I don't think if you had been very wise or very strong that He would have selected you to do this great work for Him. It is the poor empty vessels that are ap- pointed for the Master's service, not the vessels of gold and silver—these are only show-pieces. He

knows the special fitness of each, and—and I am
sure He has chosen you.'

The little Sister was very much in earnest. She
was always in earnest, and the tears were in her
eyes. Perhaps she was thinking what a dreadful
thing it would be if he were to let that money
slip. Her tears went straight to his heart; they
convinced him more than her words.

' I will go back at once and talk it over with
Jayne,' he said, jumping up and looking about for
his hat. ' You think I should be doing right,
Sister Katherine?' he asked the elder woman, as
he shook hands with her before he went away.

' I am sure that God must have put it into that
woman's heart to come to you, or she would never
have come,' Sister Katherine said. ' He is the great
Mover of hearts, and turns them according to His
purpose. I think you should see the leading of
Providence in it. It would not have been laid upon
her to make this offer if it had not been needful
for her—for her, perhaps, more than you. It may

be an offering of gratitude, of repentance, of faith. God knows! I am sure you should not deny her the blessing she is waiting for—you should not deny it a single day.'

This was quite a new view of the case.

'He should not deny it a single hour!' the little Sister said warmly. 'He should go back and write the letter at once.'

She caught both Tristram's hands in hers as he was going away; she would not let them go.

'You will promise?' she said eagerly, with sparkling eyes. 'You will promise to write to-night?'

'I promise,' he said meekly.

The little Sister could turn him round her finger. There was very little more to be said or done. He had given his promise. He had only to go back to the mission and talk it over with Jayne. He would have liked to have talked it over with Harold Beech, but there would not be time if he must write at once. Now, if Mrs. Lomax had chosen

Harold Beech for her leader, it would have been quite another thing.

Jayne was just going out to a meeting when Tristram came in. He was always going out somewhere; he never had a minute to himself. His time was filled up with services, and classes, and meetings; if he had a moment to spare, he had always got a lot of visits to make. He was due at a Bible-class now, a Bible-class for young men —mere youths. He had had dreadful trouble to get them to come at all, and he was quite sure if he was five minutes late they would go away—they wouldn't lose a chance of going away—and then he would have to do his work all over again.

'It is a splendid offer,' he said. 'There can be no doubt about accepting it.'

Tristram was ashamed to tell him about his scruples; besides, Jayne hadn't time to hear them. He had only time to murmur a few broken thankful acknowledgments of God's great goodness in having, in this time of their deepest need, sent this woman with her hands full of gifts to their relief.

He had not even time to ask her name. When Jayne had limped off to his boys, Tristram sat down and wrote his letter to Mrs. Lomax.

CHAPTER XVII.

THE HANDWRITING ON THE WALL.

'Who trusted God was love indeed,
  Tho' nature, red in tooth and claw,
  With ravine shriek'd against his creed.'

THE cheque came the next morning. It came while they were at breakfast. Jayne tossed the letter over to Tristram, and then he stood up and said grace:

'For what we are about to receive may the Lord make us thankful.'

It really was worth saying grace for. One doesn't get letters containing cheques for ten thousand pounds often in a lifetime.

Tristram's hand trembled as he opened the letter and his face flushed. He had no faith in himself;

he had accepted a great trust, and he didn't feel at all worthy of it. It is half the making of a hero to believe in himself.

Jayne was quite in a flutter. He smoothed the cheque out, and held it up to the light, and looked at it curiously through his dim glasses as if he had never seen a cheque in his life before. He had certainly never seen one for ten thousand pounds.

'Mrs. Lowry Lomax,' he repeated, reading the magic signature for the twentieth time. 'I'm sure I have heard the name before.'

It would have been very strange if he had not heard it, for it was on every tongue.

'What shall we do with it?' Tristram asked, when Jayne had done fingering the cheque, and had given it back to him.

He had no heart to finger it himself; if the truth must be told, he shrank from touching it. He had an instinctive dislike to touching it.

'I think it ought to be taken to the bank at once.

It is a risk to let such a large sum of money remain in the place an hour.'

Jayne really was afraid it would melt away.

'The bank does not open for another hour. I think I must take it to the home and show it to the Sisters.'

'By all means let them be sharers in our joy. Before you go I'm sure we ought to kneel down and thank God for it. It has come from Him, we must remember.'

Jayne plumped down on his knees as he spoke, beside the table where the cheque was fluttering softly in the breeze that came in at the open window, and Tristram knelt down beside him; that is, he turned his back to the table and his face to the chair. He couldn't thank God with that disturbing bit of paper rustling in front of him.

When he got up from his knees he put Mrs. Lomax's cheque into his pocket-book, and buttoned his coat over it and went out. He ought to have been glowing with satisfaction with that cheque so near his heart; he ought to have been reckoning up the great things he was going to do with it; but his heart was like lead, and there was a voice ringing in his ears all the way—a voice and a message.

He looked as if he had come to a funeral as he entered the little room at the home where the Sisters were sitting at breakfast. There were the same three ladies present as he had found at tea the day before. Sister Winiver's colour had come back, and her beautiful hair was hidden away beneath her nurse's cap; she was looking quite refreshed after that long night's rest. The little Sister was whiter than usual, he remarked; she could not help looking white after sitting up all night, and there was a strained look in her face, and her lips were tightly drawn. Tristram had never seen that look of depression on her bright face before, and he saw in a moment that something was wrong.

'I have got the money,' he said, when he went in; 'the cheque came this morning.'

16

He put the letter down on the table before the little Sister, and she opened it listlessly and took out the cheque.

'It has come, then,' she said—'it has come too late!' and Tristram saw that her eyes were full of tears; and then suddenly and without any warning she broke down in a passion of weeping.

Tristram looked from one to the other for an explanation, and he laid his hand soothingly on the girl's shoulder.

'Let her alone,' Sister Katherine said; 'let her have her cry out, it will do her good. She has been over-wrought. The woman she was nursing has died in the night—died for want of nourishment which she had not at hand to give her. Slipped away, as so many of them do when the fever leaves them, and there is nothing to keep their strength up. It is the old sad story.'

'The woman's life was sacrificed,' the little Sister cried passionately; 'it might have been saved! Oh, what is the use of going to people with empty hands!'

'Your hands need not be empty any longer,' Tristram said, pointing to the cheque; 'this will buy beef-tea and wine for everyone. I don't think we could spend it better.'

'It has come too late,' she moaned, pushing the cheque aside impatiently; 'why did it not come last night?' and then, seeing the pained look on Tristram's face, she dried her tears. 'I am not myself this morning,' she said humbly; 'you must forgive me being impatient and unreasonable. If you had seen the grief of that poor man— he had lost his wife and child—you would not wonder that I was upset. We want hearts of steel to witness the sights we do, and remain unmoved.'

Sister Winiver had taken up the cheque while they were talking, and was reading it beside the open window.

'Do you know who has sent you this?' she asked him under her breath.

'Mrs. Lomax,' he answered readily. Was it likely he should not remember the name of his benefactor.

'Mrs. *Lowry* Lomax,' she said, in a voice that seemed to thrill through him. Still, he did not understand.

'Mrs. Lowry Lomax?' he repeated, with a question in his voice. He really didn't care much who had sent the cheque. He had got the money, and that was, after all, the great thing. He was thinking about the beef-tea and the wine it would buy, and how it would send those poor weak things who had just recovered from the fever into the sweet, fresh country, how it would fill out their hollow cheeks, and bring back the colour to their pale lips, and the light to their dull eyes. He was thinking of the things that all that money was going to do, more than of the sender. It was going to do, oh! so many things.

Whether it were the sound of his own voice, or the look he met in Sister Winiver's dark eyes—it was one or the other, or both—a sudden swift intelligence dawned upon him, and with a sinking at his heart he remembered something. It was something he had never thought of before in connection with his benefactor.

'You don't mean——' he gasped; he could only gasp and look helplessly at Sister Winiver standing there with her eyes dilated and the scarlet spots burning in her cheeks.

'Yes,' she said, still speaking under her breath, 'it is from the woman who wrote that dreadful book——'

'That woman!'

The room seemed to go round with him; the confusion that had been in his ears all the morning took shape; the whisper that had followed him all the way from the mission was a whisper no longer. It was crying out from the wall; he could see it in flaming letters before his eyes: 'An accursed thing is in the midst of thee, O Israel!'

He wondered the Sister could not see it; he put

his hand before his eyes to shut it out, and when he drew it away the handwriting was no longer there, and someone had unloosed his collar and was sprinkling water over his face. He had been taken faint, the Sisters explained; the surprise and excitement had been too much for him.

He was himself again in a few minutes, quite himself, and on his feet, with that miserable cheque in his pocket-book—not over his heart this time. There was something else upon his heart—a cold, dead weight that he could not shake off.

He walked back as fast as he could all the way, in spite of the trembling in his legs, with a dreadful guilty, ashamed feeling, as if he had done some shameful thing. He felt exactly like Achan going out to his stoning. He had quite made up his mind what he would do before he got back to the mission.

Jayne had just returned from an early service when he went in, and he saw by Tristram's face, the moment he looked up from a notice he was writing, that something was wrong.

When a man is going to do an heroic thing he ought to look like a hero. His legs ought not to shake beneath him, and all his muscles go limp, and the very last thing that should impede his dignified utterance should be a nasty great lump in his throat.

Tristram had to contend with all these disadvantages, and, as if Nature had not handicapped him sufficiently, she took all the colour out of his white face; there was not much to take out, but she took out all there was, and substituted a chalky gray.

Jayne thought he had lost the cheque. A second glance reassured him; he had not lost the cheque, but something had happened to it. He had been the victim of a cruel practical joke.

'It—it was all a hoax, then?' he said, and he tried to throw some sympathy into his voice.

'It was not a hoax,' Tristram said. He could

not say a word more to save his life, with a lump as big as a walnut in his throat.

'You have not——' Jayne was going to say 'lost it,' but Tristram did not give him time. He was tearing open his pocket-book with trembling fingers.

'No,' he said—'no;' and he laid the cheque open on the table before him.

Jayne did not take it up, but he looked at it, as Tristram had looked at it, with a question in his eyes.

'Why have you not left it at the bank?' he said presently.

'I—am—going—to—send it back!'

He got the words out with great difficulty, but he felt better after. He felt like the old man whose tongue was loosed when he had written the name of his miraculous child.

'Send it back!'

'We couldn't keep it,' Tristram explained, speaking hurriedly, in a voice that was not at all steady;

'it would bring a curse upon the mission. Do you know who it is from ?'

Jayne looked at it doubtfully, but he did not touch it.

'Mrs.—Mrs. Lowry Lomax——' he read, and then he paused and looked over to Tristram.

'Yes—the—the woman that wrote that book.'

'That—that book that upset poor Jones ?'

Tristram nodded.

'That has upset many Joneses,' he said gloomily.

'Why did she come here ?' Jayne asked quite fiercely. 'Why did she send her money here ?'

'Why, indeed ?'

'And she asked *you* to found an order, to be the apostle of a new gospel—*her* gospel ?'

Tristram covered his face with his hands, but he did not faint now.

'Have I fallen so low ?' he murmured, and his poor chalky face flushed scarlet like a girl's.

He was dreadfully humiliated at being singled out to preach this woman's gospel. It might be the gospel of the future, God knows! but it was not his gospel.

'No, dear fellow, it is not you, it is all of us. We have failed in our duty; we have given forth an uncertain sound. We have not taken a stand. We have pandered too much to the passions of the people. We have been all things to all men in the hope of saving some. Our methods are not the old methods. I don't think anyone would have gone to St. Peter and asked him to be the apostle of such a gospel.'

And so it was settled between them that the money should be sent back. It should be sent back at once; it should not stay another moment in the place.

Jayne went out and left Tristram writing the letter to Mrs. Lowry Lomax. It was necessary that he should write a letter and explain his reasons for returning her cheque.

It was rather a difficult letter to write; it would have been much easier to accept the gift thankfully, asking no questions. It was a generous gift, in any case; it was not to be spurned ungraciously; it was very hard to say the right thing. Tristram tore up quite half a dozen sheets of paper before he wrote a letter to his mind, and then he folded up the cheque and enclosed it in an envelope. He was addressing the envelope, when the door opened and a lady came in.

It was Mrs. Lowry Lomax.

She came forward with an easy, assured, prosperous manner, and held out her hand.

'You got my letter?' she said, smiling.

Tristram got up from his chair, white to the lips, but he did not take the hand extended to him.

'I received your cheque this morning,' he said, in a voice he could not keep quite steady. 'I—I was just writing to you——'

He glanced down to the table to the letter before him, the ink of which was still wet, and her eyes followed the direction of his.

'I could not wait for the letter,' she said gaily.

'I came away at the first moment. I wanted to
hear about your plans. This is only an earnest;
there is more coming. Oh, your presses and barns
will run over; they will not hold all the gold that is
pouring in.'

She spoke eagerly, in her bright, quick way, with
her handsome face all aglow.

'I—I am afraid there has been some mistake,' he
said, 'some misapprehension. I am returning your
cheque.'

He pushed the letter forward as he spoke; he did
not give it into her hands, but he pushed it towards
her.

She understood his attitude in a moment. Her
face was pale and cold as marble, but her tone was
very quiet and restrained.

'Returning the cheque?' she said, with just an
inflection of surprise.

'I have explained my reason for returning it,'
Tristram said awkwardly, and he looked down again
at that letter.

What a coward he was under that woman's eyes, and his speech was mean and contemptible !

She took up the letter and opened it. She could not keep her fingers from trembling as she tore the envelope open, and she read it with a smile on her face—a smile of compassion and scorn.

'You know best,' she said, and the scorn on her face lent itself to her voice. 'I thought you had the interest of the people at heart ; I have made a mistake, I see.'

She tore the cheque into atoms and snowed the fragments on the floor.

'I could do nothing else,' he said meekly.

'No, I suppose not. I did not know you were so prejudiced, so bigoted to the old beliefs, or I should not have made you this offer. Still, I think you have made a mistake ; better to be venturesome for the sake of others than to be over-cautious. You must remember, the old landmarks are all removed. You cannot shut your eyes to this ; you must break some day with the old things ; you cannot go on for ever teaching what you do not believe. How do you know that God Himself is behind the offers you are making to the people? If He were behind it all, would there be all this failure, this beating about, this miserable non-success? Is this suffering, the innocent suffering for the guilty, the wrong, the wretchedness and misery, the guilt and pollution of this teeming city to go on for ever? Oh! it is time we take it in hand. We have waited long enough for help. We have prayed for centuries, and nothing has come of it; we have stretched out imploring hands to the empty skies, and there has been no relief. If we want help we must help ourselves.'

Her words cut him like a whip, and like a whip they roused him.

'I did not know that the arm of the Lord was shortened,' he said; 'it has been our support, our strength hitherto. It has never failed us yet. It is better to trust in the Lord than to put any confidence in man.'

She smiled in her superior way.

'It is no use arguing with a fanatic,' she said scornfully. 'I am sorry for the people; you will not let me help them; they will suffer, not you. Perhaps this is your creed.'

She gathered up her skirts and went out; she did not offer him her hand. She went out with her head held high, and her beautiful face smiling scornfully. He had never seen such scorn on a woman's face. She left him standing by the table humbled and ashamed.

He had let her have an easy victory. He had not stood up for his Master. He had given the battle into the hand of a woman. Where was all that fine talk about Achan and the Mammon of unrighteousness? He bowed his head upon his hands and groaned aloud: 'Oh, shame, shame, shame!'

CHAPTER XVIII.

'He fought his doubts and gather'd strength ;
He would not make his judgment blind.'

WHEN Jayne came in an hour later, Tristram was still sitting beside the table where Mrs. Lomax had left him ; he was sitting with his face buried in his hands. His attitude was one of dejection and despondency, and his face, when he looked up at Jayne's entrance, was white and stricken.

He didn't look the least like a hero. He could do an heroic thing, but he couldn't do it in an heroic way. A hero need not be a pattern of moral virtues ; it is not even necessary that he should be a paragon at all; he would be a dull hero indeed if he were superior to the ordinary weaknesses of human nature. But he ought to have faith in himself. He ought, above all things, to be loyal to his convictions. Once pledged to his faith, he ought to hold it, without doubt or question. Once pledged to it, he might make a thousand mistakes, but doubt it, never!

Tristram had been questioning the right and wrong of that hasty rejection of Mrs. Lomax's generous gift for the last hour, and his conscience hadn't quite settled the matter yet. He had been praying over it, and that hadn't made the answer any clearer. Perhaps it would make it clearer by-and-by.

'Well,' Jayne said in his cheerful way, as he limped into the room—'well, have you sent the letter?'

'The lady has been here,' Tristram said in his hollow voice. She was standing exactly where Jayne was standing when he saw her last; he was almost hoping when the door opened that she had come back.

Perhaps Jayne read all this in his eyes.

'And you gave her back the cheque?'

'Yes; I gave her back the cheque.'

'You explained, of course; what did you say?'

Jayne was almost sorry that he had not stayed away from that service; he would have given anything to have had a few words with that mistaken woman.

'I—I said that we could not accept it. If we had taken it, we could have expected no blessing on our work; like the unlawful gold of Achan, it would have brought upon us misfortune and defeat. We could have nothing to do with the Mammon of unrighteousness!'

His face ought to have been very noble while he was giving utterance to this fine sentiment; it ought not to have been white and despairing and working in that weak, emotional way.

And—she—what did Mrs. Lomax say?'

Tristram could hardly recall for a moment what she had said; he could only remember his own part.

'Oh, she thought we had made a mistake ;' and then suddenly he remembered what she had said, and his white, stricken face flushed scarlet with the remembrance of that easy victory gained by a woman. 'You ought to have been here, Jayne,' he groaned, ' to hear the charges she brought against us. You ought to have been here to meet them. They were most of them true—true in part, but she made the most of them, and twisted them in her own way. Oh, it was shameful ! it was the victory of the world ; and I—I had not a word to say.'

He covered his face with his hands; he could not trust himself to repeat all those dreadful things the woman had said.

'For her own sake, you should have said a word in season. She might not have heeded it, she was not likely to heed it ; but it would not have been lost. It would have sprung up some day. It would have borne fruit in .its time—in God's time.'

Tristram shook his head.

'You should have been here,' he said gloomily
—'you should have been here.'

It was all very well for Jayne to talk about
saying words in season ! he would have found it
hard to say a seasonable word to Mrs. Lowry
Lomax, to know exactly what to say. Perhaps,
after all, Tristram had said the right thing, and he
had not gone out of his way to say it.

It was no good wasting all the morning here ; he
had to get up and go about his work, with the
recollection of that lost ten thousand pounds
hanging like a millstone round his neck.

He had to go to the home first and tell the
Sisters what he had done. They would be drawing
upon that cheque already. There was no knowing
what demands the little Sister had not already
made upon it. Tristram shrank from telling her
more than from all the rest. He knew how she
had counted upon it. It didn't represent principle
to her ; it represented beef-tea and wine and everything those poor patients of hers needed.

He didn't know how he should tell her. It was a relief to him when he reached the home to find everybody out but Sister Winiver.

She was not so difficult to tell as the little Sister.

'I think you have done right,' she said, when he had told her what he had done. 'I don't think you could have used the money in—in mission work. You could not expect a blessing with it.'

'No,' he said, 'no; I'm so glad you see it in that light. I did not know how you would take it, the money was needed so much——'

'It was needed dreadfully!' she said, and she could not help the tears from springing to her eyes as she spoke. 'It would have done so much that will have to be left undone '—her voice trembled as she spoke; the quiver would not be kept out of it—'but I am sure you have done right. God can raise up other help. There would have been—a—a stain upon the money—it was not fit to go into the treasury of the Lord—it was like the wages of unrighteousness.'

She was not speaking to him, she had forgotten his presence; she was talking to herself, reasoning with herself.

'Yes,' he said, 'that is what I felt.'

She did not heed the interruption, but went on murmuring in a low, eager, self-accusing voice:

'How could it be otherwise? It was the price of betrayal. It was the thirty pieces that the priests rejected. They would have nothing to do with it—nothing. Oh, if you had taken this money,' she said, turning to Tristram with her eyes flashing and her cheeks scarlet, 'I would have doubled it! I would have brought my wretched dole and poured it into your lap. You should have enough and to spare. The world is full of blood-money—money that people dare not spend, and that no one will have, that carries a curse with it.'

She put out her hands with an involuntary

gesture of repugnance, as if to put something loathsome away from her.

She was trembling all over, and her cheeks were burning as if with shame ; she did not look at all like a Sister.

Tristram took her outstretched hands, which were burning like her cheeks.

' Dear Sister,' he said, ' remember there is a stream that can wash away all stains—the stains of conscience, and the stain on the ill-gotten gold of this world. There must be faith and repentance and the offering of a pure heart, and the gift will be accepted as well as the giver.'

' It can never be laid upon the altar,' she said eagerly ; ' the stained, sinful thing can never be laid upon the altar ?'

' No,' he said, with that upward look in his poor, pale face that ennobled it, and made men listen to his feeble words ; ' no, thank God ! there is only one Gift on the altar, there is no more sacrifice ; there is only one place for the stained, sinful things of the world—at the foot of the Cross.'

He did not see the little Sister until later in the day. The white, staring August sunlight was blazing down upon the hot, dusty pavement of the London court he was hurrying through as he met her coming out of an open door.

The lovely sweetness and freshness of the morning were past, and the hot August noon had scorched up every bit of shade. It was one of those intolerably hot summer days when there is not a breath of air stirring, when the skies are brass above, and the pavements of the London streets are like a furnace beneath.

The little Sister had not heard ; she came to him from the open doorway with her face beaming. She forgot all about the heat and the weariness, she ran across the road to meet him with her hands outstretched.

' How beautiful are their feet that bring glad tidings !' she said gaily ; and he saw that her eyes were swimming and her lips were trembling. 'I have just told them, the poor things! that they are all to go into the country, into the sweet, cool air, to-day, to-morrow, as soon as they can be moved. They can feel it already, blowing fresh on their faces; they are talking about the green fields and the waving boughs and the birds and the flowers. It has worked a miracle already.'

Then he had to tell her. It was like telling Mary that day in the library, only it was harder.

' Sent—it—back !'

She seemed to reel in the sunshine; if it had been anywhere but in that London court, he would have put his arm around her to support her. There was a friendly lamp-post near; she steadied herself by its aid, and waited for his answer with a swift sword-thrust of reproach in her blue eyes that went straight to his heart—his heart and his conscience, that was always getting him into trouble.

' I could not take it,' he said quickly; ' it was the price of souls. Think what evil that woman has done! She has been the ruin of thousands. I knew a man, Jones of Jesus; he was brimming over with love, with enthusiasm. He was to have gone out to Africa—he was ready to lay down his life for the Gospel—*and he read her book!*'

'Well,' said the little Sister, with that wrathy light in her blue eyes, ' what had Jones of Jesus to do with her ?'

'Well,' he repeated, like one speaking in a dream, ' he withdrew his name. He sent in his resignation to the Bishop—and—and he blew his brains out.'

'Why did he blow his brains out?' the little Sister said impatiently.

'He had found out that life was not worth living. There are a great many Joneses in the world who have made, or who think they have made, this discovery, and she—and her book—will have to give account to God for them all.'

'And—and because of Jones you sent back her cheque?'

Her lips were so dry that she could hardly get the words between them.

'Because of Jones,' he said sadly. 'He was my dearest friend. If you had seen his mother's grief when she bent over his coffin—they had to cover him up from her, she could not look upon his face, his poor face—you would not wonder that I sent back that woman's cheque. It was the price of a soul.'

The little Sister had not another word to say ; but she went back, he saw, to the poor house she had just left. Had she gone back to tell the children that the sweet, cool, green country was all a dream ?

Tristram went home and wrote a long letter to Dene. He was not fit to do any more work that day. He was so soon knocked down. He had only spirit to go back and write to Dene. She was the only one of the home party that he wrote to now. He was quite sure of sympathy from her ; he could pour out his heart to his own true-hearted little sister, without any fear of being misinterpreted. Whoever else failed him, Dene was never likely to fail him.

He told her the story of the Lowry Lomax cheque, and of the little Sister's disappointment. He dwelt bitterly on the disappointment, his and hers; and he told her about the little children with the fever in the close London court, who had felt in anticipation the cool, fresh air of the country blowing on their fevered faces.

Dene took the letter over to Mary Gascoigne at once. The London season was over, and Geraldine had gone back with her mother and Cecil to Garlands. Sir Tristram was shooting in Scotland, but Cecil had lingered near his betrothed, and Lady Cornelia had come back to rest, after the fatigue of the London season. There were other reasons for her staying at Garlands. Dene's noble suitor was coming down in September; he was coming to get his answer from Geraldine's own lips. It would be a very different wooing, among the glades of Bredwardine and Garlands, from the wooing in the heated atmosphere of a London ballroom.

The Duke had not put in an appearance yet ; he was shooting grouse with Sir Tristram on a Scotch moor, and Geraldine's maiden peace was undisturbed. She was back amid the scenes of her happy, innocent youth. The hot breath of a London season had passed over her too short a time to sully the pure mirror of her soul. She was still the Dene of old. Tristram's letter filled her with indignation and grief.

' That woman to offer him money ! and the poor little children to be disappointed.'

Mary Gascoigne was more troubled about the little children than about Tristram's rejection of the woman's cheque.

She didn't know much about Mrs. Lowry Lomax. She had never seen her upsetting book ; it was not in the Bredwardine library. There were neither three-volume novels nor yellow-backs on those sacred shelves. There were nothing but dull-looking, parchment-covered volumes that didn't promise much to seekers for recreation only. No little monthly box of books or magazines travelled between Bredwardine and London. Mary was as much cut off from the literature of the day as if she had been living in Central Africa.

' I wish we could do something for the little children,' she said, when she had read the letter that Dene brought her.

There had been a breach between the two girls; Geraldine could not forgive Mary's easy acceptance of Cecil's suit, after her rejection of Tristram. She could not understand her disloyalty; it shook her faith. She could have believed anything before she could have believed that Mary Gascoigne could have been so heartless. She had been taught to believe in everybody's goodness; she had a great deal to unlearn. She had learnt a great many things that it was difficult to understand during that brief London season; things that had been meaningless before had suddenly assumed a dreadful meaning, and among the things hard to understand was Mary's engagement.

That letter of Tristram's brought the girls together, and healed the breach as much as anything but time could heal it. Mary was full of the sick people and the little children, and the sad picture Tristram had drawn of the breathless London court.

She thought about them all the day, as she walked in the beautiful gardens of Bredwardine. All this wealth of flowers, this wide greenness, and the cool shadows of the trees, the ripple of the water beneath the bridge, and the song of the lark in the sky, and no one to heed it!

It smote upon her with a sense of shame. It was like the knowledge of good and evil; it had come upon her quite suddenly—a sense of responsibility, of being answerable to God for all these things. She had never been grateful, she remembered with a pang, for all the good things—the lovely things—that had fallen to her share; she had accepted them as a matter of course. And here were people—women and little children—dying for the life-giving breath of the country, languishing for the sight of the sweet green fields.

She could not bear the breath of the flowers on the terrace, the glow and the glory of the scarlet and the green in the beautiful grounds, the sight of the sunshine dropping down between the boughs, or the rustle of the leaves overhead. The flowers were blooming for her, and the leaves were rustling, and the sunshine dropping down at her feet, for her—her only—and God had made them for all !

A dreadful sense of responsibility came to her, like a revelation, as she stood, with that letter of Tristram's in her hands, looking out over all her wide domain.

The scales had fallen from her eyes.

CHAPTER XIX.

' A simple maiden in her flower
Is worth a hundred coats-of-arms.'

LADY BREDWARDINE had been failing lately. It was evident to everyone except Mary that she was failing fast. Love is so slow to admit what most it dreads. Her ladyship still took her daily walk in the grounds. It was always in one direction she walked now; she never failed to pay her daily visit to the marble effigy she had set up in Bredwardine Church to her late lord.

It was evident to all—all but Mary, who was wilfully blind—that these visits must soon come to a close. She could not go on, with her failing strength, taking these long solitary walks, and spending hours alone in that chill, dusky church, without hastening the end.

Lady Bredwardine was not a woman that any-one could reason with; she took her own way; she was not to be moved when she had once set her mind on anything. As her strength failed, her interest in the things about her seemed to fail too. She ceased to think about the things that used to interest her—the parish and her poor people; and Mr. Heathcote's ministrations fell on dull, unheed-ing ears.

Her daily visits to the church were followed now by long fits of abstraction. She would sit for hours wrapped in thought, with her hands folded, and her sad, hopeless eyes gazing vacantly before her. When the mood was over she would pace the room, as Dene had seen her pacing it, till the sun had sunk in the west and her strength was quite worn out. Everybody saw that this could not go on for long—everybody but Mary.

It was during one of these fits of abstraction that

Mary broke in upon her meditation with a project that would at any other time have startled her. She had been thinking for days and days of Tristram's letter; she had lain awake at nights, and thought of those poor things pining in the London court for a breath of fresh country air till she could bear it no longer. An idea had come into her mind. It was only an idea, an unformed project.

Why not let them come here?

This was not so wild a scheme as it at first appeared. There was room, and to spare, for any number of convalescents at Bredwardine without interfering with the inmates of the house. On either side the wide courtyard that led up to the entrance-gateway were blocks of unused red-brick buildings that had been built when the house was built, for the use of dependents. There were a good many dependents in those old stormy days, but the times had altered. There were no dependents now—at least, they were provided for elsewhere—and the big bare, barrack-like buildings had

LIBRARY
UNIVERSITY OF ILLINOIS

long fallen into disuse, if not decay. The rain leaked in at the roofs, and the floors were rotten with dry-rot, and bats and mice had taken up their abode in the empty chambers. They were quite useless now, they had been useless for years; but if Mary Gascoigne had sought the county—had sought the country over—she could not have found a place that would have answered her purpose better.

She went over the buildings before she broached the subject to her ladyship. She had not been over them for years and years, not since she was a child, when she used to play hide-and-seek here with her brother and the children from Garlands. She recalled the old happy time as she wandered through the gloomy old rooms. The glad voices of her happy youth seemed to follow her up and down the dusty stairs, and through the dim galleries. They seemed to be calling to her through the years, ' Mary ! Mary !' as they had called to her then, with the same love and welcome in their dear familiar voices. There was not a note of sadness in them, she remarked with a vague sense of wonder.

A door slammed suddenly behind her, and sent solemn echoes travelling through all the empty rooms. They had but one voice ; they repeated with one accord the name that had been shouted so often up and down those silent stairs, and through these deserted rooms, in the old days :

' Mary !'

It was the voices of her youth calling her :

' Mary !'

She was sure they had a message for her. There was something for her to do ; and they were calling her with the old confidence and the old love. They trusted her now, as they had trusted her then.

She knew why they were calling her in a moment. She understood it all. They were appealing to her for the children ! The voices of childhood past were appealing to her for the children of the present. Looking back on the old happy time, the

gay laughter and the merry shouts of her childhood came to her across the years fraught with a
message she could not fail to catch. They were
asking her why these halls were empty and silent,
when there were so many sad little voices waiting
to take up in their turn the song of childhood and
innocent joy, which reaches on from generation to
generation, and which no poverty or sorrow or
misfortune will ever silence while the world rolls
on.

With this question still ringing in her ears, Mary
sought her mother.

It was not a favourable time to speak to her;
she was too preoccupied with her sad thoughts to
take an interest in outside things; but Mary was
not in a mood to wait.

She poured out her little half-fledged scheme to
unheeding ears. She did not know that her ladyship was listening; she heard her to the end, and
then she got up and paced the room in her weary
way.

' What do you think of it, mamma?' Mary said humbly.

Lady Bredwardine did not answer; she only moaned.

' The rooms are no use, mamma,' Mary went on, in her low voice; ' they have not been used for years and years; nothing has been disturbed in them since we used to play in them years ago, Howard and I—and the others. For the sake of those old days—and—and those who are gone, I should like to get some little sick children down here, and show them the flowers and the fields; they would soon get well under the green leaves——'

' Yes,' said her ladyship wearily—' yes, yes; but I don't see where you would put them.'

She had not heard a word that Mary had been saying, or, if she had heard, she had not understood, and Mary had to go over it all again.

' You must ask Cecil,' she said, when Mary had finished.

'It has nothing to do with Cecil, mamma!'
Mary cried, blushing crimson; 'it is a question for
ourselves.'

'I have done with everything,' her ladyship said,
almost fiercely. 'Why am I to be troubled? It
will all be Cecil's soon. You must do nothing,
Mary, without Cecil.'

This was all Mary could get from her, and she
dared not press her closer. Ask Cecil? Why
should she ask Cecil about the disposition of her
own house? She told him of the conversation she
had had with her ladyship the next day when he
called, but she did not ask him.

'I should think you'd find the little beggars a
nuisance,' he said. 'They'd be swarming all over
the place. If you must have 'em here, Mary,
couldn't you · get a place in the village? — the
farther off the better.'

This was not very encouraging. He expressed
himself with less reserve to Dene when he got
back.

'Who's been filling Mary's head with this philanthropic rot?' he said savagely. 'It sounds like
one of Tristram's crack-brained schemes. She wants
to turn the whole place into an asylum for paupers!'

The Duke of Southernhay came down the next
day, and a party of men for the shooting, and there
was no chance of Dene getting away to hear the
rights of the matter from Mary. She did not tell
Cecil that it was Tristram's letter that had set his
betrothed thinking. She kept Tristram's letters to
herself; they would meet with no sympathy from
any other member of the household.

On the morning of the day on which the Duke
was expected, Lady Cornelia sent for her daughter
to her room before she was dressed. Her ladyship
was paler than usual, Dene remarked when she
went in, but that might be due to the imperfect
stage of her toilet.

Geraldine knew exactly why her mother had sent
for her. She sat down dutifully on a low seat
at her mother's feet, and waited for her to begin.

'The Duke is coming to-day,' Lady Cornelia began nervously. She was quite a contrast to her daughter as she sat there, with her delicate, fair complexion and light hair and fine, aristocratic profile; they didn't look like mother and daughter.

'Yes, mamma,' Dene answered dutifully.

'You know what he is coming for, child?'

'Ye—es, mamma,' scarcely less readily.

'What answer will you give him when he comes?'

'Answer, mamma?' Her cheek flushed quick.

'Yes; you know he is coming for an answer.'

'Oh, mamma, *must* I give him an answer? I have known him such a little time, and—and I have seen so few people!'

Her cheeks were crimson, and her lips were trembling, and the tears stood in her eyes. There was justice in her appeal. She had only been out of the schoolroom a few weeks, she had only seen a little bit of a London season, and she had been asked to accept the hand of the first suitor that had proposed to her. Most mothers would have been touched by the girl's appeal, but Lady Cornelia was unmoved.

'He has a right to expect an answer,' she said severely. 'He has done you a great honour. Of course, with—with your fortune, your beauty, and —and your position, you had a right to look for a great alliance; but you could not, considering your birth—you must remember that Sir Tristram is only a brewer—have expected to make such a great, such a splendid match—one of the oldest titles in the kingdom. The Duke has done you so much honour, Dene, in choosing you, when there were so many better born to choose from, that you are bound to give him an answer—there is only one answer you can give.' And Lady Cornelia screwed up her small eyes and looked exactly an inch beyond the tip of her nose.

'Oh, mamma, must I give him an answer to-day? He said he would wait,' the girl pleaded.

She could not keep back her tears. She fell sobbing at her mother's knees.

'There is nothing for him to wait for, you silly child! There is no reason why you should not love this man. Half the women in London are in love with him. He is the best match of the season. What reason is there for waiting?'

Poor Dene had no arguments ready, only her tears, and they were spoiling her pretty eyes. She could not afford to let them flow with all these people coming presently. She could see herself in Lady Cornelia's mirror as she wept. Her nose was getting redder and redder, and her cheeks were blistered, and her eyes swollen; she was looking a perfect fright. There was nothing to be done but jump up and run away and bathe those unsightly features. Before she ran away Dene kissed her mother and promised submission. She would give the Duke the answer that he had come back from Scotland to seek.

Lady Cornelia's arguments had prevailed.

CHAPTER XX.

' Passed
To where beyond these voices there is peace.'

DENE came up to Bredwardine the next day to tell Mary of her new happiness. She could hardly realize it yet. She was so bewildered with the distinguished honour that awaited her—the great honour and the exalted position—that it was no wonder the poor child lost her head.

Most girls would have lost their heads if they had been in Dene's position. Dukes are not quite so plentiful as blackberries, though they are to be picked up sometimes. Beauty has still an attraction for them, as it has for other men—beauty and wealth.

Lady Cornelia Lushington's young daughter had both. She was, though late in the field, the acknowledged beauty of the season, and she had a million of money. The ill-gotten wealth that Tristram had rejected had swelled Dene's marriage portion. The Duke of Southernhay would not have laid his strawberry-leaves at her feet if it had not been for that rejected million.

He could not have afforded to marry for mere beauty; there is beauty and to spare in the Court of St. James's, but there are not a great many millions of money going hand-in-hand with it— thrown in, as it were, as a make-weight. He had consented to overlook that stain on her birth— Lushington's Entire—for the sake of the wealth she brought him.

A Duke must live. The Duke of Southernhay had lived as, happily, few dukes live in these degenerate days. He had run through all his patrimony; he had mortgaged his estates to the last penny; the Jews had come down upon all the family heirlooms, the pictures, the china, and all the priceless art treasures that had been collected for generations. They had swept them all away. There was nothing left of ducal greatness to this last of the Southern- hays but an empty gilded cage, a tarnished reputation, and a handsome person. Yes ; there was the coronet that had tumbled in the dust.

. It may be inferred that this gilded youth had rubbed some of the gilt off before he had laid those tarnished strawberry-leaves at poor Dene's innocent feet. He had rubbed a good deal off, and the dross beneath was already showing through. He was not so very youthful, either ; the ill-spent years had left their marks, their ineffaceable marks, on his handsome face. Only a girl's innocent eyes could have failed to read there the shameful story of a shameful past. There is something in race ; the broken-down *roué* held his head up where a better man would have held it down ; and if courage and coolness to grapple with his evil star count, the Duke of Southernhay was worthy of the title he

bore. He was a brave, courageous English gentleman, very apt to take advantage of his opportunities,
and ever ready to make opportunities for himself.
He had made a great opportunity when he offered
himself as Dene's suitor.

A girl doesn't generally trouble herself about her
lover's antecedents. She leaves that to her elders;
if they are satisfied, she is. As a rule, girls are
easily satisfied. Given a handsome person, a
manner that takes with women, a great position—
well, what else is there to desire? There are
certain old-fashioned things that used to be put in
the balance—that used to weigh it down—that no
one thinks of now. The beautiful face, and the
fine manners, and the great estate—who would not
accept these and take the risk of it?

Dene had taken the risk of it, and she had gone
over to tell Mary Gascoigne the great news and be
congratulated. She had stolen away after breakfast, when the gentlemen had gone off with their
guns, and Lady Cornelia had sat down to a morn-

ing's letter-writing, to tell her thousand and one friends of Dene's engagement.

Mary was walking in the park when Dene found her; she was looking pale and anxious, if Dene had had eyes to see it. She was so full of her great news, of the wonderful thing that had happened to her, that she had no eyes for anything else.

'Have you heard any more of those poor things?' Mary asked her, when the first greeting was over.

'What poor things?' Dene asked impatiently.

'The poor things Tristram wrote about.'

'Oh, the sick children! I had forgotten all about them. One can't be always thinking about poor people; and, oh, I have such great news to tell you, Mary!'

This with a little sob. It was too bad of Mary, when she had come to tell her about the Duke, to think of nothing but those pauper children.

'Great news!' Mary repeated with a quiver in

19

her voice, and her heart for a moment stood still.
'Is it—about—about Tristram ?'

'I don't know anything about Tristram,' Dene
said pettishly ; 'it is about myself. I thought you
might care to know.'

'About yourself, dear ?'

'Yes ; I'm engaged to be married : that's all.'

'Engaged to be married ?   You ?'

'Yes; is it such a strange thing for me to be
going to be married ?   Am I such a fright that you
didn't think anyone would marry me ?'

Darling !   Mary threw two kind warm arms
around the girl and kissed her. 'Darling, I don't
know anyone good enough to marry you !'

This ought to have mollified Dene, but it didn't.
It was not at all the way she had intended Mary
to be told.   Things never do happen as one
expects.

'The Duke of Southernhay has asked me to
marry him,' she said stiffly.

'The Duke—of—of Southernhay?' Mary repeated.

She thought she had heard the name before, she was not sure ; she had a faint memory of seeing it in some newspaper scandal, in one of the few papers that found their way to Bredwardine.

' And you—you have——'

'I have accepted him,' Dene interrupted rather tartly.

Mary wasn't at all impressed by her news ; she wasn't taking it at all nicely.

' How long have you known him, dear? You can't have known him very long,' she said, in quite a shocked voice.

She couldn't understand this child accepting a lover on such a short notice.

'I've known him quite long enough,' Dene said in an injured voice. ' People don't usually dally about for years before they know their minds. I like him better than anyone I have seen, and—and I am going to be married in the spring.'

' Going to be married in the spring !'

Mary couldn't understand it ; she couldn't realize

that this little Dene, who was a child yesterday, who was a child at heart to-day, was going to marry a Duke—was going to be a Duchess.

'I suppose I ought to take you to mamma; she ought to congratulate you,' she said presently, and a shadow came over her face as she spoke. 'Poor mamma! she has been so unlike herself the last day or two; you will see a change in her, Dene.'

The girls walked silently across the grass in the sweet September sunshine. The sun was shining on their path, but there were clouds hanging over the hills—dark, threatening clouds—and the air was heavy as if with a coming storm.

'I ought to get back before the rain comes,' Dene said doubtfully, looking at the darkening sky.

'You must come to see mamma first,' Mary said, hurrying on. 'Perhaps the news may do her good. She takes so little notice of anything now; she sits for hours and hours without speaking; and when she gets up, she moans: she never forgets her sorrow for a single moment! Perhaps this news of your engagement will take her attention off from her grief for a time.'

She didn't speak hopefully. Dene couldn't help feeling, as she followed Mary across the grass, that she was getting like her mother: she was so wrapped up in herself, in her personal griefs and anxieties, that she had no sympathy left for anyone else. She was dreadfully hurt at the way Mary had taken the news of her engagement. She had quite counted upon Mary's sympathy. She had expected to be congratulated in the orthodox way, and petted, and admired, and caressed. She had expected a great deal, and she was disappointed. Disappointed was hardly the word: she was hurt, mortified; she was almost angry with Mary as she followed her—with a lump in her throat and the tears smarting in her eyes—over the grass.

Lady Bredwardine was in her own room—the room that witnessed all those weary pacings up and down at sunset. It was not sunset now, but her ladyship was tramping up and down the long, cheerless room, as Dene remembered to have seen her on that night, that seemed so long ago, when she had come over to reproach Mary for giving Tristram up.

'Dene has great news to tell you, mamma,' Mary said, when they went in; 'she has come to tell you of her engagement — she is going to be married.'

'Going to be married?'

Her ladyship stopped in the midst of her walk, and looked at the girl with her bright, dark eyes. Dene thought she had never seen such bright eyes in her life before, nor such a pale face. Lady Bredwardine was looking beyond Dene; she was looking out into the green park outside the long narrow windows, where the rain was already falling.

'She is going to marry the Duke of Southernhay, mamma,' Mary said; but Dene stood silent and trembling. She was always a little afraid of Lady Bredwardine; the black-robed figure with the white, corpse-like face and the dreadful shining eyes filled her with awe as she stood in the sudden gloom of that melancholy room, while the thundercloud gathered overhead.

Her ladyship only moaned and wrung her hands ; she did not seem to hear what Mary was saying.

'It is for life,' she said, stopping suddenly in front of the girls; 'it is for ever and ever. It is a long, long chain; longer than life, and stronger than death — oh, so much stronger than death, thank God!'

She had forgotten all about them, and was pacing slowly up and down the room, wringing her hands, and uttering every now and then a feeble moan.

'Is she often like this?' Dene asked, as she turned away with a shiver. She could not help being sorry for Mary: she could not think how she could live through it—this dull life, and this sad, sorrowful spectacle.

'She is like this for days together,' Mary said with a sigh.

' Dear Lady Bredwardine,' Dene murmured, with tremulous lips, 'I thought you would like to—to hear of my happiness, and I came over to tell you at once.'

' Your happiness?' Lady Bredwardine said sharply. ' There are things greater than happiness —things that will never melt away like happiness. There is no such word in the Bible from the first page to the last. We are not promised happiness; we are promised something higher. Covet the best gifts, child; choose the more excellent way!'

She moved slowly on, muttering to herself and wringing her hands.

This was all the congratulation that Geraldine got. She remembered long after the words that Lady Bredwardine had spoken. She watched her pacing the long dim room with faltering footsteps and her hands upraised. Long, long after, she seemed to see her wringing her hands and slowly passing on.

Mary went back with her friend, when the rain had stopped, as far as the bridge. The rain did not stop for long; the sun had come out for a few brief minutes, but when she turned to go back to the house the clouds had gathered again and a sudden storm of rain swept over the park. While she stood for shelter beneath one of the great · spreading trees, she saw a dark drenched figure walking quickly in the direction of the church. It was Lady Bredwardine.

She had left her feebly pacing the long room that looked out into the park; she was so weak· that she could only walk a few steps at a time, and then she would stop and rest; but she was walking now as if nothing were the matter—as if she were strong and well.

Mary gave a little cry, and flew along the path after her like a creature flying for life.

' Oh, mamma, stay, stay !' she cried.

She could not help crying out, though she knew that her voice could not reach her.

Lady Bredwardine had turned in at the church-gate, and was hurrying up the church path between the graves before Mary, panting and breathless, came up with her. She did not even then come quite up. Something held her back. She never knew, when she recalled long after the events of this memorable day, what held her back. Something came between her and the dark hurrying figure and separated them, and Mary fell back while her mother went into the church alone.

She had left the door—the little low door that led into the chapel—open, and the wind and rain swept in after her. She was already beside the marble tomb of the late Earl when Mary entered.

'Bernard, Bernard, Bernard!' Mary heard her murmur, and she stretched out her arms on the empty air, and with a quivering, sighing sound she sank to the chancel floor.

It was all so sudden; it had all happened so much quicker than one could write it; Mary gave a little cry and flew to her mother's aid. She was lying at the foot of the tomb—a black shapeless heap beside all this gleaming whiteness.

Lady Bredwardine's face was as white and cold as the marble figure by her side when Mary lifted her head on to her knee and bent over it in an agony of grief and dread. With trembling fingers she undid the clinging crape draperies that were soaked with the rain, and the widow's veil, that had got wrapped around her and enveloped her in its heavy folds. The bonnet came away with the veil, and then, and not till then, did Mary see how changed and worn the white face on her lap was. Her hair, which she wore long, had changed too, and hung about her throat in gray dishevelled strands that seemed to cling to Mary's trembling fingers as she strove to put them aside.

'Oh, mamma, mamma!' she moaned.

She clasped the cold hands, and her tears rained down on the white face, but there was no response.

How should she make anyone hear? How should she get help? she asked herself wildly, with a dreadful sinking at heart. No one would look for her mother here in this rain. They might not find out that she was not still in her room for hours—not until they missed the sound of her bell, her bell that she so often forgot to ring ; and then, and not till then, would they begin to search for her !

Mary could not leave her here alone while she went out into the village to summon help. She would have to go into the village ; there would be no one about in the roads on this stormy day. Anything might happen while she was away ; her mother might not be here when she came back ; she might have passed beyond all help. Mary looked up at the great windows with the tears running down the panes, and the waving boughs outside tossing their arms wildly in the stormy air, at the white-washed walls with the old familiar tombstones, at the empty pulpit and the chancel-rails, and the altar chill and bare. There was no help in these. And then her eyes travelled back to the sleeping figure on the marble tomb by which she knelt, the beautiful sleeping figure with the face she remembered so well.

'Oh, papa, papa!' she cried—she was in such distress that she hardly knew what she said, and minutes were so precious—'what shall I do, papa?'

What was the use of appealing to the cold, lifeless marble? She was kneeling like some pagan worshipper at the feet of the carven image she loved —the dear friend who had never failed her in life. She made her moan, her helpless moan.

Even while she spoke, Lady Bredwardine opened her eyes—wild, weary eyes, that seemed glazing already.

'Why are you here?' she said, and she shivered as she spoke, and gave a faint cry as she attempted to move.

'I have come to fetch you, mamma dear, dear mamma!' Mary said, in a voice quivering with tenderness. 'Oh, do you think I may leave you here a minute—a few minutes, to get some help?'

Lady Bredwardine only sighed and shivered, and closed her eyes. Was she slipping back again into

unconsciousness? Would she ever, ever open those
glazing eyes again ?

While Mary hung over her mother with this
dreadful question in her mind, there was a stir
outside, and voices fell upon her ear.

'They are here!' someone said, in a familiar
voice that sounded, oh! so sweet in the dreadful
silence.

Her ladyship's maid and one of the men-servants
had come over with wraps, and the carriage was
waiting at the gate.

They carried her back to her own place, and laid
her on the state bed where her husband had been
found dead by her side, and sent for the doctor.

The doctor did not go away again during that
sad day. He would not let Mary stop in the room—
everything, he said, depended upon quiet—but he
promised to call her if—if a change should occur.

There could be but one change. Mary could find
no rest in the house during those dreadful waiting
hours. The sky had cleared, and the sun had

come out, and the park was gleaming with the wet greenery, and the breath of the flowers was fresh and sweet. She remembered long after, when every minute of that day seemed stamped and marked upon her mind, the beautiful sweetness and freshness after the storm had passed.

The lovely light upon the park, and the old trees, and the dear familiar hills, and the tender roseate hues of the sunset, seemed to sting her to a sharper pain. The beauty and the sweetness jarred upon her. She thought of the dear, pale face upon the pillow upstairs in that big gloomy state-room, where so many Gascoignes had died. She was dying up there, and all this beauty was unchanged. The breath of the flowers she loved was so sweet, and the gold and the green of the trees, she knew them everyone, and the opal tints in the sky—there was a glorious sunset in the west—the lilacs that were flecked with rose, and the rosy hues that were paled with gray. She would never see them again.

While Mary stood watching the sunset sky, with

a sudden overpowering sense of sobbing pain, some-
body came quickly to an open window that led out
into the park, and beckoned her.

' She is inquiring for you,' someone said. ' You
must be very calm; you must not 'come in if you
cannot control yourself.'

Mary went quickly in at the open window, and
up the great staircase. She never knew how she
got up, but she put aside her passionate grief and
was white and composed when she entered the room.

Lady Bredwardine looked up eagerly when she
entered.

' Mary,' she said under her breath, ' he has been
here.' She was speaking quite calmly, with a rapt
expression on her face which was sad and worn' no
longer. The rosy sunset was shining into that
western room, and a bar of golden sunlight lay
across the bed. Her face was so sweet and strange,
with such a wonderful light upon it, that Mary's
heart stood still.

' He was here just now—he is coming again—he

said you were *right*—the old wings—Mary—you remember—you must not neglect your work.'

She looked at her child with a lingering longing in her dark eyes, now so dark and bright against the ashy whiteness of her face, and as Mary looked the smile on her face flickered, and she strove to put out her hands. Not in the old sad way—oh no! not in the old, weary, sorrowful way; that was all past.

'He is here now,' she said faintly, with her eyes shining beneath the flickering lids. 'Bernard! Bernard!'

Mary flung herself on her knees beside the bed and pillowed the dear head on her shoulder, and the golden bars of light came for a moment between her and the shining face on her bosom.

The sun had sunk behind the hills, and Lady Bredwardine was dead.

CHAPTER XXI.

'GOD ENCOMPASSES.'

> ' Not sowing hedgerow texts and passing by,
> Not dealing goodly counsels from a height
> That makes the lowest hate it, but a voice
> Of comfort and an open hand of help.'

THE winter had come and passed, and the chill, dreary London spring found Tristram still at work at the mission.

It had been a hard winter for all. There had been great suffering and privation in the East End, and the scanty fund at the disposal of that little band of workers had been utterly inadequate to meet the strain upon it. It had been a mere drop in the ocean.

The poor little fever patients had got well as

best they could; they had struggled back to a sickly life; but some of them, the weakest, had gone to the wall—that is, they had long since ceased to struggle. The story of the sweet green country with the distant hills, and the apple orchards, and the shady lanes, and the hedgerows, and the cool splash of the water beneath the bridges, were only remembered as phantoms of a fevered dream.

It was like that other story of the pearly gates, and the golden floor, and the fruits and the flowers that would never fade or decay. Perhaps they, too, would come true some time.

There had been so much to do during the winter months. There was the old machinery to keep going, the temperance meetings, and the classes, and the services, and the clubs, and the house-to-house visiting. But the winter had brought a great addition to all this work. The weather had been unusually severe, and a great many trades had been affected, and thousands of men had been

thrown out of work.   Bricklayers, masons, and .
painters are so generally out of work in the winter
that one has got used to their complaints, together
with those of the frozen-out gardeners; but other
occupations both for men and women that one
hears very little about are affected by a long frost
or unusual severity of weather.

There were many causes at work to produce
great, almost unprecedented distress in the East
End this terrible winter.   There had been great
depression of trade all through the autumn, and
the summer had been one of almost tropical heat,
and there had been much sickness.   There·were so
many reasons why people, whose salient virtue is
not thrift, and who have so little to be provident
upon, should not have prepared for the rainy day.
Their little savings, if any, had been exhausted
before the winter set in, and many of them were
weakened by disease and that languor that sickness
so often leaves behind it.   They had had to get
well as best they could in the close, pestilential air

of those sultry courts, and as soon as the tired
limbs and the nerveless hands could take up the
work laid down, they had to begin afresh. Many
had 'dropped,' fallen out of the ranks altogether;
others had dragged 'on a weakened existence so
long as the work was there to be done. When
that failed, is it to be wondered at that they aban-
doned hope, and gave themselves up to that sullen
form of misery that is akin to the recklessness of
despair? An evil spirit was abroad, and there was
a great deal of talk in certain circles about the
dangerous classes. It is so easy to blame.

The only danger that Tristram and the members
of the St. Neot's Mission apprehended was the
danger that threatened them every day, the danger
of actual starvation. They had so little to ward it
off with, their funds were so low; the sickness in
the summer and autumn had drained them to the
utmost, and the winter, when it came upon them,
found them at the lowest ebb. The little band of
workers did what they could, but the distress in-

creased week by week, and seemed to mock their puny efforts.

They opened a soup kitchen, and had to shut it up again for want of funds. Then they tried free breakfasts for the literally starving, and to the meal that was prepared for three hundred a thousand hungry claimants came, and seven hundred had to be sent away.

It cut Tristram to the heart, more than anything had done, to see the poor fellows, and the women, and the little children go out without a murmur, when he told them that he was very sorry, that he would gladly help them—God only knew how gladly!—if he could. Oh, what he would have given for that ten thousand pounds just then!

It is not much use preaching to the people of God's providence, if you cannot bring some of that providence to their doors. They are slow to see a needs-be for privation and suffering — and loss. They ask, God help them! why the poor should suffer more than the rich; why this inequality;

why Lazarus should live for ever at the gate
covered with sores, and Dives should fare sumptu-
ously every day. Many, if not all, of the starving
wretches that Tristram had been working amongst
all these months, would have willingly risked the
awful doom of that closing episode to have changed
places with Dives.

Again and again Tristram asked himself, when
this sea of trouble closed around him, whether
he had a right to refuse Mrs. Lomax's cheque.
It was to meet such a need as this she offered it—
it was for no spiritual need ; and he had refused it
because, like the manna, it had not come straight
down from above.

He told the little Sister what he felt one day,
when the scenes he had witnessed at the mission
had touched him deeply—when he had just sent
those seven hundred starving people away. He
had come away from the pitiful spectacle gaunt
and hollow-eyed—he had divided his own breakfast between them—he could not bear to look on

the sufferings he could not relieve, and he had poured out his miserable story to the little Sister.

'It may not be too late,' she said, 'if you think we ought to accept it—that we might accept it. She did not offer it for God's work; she offered it for man's work. This is man's work and God's. If God has put it into her heart—Sister Katherine is quite sure that He had—we have no right to let our scruples stand in the way of the thousands who are starving, who are perishing around us.'

The little Sister wrote to Mrs. Lomax the same day. She wrote in the name of the Sisterhood, and she said that she had Mr. Lushington's permission to write to her.

Mrs. Lowry Lomax answered by return. She never let the grass grow under her feet; she had the great virtue of promptitude. She regretted that Mr. Lushington had not seen his way before. She had sent the money he refused to a Metropolitan hospital, which had accepted it thankfully without asking any questions. Sickness and disease are of no creed, she reminded the little Sister. The man who kept the hostelry on the road to Jericho did not ask any questions of the alien philanthropist when he took those two pence in trust for the traveller who had fallen among thieves.

There was nothing more to be said. Tristram had refused the money as he had rejected that paternal million which he chose to term 'the Mammon of unrighteousness,' and it was clearly no use crying over spilt milk.

He had elected to depend on the arm of the Lord. He had gone so far as to reprove this woman, who had twitted him with the failures and the shortcomings of the old dead faith, as she chose to term it, with the assurance that 'the arm of the Lord was not shortened,' and when his heart had failed him, not his faith, and his weak knees had shaken beneath him, he had been ready to cry, '*Peccavi   peccavi!*'

He accepted the rebuke meekly; if he had not

learnt anything else in his work among the people, he had learnt meekness. He had begun to feel less confidence in himself. The failures were his, but the work was his Master's. The methods were at fault. Perhaps they were out of date. There might be some truth in what Mrs. Lomax had said, after all, that the old methods were obsolete, that God was not behind them.

It was easier to believe this than that the arm that he leaned upon had failed. The failure was his, theirs, not God's. There had been too much selfishness and individualism and love of ease ; the philanthropy that took the form of soup-tickets might not be philanthropy, after all. It might be only a sop to the conscience. What was wanted here, everywhere where men and women work and suffer, was sympathy and knowledge—a knowledge of the wants of the people that could only be gained by living among them, and a sincere desire to help and to reach the warm, living human heart that beats beneath the fustian jacket and the ragged gown.

Money was also wanted; it was wanted dreadfully all through that sad winter that tried Tristram's faith so sorely. A hundred, a thousand times he was tempted to ask himself that perplexing question, Was he right in refusing, for a qualm of conscience, the money that would have relieved all this distress, that would have saved so many of his fellow-creatures from starvation?

The question was still unanswered, and the winter had been got over somehow, and the spring was here again. The little cruse, that was so very near failing time after time, had held out through all the severe weather, and was not quite exhausted yet. The mission was still doing its work and gaining its way among the people, in spite of all the drawbacks. The temperance cause had prospered beyond the most sanguine expectations. The big corner public-house, where Tristram had addressed the crowd on that Saturday night from the costermonger's barrow, was shut up.

It was not exactly shut up, for the big doors

swung open as frequently, more frequently than
ever, but 'Lushington's Entire' was no longer
blazoned on the signboard beneath which Tristram
had given that address. The signboard was still
there, but it bore another legend now — 'The
People's Coffee Palace.'

It really looked like a palace, with its lights
without and its warmth and comfort within; and
the steaming fragrance of the cup that cheers and
stimulates—as no other cup in the world stimulates — met you every time the door swung
open.

It was a tragical little story, the story of the
transformation, and Tristram had something to do
with it, not all. The landlord of the Goat and
Compasses had not escaped the epidemic that had
claimed so many victims in the damp, unwhole-
some autumn weather. Two of his little children
had been seized with diphtheria, and no one could
be found to nurse them. Everybody fled, everybody but Sister Winiver, who heard of the sick-

ness and went through the swinging doors and
offered her help. She was always ready to go to
the worst cases. She had no fear.

The landlord of the Goat and Compasses
accepted her help gratefully; it did not matter to
him in his trouble and affliction where the help
came from. It came too late to save one little life,
and another hung in the balance. On the evening
of the day of the little one's funeral the strong man
was struck down in his prime, and Sister Winiver
had two patients instead of one.

He never knew how it came about, but in his
delirium he called for 'Tristram Lushington—the
brewer who had a conscience.' Tristram came at
once: he saw an open door, opened by God's own
hand, and he brought the poor wretch back to life.
He brought him back, under Providence, in more
senses than one. When the dread disease was
upon him, Tristram hung over his couch at the
risk of infection, and nursed him as if he had been
his own brother.

His life was spared, and the life of the child. But that was not all.

On the first day that the landlord of the Goat and Compasses could get downstairs, he hauled down the signboard over those swinging doors; and then, with his own hands—he would allow no other hands to do the work—he took the bungs out of all the barrels in his cellar. This was not all. While the beer was gurgling out of the wide throats of the barrels below, he set all the taps running above. Nor did he stop here. There were dozens of bottles ranged round the shelves behind the bar, reflecting themselves in the plate-glass that lined the walls of this palace of light, and flashing back a hundred bottles for one. Brandy, gin, whisky, rum, champagne, port, sherry, claret—there was not much claret—curaçoa, noyeau, peppermint—he gave no quarter—one and all, one after the other, he flung the bottles out into the street, taking the precaution to knock the necks off before he threw them into the gutter.

It was a memorable day in the neighbourhood of
St. Neot's Mission. It was worth a hundred
sermons. The gutters ran with wine, and the
cellars overflowed with beer—it flushed the drains
better than any Condy or disinfectant yet invented.
It was like a libation. Diphtheria and fever fled
before it. There was not a single case after that
memorable day in the whole district.

A coffee tavern now opens its hospitable doors
where the Goat and Compasses once stood, and
impulsive, open-hearted Boniface, in his white
apron, presides over the fragrant steam. He was
not such a 'bogey,' after all; he had a lurking
heart and soul somewhere beneath his unpromising
exterior, and it was given to Tristram to discover it.

The name of the house is unchanged. The
ridiculous old goat and the unmeaning compasses
have been painted out, and the old reading of the
sign has been substituted—' God Encompasses.'

There couldn't be a better sign for a coffee palace.
Tristram had only one regret when he saw his

patient taking out the bungs of those beer-barrels : he would have given anything to have taken out the bungs of all those barrels in the cellars of Lushington's Entire—the bungs out of the barrels and the vats; he wouldn't have stopped at the barrels.

Sister Winiver had gone away soon after this incident. She had gone away quite suddenly, and she had left no clue behind her. Nobody knew where she came from, or where she went. It was not a strict Sisterhood, or it would have exacted a *bene dimissit* from its members. It exacted nothing, in fact. It accepted help from all who offered, who were willing to abide by the few and simple rules. It did not put any stumbling-block in the way of any stray Magdalene who might seek to expiate her .guilt in works of charity. It asked no inconvenient questions.

When Tristram inquired of the little Sister—a few days after the Goat-and-Compasses incident— for the tender, devoted nurse who had brought this wonderful thing about, she tossed her head, and turned up her nose in a very suggestive way.

'Winiver has gone again,' she said shortly; 'I wonder she stayed so long. She generally grows restless before a month is over, and now she has stayed six! I suppose he sent for her, and she had not the strength or the courage to hold back.'

'He — who?' Tristram asked. He had heard nothing of this lady's story.

'How should I know?' said the little Sister sharply. 'She has never made me her confidante, only—there is generally a "he" in the case.'

CHAPTER XXII.

'O PERCIVAL! PERCIVAL!'

'Our bond is not the bond of man and wife;
This good is in it, whatsoe'er of ill,
It can be broken easier.'

IT had not been all loss and defeat. Even at the darkest times there had been gleams of sunshine. The most threatening of the many clouds that hung over the mission had a silver lining.

Help had come from the most unexpected quarters. The Sisters had been able, at the time of the greatest distress, to open, with some quite unsought and voluntary help, a workroom, where the wives of the men who were out of work could find employment. This was the greatest possible

boon to the neighbourhood, and kept hundreds and
hundreds of families from starving.

The machinery was so simple, and it was carried
on at such little cost, and the work was constant.
No one knew exactly how it came in, but it came
in regularly, not too much at a time, and did not
fail through all the long trying winter. It was
work that all could do ; it did not want skilled,
trained labour, and it was paid for the moment it
was completed.

Oh, it was lovely work !

There were stockings to knit by the hundred.
Every woman knows how to knit a stocking—or
ought to know—and those who didn't, or who had
forgotten the way, were taught. Stockings, and
jerseys, and vests, and mufflers, and big, huge
steering gloves for sailors far away on the North
Sea. It was a beautiful thought of some generous
soul—a double work of charity that brought a
double blessing.

Then, there were men's shirts—shirts by the

score, piles and piles of shirts; the difficulty would seem to be to find men to fill them: shirts, and vests for men, and warm petticoats, and useful frocks, and working aprons for girls going out to service. There are girls going out to service from every village in England and Scotland—and, let us hope, Ireland—not by any means forgetting Wales, and every one of these needs to be equipped with certain things to make a start in life. There are hundreds of old men and women, too, who suffer from cramps and rheumatism, and aches and pains that only warmth can relieve, everywhere, everywhere. We are all human, and we all need the same flannel (with a difference in the quality).

There are young children, babies without number, that one's heart yearns to cover up from winter's cold in warm, weather-defying garments. In every parish there is the same need, and when Christmas comes round, thank God! the wants of the poor are seldom forgotten. Some good women are working for this end all through the year, un-

mindful that they are thus robbing their poorer
sisters. Let them stick to their own dainty work,
and employ the poor to work for the poor, and
thus bring a double blessing.

The Sisters' workroom was full all through that
hard winter, and those for whom room could not
be found were allowed to take the work home with
them.

They were not all skilled hands, by any means ;
there were many women on the benches who had
not done a stitch of sewing for years, who had
almost forgotten the way. Their fingers were
stiffened and coarsened by rough labour, and they
could scarcely hold a needle. There were other
old crippled fingers, too shaky and palsied to be of
much use, and there were, alas ! some young
women, with babies in their arms, who had never
done a stitch of needlework in all their useless
lives.

One meets with strange people in the East End.
A woman who had never threaded a needle !

The Sisters made no difference : they employed them all. There was one poor old creature, nearly blind, who came day after day, week after week— her seat was very near the stove—who plodded on at a shirt, a coarse rough shirt, that her crippled old fingers could hardly hold. She would take no other work ; she had made a shirt in the days of her far-off youth, and she thought about it, maybe, as she fumbled over these clumsy button-holes. The feel of the coarse calico, and the unforgotten stitch, may have brought back to her those old days and the memories that hung about them.

The little Sister used to watch her smiling as she sat at work, and the look of pride which lit up her poor old face, as she brought up the finished garment for the Sister's examination, was worth going a mile to see.

'You wouldn't ha' thought I could ha' done it so well at my age, dearie,' she said with some pride ; 'I'm nigh eighty, an' I thought I'd a-forgotten the

way, but I felt like a gal again as I made they
buttonholes.'

The Sister looked at it through a mist. She
was thinking of the threescore and ten hard
years that that bit of coarse sewing had bridged
over.

'Like a gal again!' she repeated to herself softly
as she examined the clumsy work, but she said
aloud: 'It is done quite beautifully, Betty. It is
not often one sees such work.'

This was quite true. The poor old creature
hobbled off, smiling and contented with some fresh
task; and—and the little Sister, when there was
no one nigh, unpicked those clumsy stitches and
made the shirt over again. It was a shameful
waste of charity, but she would not have let the
patient, painstaking old soul know it for the
world.

When the new year came, and the winter work
was over, quite a godsend happened to the working
party that kept them employed until the spring,

when the dark days were all over and the men went back to their work.. A lady somewhere down in the country—a nameless lady—had given the most wonderful order. She had sent material for a hundred little red cloaks, and for a hundred cotton gowns, a hundred flannel petticoats, a hundred of every kind of garment that a little girl could possibly want, and she had asked the Sisters to make them up to fit all sorts and sizes of little girls from four years old upward.

She had not stopped with the girls. She had remembered the boys: a hundred little coloured shirts, and a hundred pairs of knitted socks and vests—nothing was forgotten. There was employment for any number of hands. There were bales of worsted, and rolls of calico and print and flannel, and yards and yards of bright scarlet cloth. It made the women's dull eyes brighten to see it. The lady—the nameless lady—the Sister told them, was going to turn her beautiful house into a children's convalescent home when the summer came

round, and all these lovely things—the little shirts,
and the frocks, and the delightful red cloaks—
were for the children to wear. Oh, happy, happy
children!

The Sister told Tristram something of this one
day when he came in, as usual, to say a few words
to the working party; but she did not tell him the
name of the lady.

He smiled—he could not help smiling like the
mothers who were stitching round the table—when
he saw the pretty red cloth. It seemed to brighten
up the dull, bare room. What a bit of colour it
would be by-and-by in a hundred poor homes!

'What a number of people she will make happy!'
he said, speaking of the lady, the nameless lady.
'What a number she has already made happy!'
And he glanced at the smiling faces round the board
—poor, pinched faces many of them; but that bit
of scarlet they were sewing upon had brought, or
had lent, a colour to the palest face among them.
'May God bless her for her double gift!'

A murmur went round the room, a quite audible murmur, as if the workers were repeating the benediction.

When the address and the prayer that followed it were over—in which the dear lady was not forgotten—Tristram went out, and the little Sister walked back with him as far as the door of his night-school.

The little Sister, he noticed, was paler than usual, and there were traces of recent agitation on her tell-tale cheeks. He could see that she had been crying. She told him what had happened as they walked along; she did not wait for him to ask.

'You remember about—about my keeping that money back, that I might send Percival to college?' Her voice shook perceptibly, he noticed, as she spoke.

'Yes; I remember all about it,' Tristram said, looking at her sharply with a question in his eyes.

'Well, he has given me up.'

She said it quietly, as if it were some everyday

thing; but he could see her lip tremble, and if there were tears in her eyes, the kind gathering dusk hid them.

'Given you up?' he repeated.

They walked on in silence, and Tristram was trying to picture to himself what kind of man this could be who would take a woman's money and give her up. He couldn't give up the education she had given him when he gave her up.

'Percival was quite right to give me up,' she said, speaking hurriedly, as if she were trying to excuse him to herself. 'He had found out that he did not love me well enough; that there had been a change in his feelings, or he had not understood them aright at first; he had mistaken friendship for—for love.'

It was a dreadfully humiliating confession for a woman to make, but the little Sister made it bravely, keeping the tears in her eyes from falling.

'Has he only just found it out?' Tristram said dryly.

'He has only just found courage to tell me. I —I thought his letters had changed. There was something wanting in them; there was not the old ring. Oh, it was fortunate he found it out in time! It would have been dreadful to have found it out after. Think of a marriage—a life-long tie —without love!'

Her tears were falling now, and the growing dusk hid them, but her voice shook like a leaf in the wind.

'How long has he been at Cambridge? When does he take his degree?' Tristram asked quite irrelevantly.

'Oh, he takes his degree in June. He has been up three years. There is only one more term. He has done so well; he has got several pupils. He will be able to pay his expenses next term—without —without me. He will accept no more help from me.'

Tristram could hear that she was sobbing still. He would have liked to have a few words with

Percival just then. He would have liked to speak his mind to that conscientious undergraduate who had just found out his own mind.

He had been a long time finding it out—all the years that he was working for his degree, while he was living on this woman's bounty; and when his degree was assured, and her help was no longer needed, he had suddenly discovered the true state of his feelings.

Tristram left the little Sister at the door of the night-school. She had a patient to visit close by, but he did not tell her what he thought of the conduct of her lover. He could not trust himself to speak of it.

There were a lot of youths round the door of the night-school—tall, hulking fellows, almost men, of that dangerous age when the restraints of childhood are removed, and reason and judgment have not begun to exercise their sway. It was an encouraging feature to see that they did not slink away, as they once had done, when he came down the court.

They pressed round him now, and called him by his name, one after the other, 'Mr. Lushington! Mr. Lushington!'

He held out his hand and shook hands with several of them—'How d'ye do, Ben? How d'ye do, Jim?' And he passed through them into the hall.

It was really only a cellar; it could not be dignified by the name of a hall. It was the basement of a house that was let out in tenements, and a flight of stairs led down to it from the street: a long low room, with a sanded floor and white walls and roof, and a big blazing fire crackling in the ample grate. It was well lighted and well warmed; light and warmth go far to ensure the success of an enterprise among a shivering, homeless population. There were a few texts on the walls, and some homely pictures from illustrated periodicals. There was the delightful 'Dirty Boy' that the proprietors of a certain soap have made famous, and a lovely urchin blowing soap-bubbles, and an

old-fashioned print of Sir Roger de Coverley going
to church, and some likenesses of the Royal Family,
and a Scripture-print of Christ blessing little
children, and the cleansing of the ten lepers, and
Moses lifting up the serpent in the wilderness.
Everything here was suggestive, and preached its
silent lesson.

There were some periodicals on the long tables,
and some picture-papers, and there was a bagatelle-
board, and draughts, and dominoes, and some
games; but, above all, there was a piano.

The boys pressed Tristram down on the stool
beside it, and crowded round him while he played.

'What shall we sing?' he asked.

He wanted to sing something to let off his anger,
his hot indignation against that 'cad'—he called
him a 'cad'—who had betrayed that dear woman.

' "Comrades!" " Comrades!" ' they cried with
one accord.

It did him good to sing something with a heart in
it, with a genuine human ring—something that

wasn't sneakish, and mean, and caddish. The cad has many varieties, and he doesn't always wear a fustian coat.

The London roughs, who ought by rights to have been out 'larking,' and smoking cheap cigars at music-halls, or picking pockets in a crowd, joined in the hearty chorus :

'Comrades! comrades! ever since we were boys,
  Sharing each other's troubles, sharing each other's joys!'

Tristram was so disturbed that he could not give the usual address that night; he could not put aside in a moment his anger and indignation. It really looked as if he were going to let the sun go down—and rise again—upon his wrath.

They had quite a concert, these London roughs, among themselves. They chose their own songs, and Tristram played for them. It quite touched him to hear them singing. He remarked with a sense of wonder, as if the age of miracles were quite over, as if it were a strange thing that there should be results—actually results !—that the songs they chose had all the true ring in them, and that they sang them heartily, with an earnestness and enthusiasm that brought the tears to his eyes.

Only yesterday, it seemed, they had been among the hopeless classes—they had been given up—and now, to-day, like the outcast of old, they were sitting at the feet of the Great Teacher, clothed, and in their right mind.

Before they went away Tristram gave them a parting word of encouragement.

'Look here, dear fellows,' he said, and they could see that he was moved as he spoke to them; he had not learnt the art of concealing his feelings. 'I am only a young man like yourselves, and I have the same temptations. If I have had strength to overcome them, if there is anything in my life that is true and earnest, believe me, it comes through the Master whom I serve. Let Him be your Master through life, as He is mine.'

They listened to him in silence, and one by one,

as they filed out of the hall, he gave them a hearty
grip of the hand and a ' God bless you !'

The night air seemed full of benedictions as they
passed out into the street.   There was no ' larking '
and there was no noise.   They might have been
going out of a church.

If Tristram had done nothing else here in the
East End, he had investigated that interesting
specimen called a ' cad,' and had discovered his
lurking heart and soul.

He had found him to be human, after all, and to
have real blood in his veins, and with a responsive
chord in his coarse nature, beneath the unpromising
surface, as true as—and more easy to move than—
the finely-strung machinery in the breasts of men
of sentiment and ease.

When Tristram went round to the little house
with the grape-vine over the front the next morning, there was no one at home but the little Sister.
The grape-vine was budding, he remarked, as he
went up the steps.   It was quite out of place here

in the midst of these courts and alleys. It ought
to have been climbing over a cottage in the suburbs,
where there was fresh air and sunshine. It did its
little best to flourish in this uncongenial place.
It put out its green leaves in spring, and its few
and scanty bunches of hard green grapes in
summer, and it made the poor shabby house quite
a cheerful feature in the unlovely street.

The little Sister was writing a letter when Tristram went in. She had stayed at home to write
this letter, and her eyes, he remarked, were red, as
if she had been crying, and the pages before her
were blistered as if her tears had fallen upon them.

'I am writing to Percival,' she said. 'I could
not trust myself to write to him before. I might
have been tempted to say things I should be sorry
for after. I would not say anything to hurt his
feelings for the world!'

'No—o,' Tristram said, raging inwardly. 'I am
sorry I came in to interrupt you. I'll come in
later on, when—when you've finished it.'

He went so far as the door, and then he turned and looked back, and saw her bending over this wretched letter, and her tears dropping upon it. The sight of her distress moved him; he could not bear to see a woman's tears. He was dreadfully sorry for her.

Something made him go back and say a word of comfort to the poor broken-hearted little soul writing her miserable letter. He put his hand kindly on her shoulder and said a few comforting words, a text or two; but his sympathy had not the desired effect. He had much better have left her alone.

She broke down completely.

'O Percival! Percival!' she moaned, and she hid her face in her hands and sobbed aloud. 'O Percival! Percival! Percival!'

Tristram ought to have come away and left her to her grief. Such griefs are sacred; they are not for strangers to pry into. It was like baring her inmost heart.

He could not bear to go away and leave her

there. The sight of her grief touched him; he
could not find it in his heart to leave her. The
sight of the little lonely figure weeping at the table
moved him as nothing had ever moved him before.
He knew her worth—what a dear, precious little
soul she was. She was worth a thousand—a
million—of that mean cad who had thrown her
over.

Sympathy is akin to love. There is only a step
between. In a moment Tristram had made up his
mind.

'Grace,' he said, in an odd jerky voice that he
hardly recognised for his own—'Grace!'

The little Sister's name was Grace. She looked
up at him piteously, and he took her wet,
trembling hands in his.

'Grace!'

He never knew how it came about, but he had
got his arm around her, and her head was resting
against his bosom.

'Dear Grace,' he said, bending over her, 'could—

could you love me ? I am a poor fellow, I am not
like—like Percival—but I would try to fill his
place more worthily.'

'You?' she cried, 'you? Oh, Mr. Lushington
—Tristram—do you mean it ?'

She was white and trembling, and looking up at
him piteously through her tears.

'Dear Grace!' was all he could say, 'dear, dear
Grace! We are of one mind. I—I am sure we
could work together.'

There was a strained look on her face, but her
eyes were soft and downcast, and her lips trembling.

'You don't mean,' she said, in her unsteady
voice and with her cheeks crimsoning—' you don't
mean, Mr. Lushington—that you'd be willing to—
marry me—after—after that ?'

His only answer was to draw her rosy face to his
bosom.

'Dear, dear Grace !'

The blurred, blotted letter to Percival was

not sent after all. It was a great waste of tears.

There was not a single blister on the neatly written page in which the little Sister gave back her lover the troth he had slighted.

CHAPTER XXIII.

'A LITTLE RIFT WITHIN THE LUTE.'

' It is not worth the keeping; let it go.'

MARY GASCOIGNE had not been idle during these winter months. When the first desolating grief for her loss was over, she set herself to fulfil the last wishes—the last commands—of the dear ones who had passed out of her life.

It was a sacred duty, and she· took it up reverently, thankfully—oh, so thankfully! She did not know what she should have done without it. To have sat idle, with folded hands and eyes faint with weeping, with that strong yearning and passionate pain in heart, that was so akin to despair, would have been dreadful !

There is nothing like work to charm away pain —mental pain. To accomplish a task, a legacy bequeathed by faltering lips and failing hands— perhaps the only legacy—is the best balm for the still-quivering wound.

Mary Gascoigne had plenty to do. Her hands were quite full for months, all through the long dreary winter. There were those old dependents' buildings, whose use had long passed away, to be restored and made ready for occupation by the spring. There was a great deal to be done to make them ready after all these years of neglect and disuse. The roof had to be made water-tight, and the floors repaired, and the walls painted and dis- tempered (that is to say, coloured with some bright, warm, cheerful colouring), and the whole place had to be furnished.

It was Mary's work through all the dark winter days providing for the comforts and conveniences of those old rooms. The great house was turned inside out to provide the things that were needed.

The old storerooms and lumber-closets that had been shut up for years were overhauled and their contents brought to the light, and the vast, gloomy, desolate bedchambers that no one ever slept in were rifled of their useless fittings.

It was better to turn them to the humblest account than to let them slowly decay and fall to pieces in those dreary chambers. The worm would make short work of them—the silent worm and the lively moth. They would perish more surely in the misusing.

Mary had them all brought out to the light, and carried over to those new old rooms when they were ready to receive them. It was quite wonderful how bright and cheerful they looked when all the cobwebs were swept away, and the old window-panes were polished, and the spring sunshine poured in. They only wanted the noise of little pattering feet and the glad music of young voices to bring back the old tide of life that had ebbed so long ago. When the rooms were ready, swept and

garnished, then Mary sent those bales of cloth and
calico up to St. Neot's Mission to be made into
fitting garments for her little flock. It would
never do to have the children down here in their
rags and squalor, and with their poor feet upon the
ground. They would be a blot on the bright landscape; they would be out of place amid these
lovely surroundings.

She had been thinking about it all through the
dark days of winter, picturing to herself those red
cloaks flitting among the greenery of the park.
She would be able to see them ever so far off—and
—and perhaps other eyes, looking down, might see
them. God knows! She liked to hope they were
not far off, those dear eyes that she missed. She
talked over her plans with Cecil, but he did not
enter very keenly into them. He thought it would
be an awful nuisance having all those little beggars
about.

'It will take a lot to keep it up, Mary,' he
remarked one day when he had ridden over to see

her, and she had pointed out to him with pride the two blocks of buildings on either side the clock-tower that had been got ready for her young charges.

The doors and windows were shining with new paint, and there were blinds to the dull old windows, and white muslin curtains were fluttering in the breeze. The spring was here again with its fresh greenery, and the young buds in the avenue were bursting, and there were already primroses in the park.

The snowdrops had gone, and the daffodils were in bloom, and the clouds were sailing high above the tree-tops. There had been a good deal of building going on lately. The rooks had been repairing the old nests in the elm-trees for weeks past. Mary used to watch them blown about in the wind, carrying great twigs that seemed much too heavy for them, to repair the old breaches. It was like carrying the old furniture over to those newly-restored rooms. The cawing rooks overhead seemed quite in sympathy with her. By-and-by, when the work of restoration was over, there would be the feeble twitter of the young birds in those old unsightly nests, growing stronger day by day. By-and-by there would be feeble footsteps and weak voices in those newly-garnished rooms, growing firmer and stronger—oh, so much stronger, please God!—day by day.

'Oh yes, it will cost a lot to keep it up,' she said. 'I have thought of that; I have thought of a way, Cecil.'

She paused by one of the open doors of the building, but he would not enter; he turned away in the direction of the house, and passed in with her at the wide swinging hall-door. The sun was shining in as they entered the house, and lit up the great gloomy hall, with its treasures of old armour and carvings, and the family pictures on the walls.

Cecil paused at the foot of the wide staircase and looked up with some feeling akin to pride. It would be his shortly, it was almost his now—this beautiful old place with its heritage of generations of nobility and culture that no vulgar wealth could buy.

It was a grand staircase; there was not another like it in the county. It led up by two broad flights of stairs to a gallery above, lighted by a beautiful deeply embrasured window, with the old diamond panes filled with escutcheons of the Gascoignes. He quite felt as if they were his own ancestors, as he walked up the wide carved staircase, with the Gascoignes on the walls looking down upon him out of their massive gilt frames.

There were other distinguished personages here in this grand company besides the ancestors of the race; there were the sister Queens who had slept beneath this roof—a fair, pink-eyed Anne, with her baby son, whose innocent, untroubled brain was never to be disturbed by the affairs of State; and the dark-haired, stolid Mary. Cecil surveyed the royal portraits with some pardonable pride, as he walked through the splendid suite of state rooms by Mary Gascoigne's side. It was not every noble family in the county that could boast of entertaining royalty : not hiding a hunted fugitive with a doubtful history for a night, but entertaining, with befitting state, the crowned heads that deigned to rest beneath their honoured roof.

Cecil couldn't understand why Mary took him through these gloomy state-rooms to-day. Nobody occupied them now : they had been shut up all the winter ; they struck him with a chill 'like going into a vault. The furniture and the chandeliers were swathed in holland wrappers ; everything was covered up, except the pictures on the walls, which were used to this sort of demi-state, and were not at all disturbed by it.

'Nobody ever uses these rooms now, Cecil,' she said, stopping in the middle of the great drawing-room, and looking round with a faint flush on her pale face, and her lips trembling. He saw that her eyes were full of a vague yearning and entreaty —that she had a reason for bringing him there.

He could not think what she was going to say.

'It is a pity to keep them shut up, Cecil,' she went on hurriedly; 'so many people would like to see them—people we don't know, strangers who travel about to see old places and beautiful things. It is like a charge to have these things that so many want to see; it does not seem right to cover them up here, and lock the doors upon them, and refuse to let others enjoy the pleasure that we no longer take in them.'

He could not think what she was driving at.

'Oh, you'll take a pleasure in them by-and-by, Mary,' he said awkwardly; 'when—when you've got over this. You only want to fill the house with people, and the old place 'll look like itself again. Take off all those wrappers, and throw open the windows, and let in the sunshine. You wouldn't know the place if there were a lot of people about.'

'That's it,' Mary said eagerly, with a pink spot coming into her cheeks, and her eyes brightening. 'I want to fill the place with people. If it were known that we had thrown the house open—the grounds, and the state-rooms, and the library—we should have all the county here. They wouldn't mind giving their shillings — giving their half-crowns: I don't think some people would stop at half-crowns, if they knew what a good cause it was for—to see the house, and the pictures, and the grounds.'

'Their half-crowns to see the house! Mary, what are you saying?'

He thought she had taken leave of her senses.

'Why not?' she said eagerly. She was so full of her scheme that she did not see the cloud that was gathering on her lover's brow. 'Most people throw their places open now in the summer months, if they have anything to show, and the money that is given helps some good work. It is a way of raising money that hurts no one, and it is not a charity. It pleases those who give; they would not come here unless they wished to give their mite, to help in this noble scheme.'

She called it a noble scheme—it was not hers now; it was carrying out the wishes of the dead.

'You would never throw *this* house open, Mary!' Cecil said, with some dignity.

The blood of all the Lushingtons rose at the thought.

'And why not?' she demanded, looking into his flushed face with her clear eyes.

'Oh, it would never do, you know; what would people say? Fancy the guv'nor throwing open Garlands!'

Mary could not help smiling at the idea of Sir Tristram throwing open Garlands. She could not fancy people coming from a distance to see those gilded saloons, with their overpowering upholstery and their modern pictures. If it had been the town house, where all the *bric-à-brac*, and the Wardour Street furniture, and the Old Masters from Christie's were to be seen, it would have been different.

Cecil saw her smile, and caught her hand in his.

'I say, Mary,' he said thickly—he was agitated in spite of himself; he was shocked at the suggestion of taking money at the doors, like a show; he couldn't control his feelings—'you must give up this—this wild idea. I—I couldn't hear of people paying their shillings—their half-crowns— to see the place. Let 'em come, by all means, if you wish it, but don't charge 'em anything. Think what they'd say in the county! I should have fellows telling me at the club that they'd just been down to my show. Oh, I don't think I could stand it!'

'You forget, Cecil,' Mary said with some dignity, 'that this is my house—that I am carrying out a sacred charge. I am sure that papa——' her eyes filled with tears as she spoke; she could not trust herself to mention her mother's name. 'I am sure that papa, who was so wise and noble, would not see anything unbecoming in this. It is for a good cause, a noble cause, and it is very near my heart. Everyone would understand, when they saw the dear children in the park, why the charge was made. It could not be carried on without money, and people would be glad to help. It would be giving them an opportunity. People are only selfish from thoughtlessness and want of opportunity, and now they will see the children, and it will come home to their hearts.'

She couldn't have convinced him if she had pleaded for a year. He went away with a cloud on his handsome face.

'If you must have the little beggars here, Mary,' he said when he went away, 'I'd rather pay the cost of them myself, if it'll be any pleasure to you, than make a show of the place. It would be the talk of the county.'

He went back and told Lady Cornelia all about it; he did not tell his father—Sir Tristram was suffering from gout, and he was unusually irritable. He did not know what would happen if he were to tell Sir Tristram. A good many things had occurred to upset Sir Tristram lately. His eldest son had written to him and remonstrated with him for allowing, for giving his sanction to, Geraldine's engagement to the Duke of Southernhay.

Tristram had taken the matter up. The great connection had not dazzled him. He had heard all those stories about the Duke, the old ugly stories that were on every tongue, of that shameful past that, if he had been a man of humble birth, would have been a barrier to the society of any pure woman. He had felt it his duty to interfere.

Sir Tristram had resented his son's interference; he had by his own act cut himself adrift from his family, and he had no claim to be admitted to their councils. There had been a further widening of the breach that already divided father and son. Geraldine was forbidden to hold any correspondence with her brother, and Tristram's indignant letters of remonstrance were returned unread.

CHAPTER XXIV.

VANITAS VANITATUM.

'Sun comes, moon comes,
Time slips away.
Sun sets, moon sets ;
Love, fix a day.'

DENE had at last fixed the day; at least, Lady
Cornelia had, which was the same thing. She had
done most of the wooing; she had named the day,
and she had selected the trousseau.

Dene had quite as much to say in each of these
momentous concerns individually as she had in all.
Lady Cornelia arranged everything. She was
really having a very good time: dictating to dukes,
receiving the congratulations of Royalty, and up to
her neck every day, and all day, in Mechlin and
Duchesse satin, and point d'Alençon, and orange-

blossom. It was a disputed point for quite a
month whether the bridal veil should be of airy
fairy Mechlin or of priceless Alençon.

It caused Lady Cornelia sleepless nights, and
Dene would not decide either way. She hated
both. She would have liked a soft simple white
tulle veil, such as she wore at her confirmation. She
had no idea of being covered up in old dead yellow
lace that looked like grave-clothes; that had been
shut up, more likely than not, in a vault for more
than a century; that had a musty smell about it,
and a history, to begin with—a long sad history of
centuries of loss and sorrow and disappointment.
She was young and sanguine, and she shrank from
the sad relics of past failure.

Lady Cornelia had no patience with her
daughter's whims. She selected the deadest of the
disputed laces immediately. The bridal veil was to
be of point d'Alençon.

The gowns had been settled long ago. There
were rich trains by the score for Dene to trail after

her and practise before the glass in. She had no need to wear a sheet now. She could drag as much plush, and velvet, and rich satin, and costly lace behind her as her heart desired. She could stand for hours and hours before the glass trying on lovely gowns—gowns for breakfast, and dinner, and tea, and luncheon, and visiting, and fêtes, and receptions, and balls, and theatres—to say nothing of Court gowns with trains that were a burden to carry.

All these, and more, till her heart grew sick with their beauty and softness and lustre, and her limbs, her strong young limbs, trembled beneath her with utter weariness, while the *modistes* knelt around her pinning, and stitching, and arranging. She could have stood the whole morning once without getting weary, trying on gown after gown, feasting on their beauty and daintiness, and she could not stand for an hour now.

O vanitas vanitatum! She had got all that her heart could desire, all and more—but the desire had failed.

She could no longer plunge into a new gown as she used to do in the old days at Garlands; she put them on languidly now, and she took them off with a decided feeling of relief.

The wedding-day was fixed, an early day before Easter, and the breakfast was ordered, and the trousseau was nearly ready. Dozens of pale-faced women were working day and night at it, sewing at it day after day till they were nearly blind, and falling asleep over it sometimes, and dreaming of the fair young bride who was going to be so happy and rich, and have everything that the world could give; wondering dimly, in a blind, confused way, what she had done in her short youth to be so signally blessed, and what — what they could possibly have done, what horrible blunder they could have committed, that they should have to sit here and stitch all the rest of their lives.

Dene had to be up in town a good deal on account of that tiresome trousseau. She never could understand why she wanted so many gowns, or why Lady Cornelia insisted on her trying them all on. She missed Mary dreadfully just now when she was hungering for sympathy, and she hated town at this time of the year. She was always longing for the woods round Garlands, where the early celandine and the primroses were blowing; and for the old orchards that were full of daffodils in March; and she wanted to hear about Mary's plans, and to see the new old rooms where the little sick children were coming by-and-by.

Cecil came up to town after that interview with Mary. He came up to consult Lady Cornelia; as we have shown, there were reasons why he should not worry Sir Tristram.

'It's too bad,' he said gloomily, 'to expect a fellow to put up with those little beggars about the place, and then—then to throw his house open at a shilling a head! You must reason with Mary, my lady; you really must go down to Garlands at once, and talk to her.'

Lady Cornelia promised she would go down. She could not go for a few days, for a week perhaps, on account of Geraldine's trousseau.

' Hang the trousseau !' the young man exclaimed with some heat. 'If you don't go down at once, mother, she'll fill the house with brats ; you can't say where she'll stop. She's bitten, I believe, with the same craze as Trim. There is no knowing what she will do when she once begins this sort of thing. You must nip it in the bud, mother.'

With some reluctance Lady Cornelia promised she would go down the next day, on condition that Cecil returned to Garlands with her, and between them they would make Mary listen to reason.

Before she went her ladyship told her son a dreadful secret that had been burning in her breast for days. Tristram had filled up the measure of his misdoings by falling in love with a common-place young person in the East End. In the same letter in which he had taken upon himself to censure his father for countenancing Geraldine's

marriage with the notorious Duke of Southernhay
—he called his future brother-in-law 'notorious';
he did not mince matters—he informed him of
his engagement with a lady working in the East
End, one of the Sisterhood attached to the
mission.

Sir Tristram was furious. The unwelcome
intelligence had brought on an attack of gout.
He was confined to his room, to his chair, where
he raved all day like a madman, and frightened
all the people about him out of their wits.

He was too angry to write to his son; besides,
he could do no good by threatening. He could not
disinherit him : Tristram had disinherited himself
already. He could only let him go his own way,
and drag the great name of Lushington's Entire
deeper and deeper in the dust.

'Nothing need be said about this crowning folly
of Tristram's,' her ladyship said to her son, 'until
after Geraldine's wedding. When she is safely
married I shall breathe more freely. My nerves

have been a good deal upset lately, since Lady
Bredwardine's sudden death. I don't think I have
recovered the shock yet. I am always dreading
that something may happen to stop the marriage.
I don't think we will say anything about this whim
of Mary's or—or Tristram's folly, until after the
wedding.'

'I don't see that you've got anything to be
nervous about, mother,' her son said rather ungraciously. 'Southernhay isn't such a catch, after
all. He's got the best of the bargain. A million
of money isn't to be picked up every day, and
Dene's good enough for any man—a deuced deal
too good for him!'

The young man went away muttering to himself,
with an air of being able to say something more on
the subject of the Duke's deserts if he had the
mind to, but her ladyship did not encourage him
to pursue the subject.

She went down to Garlands with him the next
day, and left Dene at the mercy of the dressmakers,

and Sir Tristram with his leg swathed up in flannels in the charge of his physician and valet. He couldn't have walked across the room to save his life. He could only sit in his chair, rich man as he was, with his millions of money, groaning with pain, and bellowing out oaths when a twinge was extra severe, like any pauper. He had a cellar full of wine, to say nothing of those vast storehouses of Lushington's brewery full of beer, and he could not drink a drop—not a single drop ; he had a larder full of dainties that only rich men can command, and he could not touch a single morsel. He could take nothing, nothing but a basin of slops—like a pauper. He had everything that wealth could give ; nothing was denied him—purple and fine linen, and sumptuous fare, and a house full of silver and gold, and all that gold and silver would buy ; and he was sitting here, cursing and swearing, and groaning like — like a pauper ! Truly, we are all one flesh !

Lady Cornelia had gone off in a hurry. She had

forgotten her usual caution ; perhaps her nerves, as she said, were unstrung. She seldom forgot things, but she quite forgot before she went away to leave any instructions about the letters. A great heap of letters that had come by the morning post lay unopened on Sir Tristram's table, and among them, on the top, was one for Dene.

She saw it as she passed through the room to inquire for Sir Tristram. She could not understand why it had been brought there, and she tore it open and read it before she went into the adjoining room.

The writing was not familiar to her ; it was a woman's writing, and the device on the seal was the motto adopted by the St. Neot's Mission. Her heart sank as she read the letter, and the colour faded out of her cheeks.

Tristram was ill. He had been ill a week with fever and delirium, and his strength was failing. The doctors feared the worst, and had begged the Sisters to communicate with his friends. The letter had been written the previous night, and he might even now be——

Dene did not allow herself to frame the thought into a word, she flew with the open letter into her father's room.

'Oh, papa, papa!' she cried, bursting in unfeelingly; she did not use the slightest caution in approaching the invalid. 'Tristram is ill—dying, perhaps—and there is nobody to go to him!'

Sir Tristram greeted her with a volley of reproaches for meddling with his letters, and shouted to her to shut the door which she had unwittingly left open.

'How do you know he is ill?' he demanded.

'Here is a letter from a lady, from one of the Sisters who are nursing him. She says——'

'Hang what she says!' Sir Tristram interrupted with an oath. 'It is a plant—it is all a scheme for making herself known to the family. Nursing him! of course she's nursing him! A brazen, indecent hussy to have the impudence to write to you!'

'Oh, papa! what else could she do? She could not let him die without letting us know.'

'Were there no men about the place who could have written? Is it a woman's mission? I did not know that my son had joined a Sisterhood.'

Sir Tristram refused to hear any more about it, he would not even look at the letter. He frightened Dene out of her wits when she came over to kiss him and implore him to let her have the carriage and go to St. Neot's with her maid, and see how matters really were. Her dress happened to come within an inch—within half an inch—of the much-bandaged foot as she bent over him, and Sir Tristram lifted his crutch impatiently and hurled such a volley of oaths after her that she fled in haste from the room with her fingers to her ears.

The poor child had no heart for anything all through that dreadful day She refused to try on a single gown, and she would not see the Duke when he called; and after lunch she surprised her maid by declaring her intention of walking in the park.

It was a dismal afternoon with a wet west wind blowing, and a white mist creeping up from the river ; a dog would not have gone out on such a day. It had taken Dene all the morning to make up her mind, but she had made it up at noon.

It was no use asking Sir Tristram's permission ; she would not have asked it for the world. It was no use waiting till Lady Cornelia and Cecil came back. Tristram might be dead before they returned. He might be dead—dying now. Dene's little tender heart could bear the suspense no longer. She summoned up all her courage, and she went out with her maid into the mist and the rain. At the corner of the square she found a cab, and they drove together to the East End.

She had never been in the East End before, and the sight was new to her. A drizzling rain was falling, and the streets looked duller and grayer than ever. She had never seen anything look so dull and hopeless as these East End streets. She had been used to brightness all her life, brightness and flowers and sunshine; she had never had anything to do with gloom.

The squalid streets, and the hopeless, helpless apathy on the faces of the women, struck her as she looked out of the window of the cab from the midst of her warm furs. She shuddered and drew down the blind; she could not bear to look upon all this misery. She did not wonder that Tristram was ill; she only wondered that he had borne it so long, that he had not broken down before.

There was no one to receive her at the mission; Jayne had gone out, and the other workers were away. Everyone had his work to do, and when one of the scanty band fell out of the rank another had to take his place.

The old lady who did the ' chaws,' as she termed it, of the establishment informed Dene that the gentleman upstairs was mortal bad. The Sisters had been up with him night after night; he would certainly have died if it had not been for the Sisters' nursing. He had caught a bad sort of fever in

going about the courts and alleys of this crowded
place : he was bound to catch it, for he had not
spared himself night or day. He had sat up for a
week at a spell with a bad case—a man, a confirmed drunkard, whose wife and child had died of
it, and he had brought him through, and then he
had been stricken down himself.

'He wouldn't be warned,' the old lady said,
shaking her head and wiping her dim old eyes,
that Dene saw were red with weeping; 'he would
go his own way. He gave himself up for a drunken
wretch whose life was not worth saving. It was
like throwing his life away.'

The old woman told Dene all this while she
waited in the room below for the Sister who was
nursing Tristram to come down.

The Sister came down at last. She had been
unable to leave her patient before, she explained;
he was wandering in his mind, and she could not
leave until he had dropped asleep.

She was looking at Dene with an eager interest

in her dark eyes, and the colour was coming and going in her cheek as she stood by the table talking to her. Dene could not help remarking how bright and dark her eyes were, and what a beautiful proud smile she had when she thanked her in broken words for her kindness to Tristram. It was Sister Winiver, who had come back.

' It is no more than we do for the least,' she said coldly. ' Why should we make a difference? Your brother has not spared himself; he has left us all a lesson. If—if he is taken, he will not have lived in vain.'

' You think—he will not recover ?' Dene gasped, and all the colour dropped out of her cheeks.

' I did not say he would not recover. He is very ill, he has been delirious for days ; but there is still hope—while a spark of life remains there is always hope. The age of miracles has not passed.'

This was not reassuring.

' You will let me see him !' Dene sobbed. ' You will not let him die without my seeing him ! I am his only sister, and we have been so much to each other.'

'He would not know you if you saw him,' the Sister said; 'he has not known anyone for days, not even Sister Grace; and, besides, the fever is infectious.'

Dene had not noticed that the Sister had put the table between them, the table and a draught of air from the door.

'If you are not afraid of taking it, why should I be afraid?' the girl said eagerly. 'He is more to me than to you; if any one runs a risk, I am the one who ought to run it.

'If you went up into that chamber you would not be able to go back; you would carry the infection in your clothes, you would carry disease—and death—into the midst of all your ease and pleasures. You are about to be married, I am told; you have others to consider besides your-self.'

There was a hard, scornful ring in the Sister's

voice that Dene could not understand, and her cheeks were scarlet.

'What is the risk to me?' the girl said, flushing too, a scarcely paler red. 'Tristram is dearer to me than—than all the world.'

She was eager and earnest, she would not be put aside, and she followed the Sister up the stairs when the old woman came in hurriedly to tell her that her patient was awake.

The Sister stopped outside the door of the sick-chamber, and warned her for the last time. Her eyes were cold and hard and unpitying, but as a mere matter of duty she warned her.

'Remember,' she said, standing with the handle of the door in her hand, ' the risk you are running. If you do not think of yourself, think of your lover!'

'I can think of no one but Tristram ; and—and I am sure he wants me,' Dene pleaded. 'You do not think I could let him die here among strangers, without any of his own about him ?'

She was not to be persuaded; she would not listen to reason. She could hear Tristram's voice inside, it sounded quite strong; but she could not catch what he was saying, the words were wild and running together.

The Sister could not wait another moment.

'Remember, I have warned you,' she said impatiently; but her warning was lost upon Dene, who had pressed into the room and was kneeling beside the bed.

'Oh, Trim! Trim!'

CHAPTER XXV.

'The grand old name of gentleman,
Defamed by every charlatan,
And soil'd with all ignoble use.'

THERE was great consternation in Chesham Place when Lady Cornelia came back the next day. The cab had been sent home empty; at least, the maid had come back in it, but Dene had remained behind.

Sir Tristram had been much worse after that interview with Dene. His physician had to be sent for in haste, and he had given him an anodyne, and enjoined quiet, perfect quiet, beyond everything. The frightened servants hadn't dared to tell him of Geraldine's absence. When Lady Cornelia came back the next day she was greeted with the unwelcome news. She was not only angry, she was in despair. She was quite sure that the Duke would not look with complaisance on this quixotism of his *fiancée*. He would think that it was in the blood.

Her ladyship had a severe *crise de nerfs* when the painful news was broken to her, and she sent Cecil in the carriage at once to fetch his sister home. Above all things, it was necessary that it should not reach Sir Tristram's ears. He was still in a critical condition; physicians were going in and out of his room all the morning. They looked bland and smiling when they went in; they looked bland still, bland and solemn, when they came out. The patient must be kept perfectly quiet; there must be no distractions, at the peril of his life.

No one could understand what could have called Lady Cornelia and her son away at such a critical time, and her ladyship did not choose to explain.

If she had stayed at home this shock might have been averted.

She might just as well have stayed at home, for all the good she had done. Mary had not listened to reason. She had taken her own way, and she had refused to be guided by Lady Cornelia's counsel.

' It was a sacred charge,' she pleaded. She owed it to the dead to carry out their wishes. It was her mother's dying bequest—her mother's and the late Earl's. Mary quite believed that Lady Bredwardine held communion with her dead lord, and that in some mysterious way he made his wishes known to her. She was quite sure that she was carrying out the wishes of both her parents in this philanthropic scheme of hers, and in throwing the house open to provide the funds to carry it on.

Lady Cornelia had come away in a huff. She could not understand Mary's obstinacy. She went so far as to advise Cecil to break off the engagement if Mary continued obdurate.

'Your house would never be your own,' she said,
'with all those pauper children running about. I
don't know what has come to Mary—or to Tristram. People never thought of such things when I
was a girl.'

This was quite true.

Cecil's visit to the mission was as useless as his
journey to Bredwardine. Dene refused to come
back. She was helping the Sisters to nurse her
brother, and she would stay with him until the
end. The end might not be far off; the doctors
were expecting a crisis. When—when it was all
over, she would come back. There was not a word
said about her approaching marriage, or the Duke,
or the trousseau, which the dressmakers were in
despair about.

She had forgotten all about them. She only
remembered that Tristram was ill, and needed
her.

'He has recognised me once,' she wrote to her
mother, in a missive her ladyship immediately

burnt, ' and, oh! you should have seen his beautiful smile when he saw me sitting by his side !'

Dene's *fiancé* was in despair. The wedding-day
was approaching; the preparations were nearly
completed; the lovely bridesmaids were anxious
and tearful; the wedding-presents were pouring in
—and the bride was away in the East End nursing
a fever patient. She was more than likely to get
the fever herself—fever and diphtheria, and heaven
knows what !

Remonstrance was useless; she was deaf to
reason. A hundred wild horses would not drag her
away from her post, and no one was brave enough
to enter that infected chamber and carry her away
by force.

No one was brave enough but the Duke. Armed
with Lady Cornelia's consent, he went to the East
End fully prepared to carry off his lady-love out of
the clutches of the destroyer. He went in his
grand ducal carriage—with plenty of disinfectants—
and a pair of thoroughbreds that were a sight to see.

Dene refused to come down to her lover; she was quite sure she would give him something if she came down, and she sent a message to him by the dear old lady. But the Duke was not so easily got rid of. What is the use of being a Duke if bolts and bars do not fall open before you?

He followed the old lady up the stairs into the chamber where Dene and Sister Winiver were nursing the sick man back to life. Tristram had recovered consciousness the last day or two; the delirium had passed, and he would lie for hours holding the hand of the dear little sister that he had lost so long. That cool, tender hand-clasp seemed to bring him back to life. He had been drifting away on a wide sea until Dene had stretched out her little cool hand through the darkness and brought him back to the shores of life. He could not let her hand go now; it was something to cling to when the light was low and everything seemed slipping away.

He was still holding Dene's hand when her lover

came into the room, and Sister Winiver, who took her turn with the little Sister in nursing Tristram, was bending over him with some nourishment in a spoon.

She was so occupied with her patient, getting the nourishment down his unwilling throat, that she did not look up when the unexpected visitor came into the room ; and, besides, she had her back to the door.

Dene gave a little cry when her lover came into the room, and Tristram opened his eyes. She got up from her seat by the bed, and went over to the door quickly to put him out. Every moment he stood there was fraught with danger.

' Oh, go back ! go back !' she said, putting out her hands before her as if to drive him away from the bed ; 'you ought not to be here ! Oh, you don't know what a risk you are running ?'

He looked at her with undisguised admiration in his handsome *blasé* face, and real tenderness in his voice.

'My darling, my darling !' he said, and he took her outstretched hands in his.

Sister Winiver's hand that was holding the spoon to her patient's lips trembled at the sound of the strange voice, and she looked round and saw Dene in·her lover's arms.

'What is it? Who is it?' Tristram asked impatiently.

There was no answer to his question but the Sister's whitening face. The spoon had dropped from her nerveless hand, and she fell with a little quivering sigh to the floor.

Tristram started up in bed ; a light had suddenly dawned upon him. He could not have raised himself an inch a moment before. Dene was in her lover's arms, and—and Sister Winiver was in a heap on the floor. The room had already begun to go round with him, and he reached out his hand through a mist.

'You villain !' he said, or shouted, rather; 'it is you—you villain !'

He fell back on the bed like a log, and Dene flew to him, and it was a long time before he opened his eyes again—so long that she despaired of his ever opening them; and there was no one to call for help. Sister Winiver was in a dead swoon on the floor. Dene had her hands full bringing her two patients back to life, and when she remembered her lover, and the errand he had come upon, he had gone.

The Duke had fled at that unexpected recognition. He had not waited for an explanation.

Tristram called Jayne up to his bedside before the day was over and dictated a letter to him. He was too weak to hold a pen, but he could dictate a letter. He could not rest until that letter was written.

It was to the Duke of Southernhay, who had proposed to do such honour to his family. It was a letter of few words, he had not strength to dictate a single sentence more; but it was to the purpose.

It informed his Grace that a shameful chapter in

his chequered history had been unveiled : that the victim—innocent or guilty, it mattered not—of that notorious *esclandre* was here ministering to Tristram by his sister's side. It went on, further, to threaten immediate and public exposure if the Duke did not at once, without an hour's delay, renounce his claim to Geraldine's hand.

Lady Cornelia was startled the next morning by receiving a missive bearing the splendid ducal crest of the Southernhays. The Duke formally released Geraldine from her engagement. He did not give any reason for the step ; he merely begged Lady Cornelia to assure her daughter of his highest admiration and esteem, and to consider herself free —free from her engagement.

Her ladyship really had a very alarming *crise de nerfs* this time—and the family physician had to be called in. He advised that Sir Tristram should be kept in ignorance of what had happened—at least, for the present.

While he was still in the house a cab drove up to

the door, and a lady in a Sister's dress got out. It was the little Sister. She was not alone; she had brought Dene back. Dene had been stricken with fever, and the doctors had recommended that she should be taken home without delay. She would have had no chance of getting well in that close, vitiated air, and they had brought her back.

The girl was flushed with fever, flushed and pale by turns, and shivering as if she had received a shock, and her head was wandering already. This was no time for explanations. Dene did not know her mother when she came to her bedside. She could only hold out her hands, her poor hot hands, and implore someone to ' go back ! go back !'

Lady Cornelia had to be forbidden her daughter's room ; her complaints and laments only disturbed the patient. The little Sister could give her lady-ship no satisfactory explanation. A gentleman had called to see Miss Lushington the day before. He had forced his way into her brother's sick-room, and he had created a good deal of confusion. Her patient had had a relapse in consequence, and one of the Sisters had been carried away ill, and Dene had since sickened of the fever.

Lady Cornelia looked at the Sister curiously out of the corners of her small, half-closed eyes, while she was giving this meagre explanation. The young person spoke with a great deal of confidence, she remarked ; she was not in the least nervous or shy —the presence of the *grande dame* did not move her in the least, and she spoke of her ladyship's daughter as Dene.

Could this be the Sister that Tristram was going to marry ? A little bit of a creature with a pink face, and fearless blue eyes like sword-blades, and fluffy hair, and no features to speak of, and with not the least respect for dignities. Could this be the future Lady Lushington ?

Lady Cornelia's heart stood still.

Dene's illness was a very serious affair. There had been a shock to the system in addition to the fever, and for days the delirium ran high. They

cut off all her beautiful hair—the lovely little dark
rings that used to cluster round her bright face.
It would be a bright face no longer, if the fever
were cheated of its prey, and she drifted back to
the sad shores of everyday life.

It did not seem at all likely for weeks together
that she would ever drift back. The doctors came
and went, and there were relays of trained nurses,
in beautiful becoming caps and aprons, going in and
out of the sick-room all day, and every sound in the
great house was hushed, even the sound of Sir
Tristram's curses and groans He remembered
long after how he had sent the poor little thing
away in terror and weeping, when her skirt had
brushed by him on that miserable day.

A paragraph went round the society papers in the
early days of Dene's illness, that the marriage had
been postponed—unavoidably postponed. Everybody quite understood the reason for the postpone-
ment, and there were daily bulletins in the papers
of the condition of the little bride ; but no one could

understand why, at this critical time, the Duke of
Southernhay should go away.

Lady Cornelia kept her own counsel. It was
better for the matter to drop quietly than to make
a scandal. Everybody would soon forget all about
the engagement: there would be no need of an
explanation by-and-by.

In the present state of things she dared not tell
Sir Tristram. She locked up the Duke's letter in
her desk, and the secret in her bosom. It would
be time enough for explanations by-and-by.

Mary wanted to come up and nurse her friend,
but the doctors gave strict injunctions that only
the trained nurses they sent in should be about the
patient — no strangers or relatives; no one who
would be likely to set the train of memory working
afresh, and recall the incidents of the shock that
had prostrated her. Rest, perfect rest, and still-
ness, and silence, were enjoined above everything
else.

The wet, windy spring days wore on; the daffo-

dils in the orchards were no longer in bloom ; the
kingcups in the meadows were over, quite over,
and the early celandine had given place in the
woods round Garlands to bluebells and cowslips,
and the primroses were paling in the lanes.

A change had come over all the world, when
Dene, changed too, and saddened, a mere shadow
of the old, bright Dene of her childhood, was
brought downstairs.

Sir Tristram came into the morning-room to see
her, as she lay, like a little white snowflake, on the
couch that was drawn up beside the fire.

He was dreadfully shocked at the change in the
small white face on the pillow ; he would not
have known it for Dene's but for the wistful dark
eyes.

' You will soon be picking up again, now that you
are downstairs,' he said awkwardly, as he bent over
her and kissed her. ' We shall soon have Southernhay back, and hear the sound of wedding-bells.'

' No, papa,' she said quickly, ' not that—any-

thing but that!' and then she began to cry hysteri-
cally, and Sir Tristram saw that he had put his foot
into it.

'Confound it!' he said to his wife, when she
had carried him off into the adjoining room; 'why
didn't you tell me there had been a split?'

'I thought you knew, dear,' Lady Cornelia said
sweetly.

'How the deuce should I know? I thought it
odd Southernhay hadn't written.'

'He isn't likely to write,' Lady Cornelia said,
repressing a sigh.

'Not likely to write! You don't mean it's so
serious as that?'

Her ladyship nodded her head.

'Good heavens! you don't say it's off?'

'It's been off ever since—since Dene came back.'

Sir Tristram sank back in his chair and gasped.

It is not wise to let people afflicted with gout
gasp. Men seldom gasp unless the situation is
grave. Lady Cornelia thought that she couldn't

have broken it more gently to Sir Tristram, but she was nervous as to the result.

'You don't mean she has—thrown the Duke over?' he said, with a catch in his voice that did not escape her ladyship's sensitive ear.

How *could* she tell him that the Duke had given Geraldine up ?

He would never have understood things ; he would have raged and fumed, and he would have brought on a fresh attack of gout. He had an enemy always lying in wait for him. Sir Tristram could not afford, like a less fortunate man, to indulge in the luxury of being angry. He had to take life easily, quite easily ; he could not afford to get into a passion.

Dene was far too weak to be bullied. She was too weak for explanations. She could only, for many days, lie on the couch, drawn up beneath the window, where the warmth of the sunlight fell upon her, and watch the clouds sailing by, and the little black London sparrows twittering beneath the eaves.

By-and-by she was able to be taken down to Garlands, and the fresh breezes of her native hills, and the breath of the sweet green country, with the orchards and the hedgerows in all their summer prime, wooed her back to life.

CHAPTER XXVI.

' A childly way with children, and a laugh
Ringing like proven golden coinage true.'

THE spring was back again—the sweet spring days—
the flowers blooming in all the woods, the grass
green again in the meadows, the orchards white
with blossom, and the lilac nodding over the garden
wall.

It had all come back—bud and leaf and blossom
in unbroken sequence. There was nothing wanting. The silence and the leaflessness were over ;
the birds were back again in the branches, singing
their glad pæan of praise, telling the old new story
of the resurrection and the life.

The sparrows were back in the London courts, building merrily under the eaves, and the sunlit clouds were sailing over the dull, gloomy London streets, and, behold ! there was darkness and gloom no longer.

There was a voice in the sweet west wind—a glad, glad note in the lark's song, going up into the blue, and coming down into the smoke and the mist, as if it brought back a message of joy with it.

Tristram was back again at his work. His illness had made a terrible break in it; at least, he thought so : he could not understand how it could go on without him. It had gone on, nevertheless; it did not seem as if he had been missed. It hurt him to feel that everything could go on very well without him. If he had died it would still have gone on.

Perhaps, after all, the work was not his; it was God's work. He had been only the clay in the hands of the Potter. The failures had been his, the work had been his Master's, and he had marred it by his eagerness and ignorance.

All his schemes and his efforts for the re-
generation of the world had not come to much.
Drunkenness was still rampant—drunkenness and
destitution, with all their attendant evils. A public-
house had been shut up at one corner, but a music-
hall had been opened at another; the thousands
who had been fed in the hard days of winter were
all hungry again—as hungry as ever. Free meals,
soup-tickets, coal and blanket distributions, had
only afforded temporary relief. The distress was
still there as great as ever, and all that had been
done for the people, when it stopped, only made
them poorer than before. Clearly the old methods
had failed. Other means must be found for dealing
with the hard problem.

It made Tristram's heart ache when he reviewed
the work of the past year—its high hopes, its heart-
burnings and failures. Charity administered wholesale had failed. It seemed to him, looking round
upon the poor tale of results, that everything had
failed. He had looked for immediate results; he

had been in such a hurry to regenerate the world, and the world had not been regenerated. Relief administered wholesale had only created more destitution than it had removed. The feeding of the destitute children had only weakened the responsibility of the parents, and it had set more money free to be dissipated in drink.

Perhaps it had not been all failure. There were other forces making for good in the world. God had not left Himself without a witness. Even in the midst of all the suffering and distress of the past winter there had been compensation. The suffering and the privation had called forth the special virtues of the poor—patience, helpfulness, love, sympathy. Patience was never wanting— patience and submission—and helpfulness and sympathy—the poor ever help the poor—and love. Love was always there—love ready to bear and strong to save. Perhaps this was to be the power that was to regenerate the world.

There had been changes at the mission during

Tristram's illness. New workers had come, and old tried colleagues had gone away to other spheres of work. A branch had been established in a distant part of the parish, and a plot of waste ground had been secured for a new mission-room, but there was a great difficulty in the way of funds.

The hands of the workers had been crippled all the winter, and here they were undertaking more than they had ever done before, and running into expenses there did not seem any likelihood of their being able to meet.

The call had come so directly from without, and it was so urgent, that the mission could not put it lightly aside. Meetings had been held by the workers through the winter months in a densely-crowded neighbourhood, nearly a mile away from St. Neot's Mission, and the services had been largely attended. Often crowds had to be refused admittance, as the building where the meetings were held was insufficient to provide accommodation for the numbers that sought to press in directly the doors were open.

This was distinctly encouraging. It was more encouraging when the people later on petitioned that a larger room might be built, and offered to bear a portion of the expense. Still, the mission did not see its way. At the first service that Tristram was able to take after his illness, when he was still looking worn and weak, something quite remarkable happened. He had given his first address at this small, distant mission-room, as his voice was still too weak to fill the great hall where the meetings were usually held. A whisper had got about that he was going to speak that night, and long before the doors were open there was a patient crowd waiting outside large enough to fill the limited space twice over. How they crowded in when the doors were opened was a sight to see. Every seat, every square inch of room, was filled in no time, and there was a huge crowd blocking up the doors and reaching half-way across the road.

When Tristram appeared on the platform, pale and weak, and moved out of himself by this unexpected reception, a murmur ran through the crowd, and the men with one consent rose up in their places to greet him, and some of the women present began to weep. He had not strength to say very much ; but when the meeting was over, before he left the platform, a man in the middle of the crowd pressed forward to shake his hand—a rough-looking working man, with a bit of blue ribbon in his buttonhole and a crape band round his arm. It was the man he had nursed through the fever.

'God bless you, sir !' he said in a broken voice, grasping Tristram's thin white hand in his great palm—'God bless you and reward you !' And he passed his ragged sleeve across his eyes as he came down the steps of the platform.

Everyone there knew the story of the man's loss —and gain, and what Tristram had been to him in his trouble. There was a good deal of handshaking that night—more than Tristram could well bear. They nearly shook his arm off. But that was not all. A deputation waited upon him the next day composed of the working men who had attended the meeting, offering to build a mission-room themselves, and provide what they could of the material.

Tristram could hesitate no longer. His heart went out to the dear, hearty fellows as it had never gone out to them before. He had never dreamed of awakening such enthusiasm and loyalty and eager co-operation. The men were as good as their word. One man gave the beams for the roof; another the wood for the floor; a third, a plumber, gave the gas-fittings; a mason gave the bricks from an old wall; a poor working man gave the sashes for the windows—old sashes that his master had given him; and another gave the doors. Every inch of material used was either given or supplied at cost price. It was like the building of the Temple. The people brought freely of their humble store— brick and timber and lead-piping—and every man worked with a will.

It was spring when the new mission-hall was begun, and it would be finished by August.

While the work was going on, Tristram was occupied with plans that affected himself—himself and his future. It was desirable that a ' settlement' should be established in this new quarter as a centre for mission-work, and everyone was unanimous in pressing Tristram to take charge of it.

There was someone else to consult now. The little Sister had to be consulted.

He was to be married in the autumn ; there was nothing to wait for. A man can do so much more with a wife to help him. He had learnt to rely so much on the little Sister that he could not undertake this new responsibility without her to share it with him. They could do so much working together, each making up the deficiencies in the other, strengthening each other's hands, and knit together in one common bond.

The Sisters were loath to give up one of their number. They could ill spare the little Sister now; their numbers had sadly dwindled since the winter. Sister Winiver had left them again—gone away, as she had come, suddenly, and without any warning. She had been found missing a few mornings after that unexpected meeting in Tristram's room. She had gone away silently in the darkness, and she had left no explanation behind; only her nurse's dress and apron neatly folded up upon the bed, and a few trinkets—not very valuable trinkets—laid upon them. It was all that she had of her own to leave for the mission. Tristram remembered when he saw them what she had said on that day when he returned Mrs. Lowry Lomax's cheque, about the money with the stain upon it that was not fit to go into the treasury of the Lord.

' Will she ever come back ?' Tristram asked sadly. He had not much hope that she would ever return. The Duke of Southernhay had gone abroad, and rumour had said—rumour is always

ready to repeat a slander—that he had not gone
alone.   .

'If she comes back we shall certainly not take
her in!' the little Sister said, with crimsoning
cheeks and flashing eyes.

'Hush!' Sister Katherine said softly from the
depths of her great chair; she could not get far
away from that big chair now. 'It is not for
us to judge her. She will come back again some
day—and—and we will take her in when she
comes.'

The little Sister wrote to Dene and told her all
about the new 'settlement.' She told her something besides. She told her that when Tristram
went to his new post he would not go alone. She
often wrote to Dene after her illness. They had
seen so much of each other while she was staying
at the mission, nursing her brother; but the little
Sister never said a single word about Sister Winiver
in any of her letters.

Dene told Mary all about Tristram's engagement.

She could not keep it back any longer. Mary must know some day. It was already June when Dene showed her the little Sister's letter.

'I am sure she is worthy of him,' Mary said, in a voice that would not keep quite steady. 'They will work together. She is a noble woman! She has given up all, everything—she has kept nothing back. Tristram could not help loving her.'

It was Whitsuntide and June, and Mary had the first batch of her convalescents down the next day —pale-faced, sad-eyed little waifs and strays from London courts, wandering silent and amazed amid the sunny lawns of Bredwardine.

The scarlet cloaks and the print frocks had been brought into use. They brightened up the wide green landscape. It was as if a garden of bright exotics had burst suddenly into bloom.

Cecil came over one day when the children were playing in the park; the first shyness had disappeared, and they were silent no longer. Already the colour had come back into the little, pale faces, and their eyes were no longer sad. They were bright with the brightness of returning health, and the weak voices were no longer weak; they were shouting for joy—oh, such a glad, glad shout!—as Cecil came riding through the park.

At first he did not know what this meant, the shouting and the laughter; but when he saw the red cloaks and the children at play, it dawned upon him.

' Oh, this will never do,' he said ; ' I could not put up with this, not—not to be owner of Bredwardine.'

He had expected to meet Mary in the grounds on this bright June day, but she was nowhere to be seen, and, throwing a rein to a groom, he went into the house. There was quite a large party already in the house; the hall was full, and he had to press his way through the crowd—a vulgar crowd. It was Whit Monday, and a large party of excursionists had come over to see the house, and they were dropping their shillings into a box!

He would have strode through them up the staircase, but the housekeeper barred the way.

'For the Convalescent Home, sir,' she said, gravely presenting the box.

It was too much for Cecil, and he turned away. He wondered that the old Gascoignes on the staircase didn't come down out of their frames.

He passed out through the common crowd with a deep red flush on his face. He never thought that anything could hurt him so much. It was a deeper humiliation than that never-to-be-forgotten sight of Tristram addressing a London crowd from a costermonger's barrow.

The groom had taken his horse away, and he had to walk round to the stables to find it. On the way he met Mary, with two little red-coated waifs clinging to her gown, and one, a tiny creature, a mere baby, on her shoulder. She was running and laughing as he had never seen her laugh since the days of her own childhood—laughing and playing with the little group; and when they had pulled her down upon the grass, they sprang into her arms, kissing her and being kissed. A laughing, happy group, a sight so sweet and innocently happy, so full of God's great mercy and compensation! It would have moved most men, but it did not move Mary's lover.

She saw there was something amiss as Cecil strode towards her with that dusky red flush on his face and his lowering brow. She got up from the grass, but she did not let go the hands of the little ones who were clinging to her.

'I have just come from the house,' he said in a voice that he could hardly control.

'Yes?' she said quietly, pressing unconsciously the little hands she held in hers.

'I—I can't stand it, Mary,' he said, with a catch in his throat.

'No—o,' she said slowly.

*   *   *   *   *

There was nothing more to be said. It was all over, and she had made her choice.

When he rode back she was still there, on the grass where he had left her, with the children about her—a solitary woman with the children clinging to her.

CHAPTER XXVII.

' Dust are our frames, and gilded dust our pride.'

IT really was all over. Cecil had given Mary Gascoigne up. He couldn't stand her quixotism. He didn't know where it would lead her. She might join the Salvation Army, and wear a poke bonnet and carry a tambourine. She might devote herself to hospital work, and go about in a nurse's gown and a tall white cap. There was no saying what she might not do.

When women are bitten with a mania they are bitten much more severely than men. There are no enthusiasts like female enthusiasts. Take a

woman out of that fatal selfism which is at the root
of half the evils of society, and her arms are wide
enough to embrace the whole world.

Mary Gascoigne's arms were wide enough to
embrace a wider community than the little flock
that came in relays to her convalescent home.
She had done all that she could do here. She had
provided for the care and comfort of the numerous
family, and she had thrown her house open to
strangers to provide funds for their maintenance.
There was nothing to keep her here.

Dene had told her all about the Sisterhood in
that little house where the grape vine grew over
the front. She had told her what good work the
Sisters were doing in that crowded neighbourhood
where there was always destitution and suffering to
relieve. She had told her of their scanty means
and their dwindled numbers; she had heard that
another Sister had left since she had been taken
away, and that now, when the little Sister should
go away in August, there would be none left to

carry on the good work, that the home would be
shut up for want of workers.

'She—goes—away—in August?' Mary asked
breathlessly, with the pink colour coming and
going in her cheeks.

'Trim is to be married in August,' Dene said
with a sigh; and—she was still weak—she could not
keep the tears from brimming in her eyes. 'They
will go away for a holiday. He has not been away
a day since he went there in June—and—and when
they go back they will settle in their new home.
The big mission hall that the people are building
for him will be ready by then, and they will begin
their work together. I suppose it is a great
work?'

She spoke sadly, with a note of interrogation in
her voice. She did not seem quite sure of the
answer.

'Of course it is great work,' Mary said eagerly.
'There is no greater work in the world than helping
one's fellow-creatures. It is a privilege, a blessed-

ness, higher than happiness—oh ! so much higher and nobler than mere selfish happiness—to give ourselves for others.'

Mary was thinking of the saints of old, of the men and women who endured reproach and persecution, and who found even in dungeons and on racks a joy passing the joy of harvest. She had not read those old lives of the saints in vain.

Dene sighed.

'Trim has made a dreadful mistake !' she said to herself as she looked at Mary's rapt face and her quivering lips. 'It—it is a pity the home will have to be given up,' she said aloud. 'The Sisters were doing such good work there.'

'Must it really be given up? Would it not be possible to keep it on if someone stepped into the place of—of the Sister who is going away ?'

' There does not seem anyone likely to step into her place. It is not an easy place to fill. It is in a shocking neighbourhood, where the people are always falling ill of dreadful complaints, and where they are always poor and out of work, and the men, and sometimes the women, are often getting drunk. She seemed to bear a charmed life, going in and out among the people, and doing such unpleasant things. Oh, I don't think they will ever get any-one to fill the little Sister's place !'

Mary Gascoigne was not so sure of that. She went up to town the next week. There was nothing to keep her here at Bredwardine ; nobody to miss her when she went away, nobody to welcome her when she came back. She might as well go to town as anywhere else ; there was no one to ask her where she went or why she went.

When a woman has no ties, has nothing but a lonely, desolate life to look forward to, she takes to dogs, or cats, or parrots, or babies—not often to babies—or to going about the world with a rusty black bag and a bundle of tracts. Failing these resources, she joins a Sisterhood and nurses the sick. A woman must have something to love, and if she is fated never to become a wife or a mother, what is she to do with her life, with her affections? They are hers still; she cannot get rid of her affections. How is she to find a safe channel for them if the love of husband or children is never to be hers? Fate decides the question for most women, and condemns them to a hopeless, selfish existence, ending often in confirmed invalidism, hypochondria, and not infrequently insanity.

Mary Gascoigne did not wait for fate; she decided for herself. She went one fine July day to the East End, and saw the little house with the grape-vine over the front and Sister Katherine sitting in her chair. There was no one else at home. The little Sister was out about her work in the parish, and Sister Katherine was here at her post, ready to receive 'the mothers,' or the working girls, or anyone else that needed her counsel or help. Mary learned from her all she came to know about the work of the Sisters. They would be sadly missed if they ceased to labour here. When the little Sister was married—one of the number,

Sister Katherine informed her, was shortly to be married to a man who was doing a great work in this place, who had made great sacrifices for conscience' sake—the Sisterhood would be broken up, unless someone should come forward to fill her place. They had recently lost two other members —one through illness, 'and one—one who had gone away.'

The little Sister did not come back until late in the day. When she came in with Tristram, she found Sister Katherine full of the visitor who had been there during her absence: 'A sweet young lady, with the most beautiful face in the world, she said in describing her. 'She is coming here in August, when you go away from us, Grace ; she is coming the very day. We shall not have to break up the home, after all. I knew that our extremity would be God's opportunity. I knew that His promise could never, never fail !'

'Who is this Providence that has dropped down from the skies?' the little Sister asked in her bantering tone. She was not quite pleased at her place being filled so easily. 'I hope you did not forget to ask her name, Katherine?'

'She told me her name before she went away. We are to call her Sister Mary. I did not ask for any other name.'

Everything seemed settling into place. When the little Sister dropped out of the rank, another was ready to take her place. The great mission-hall was nearly completed, and the house was being furnished. The little Sister insisted on furnishing the house herself. She had still a little money left that she had not given up to the work of the home —the money she had put aside for Percival's degree —the perfidious Percival!

She had that two hundred a year still. It would keep them from being a burden on the funds of the mission; and Tristram had Dene's little legacy. A year ago he would have thought it ridiculous, the height of folly, to marry on such an income; but now it seemed positive wealth. They were still deep in store lists and furniture catalogues, when an event happened that threatened to upset all their plans. A telegram reached Tristram that his father was dying.

He set off at once to Garlands, and he reached there in time to see his father once more alive. Sir Tristram's old enemy had again attacked him, but this time in a more serious form ; the gout was not confined to the limbs now, and any moment, the doctor had warned her ladyship, it might be fatal. He had not thought it his duty to warn Sir Tristram to set his house in order ; it is scarcely a doctor's part.

Perhaps, with that strange prevision that comes before the end, the Baronet realized that the end was not far off : perhaps he read it in the anxious faces round his bed. He had sent for his lawyer just before Tristram arrived, and he had added a codicil to his will. When he had done this, poor gentleman ! he thought he had done all. He had not been ill long enough to be changed by pain or weakness, or troubled by apprehension. As men live so they die, and Sir Tristram proved no exception to the rule. It had been necessary to administer narcotics after that interview with the lawyer, and he was still under the influence of the anodyne when his eldest son reached Garlands.

The house was in a state of confusion when Tristram arrived—that is, in as much confusion as a perfectly ordered household could be. Nothing short of an earthquake would have disturbed the regularity of that magnificent establishment. The dinner-hour had been altered, but the meal had not been put off.

A great London physician travelled down with Tristram, and they drove from the station to the great house together. The red sunset light was shining on all the many windows as they drove up. It looked from a distance as if the house were illuminated. Tristram long after remembered that home-coming, the beautiful familiar landscape, and the shining windows that seemed to betoken the presence of some unusual guest.

The great man who had been summoned in haste from London went up to the sick-chamber at once, and left Tristram waiting in the room below. It was his father's study; everything in it was familiar to him. It brought back his happy childhood, as he stood there looking round at the dear familiar objects he had known and remembered all his life : the whips on the wall, the guns and fishing rods; the bookcases well filled, no breaks, no irregularities; the directories, and Bradshaws, and Army Lists on the table; the perfectly-appointed writing-table; the unopened letters that had come yesterday and to-day; the blotting-pad he had last written upon; the pen he had last used. These things smote upon Tristram like a blow. They seemed to reproach him for having been wanting in duty to the kind father who had never denied him anything in his life.

Was it possible that he had been wrong, after all; that in his eager haste to transform the world he had been inconsiderate, undutiful?

It was too late to ask the question now. As he stood looking out through one of the shining windows, with a strange mist before his eyes, at the same hills and the same beautiful river that his father had watched from that window for so many years, the great doctor came downstairs. Tristram heard his step and looked up, trying to read the verdict on his face.

' I think you had better go up at once,' the great doctor said kindly; ' he is conscious, and is asking for you.'

Tristram went up the wide staircase like one walking in a dream. Sir Tristram was propped up in bed, and his face was turned towards the door. He was watching for his son. He looked up with a tender smile of recognition as Tristram came to his side !'

' My dear boy !'

The misunderstanding of months was bridged over in those words.

' I have been in fault, sir,' Tristram said humbly,

as if he were still a child; 'I—I have not con-
sidered you as I should. Forgive me, father, if I
have done wrong!'

'My dear boy!'

His voice was weak; he could not say much, but
he pressed the hand that Tristram held in his, and
then with an effort he raised himself in the bed,
and looked round upon those standing near—his
wife and children and the medical attendant—and,
in a voice that rang through the silent room, and
thrilled every heart, he said slowly, and with strange
deliberation:

'You have done—quite—right. If—I—had—
my time—to—go—over—again—I would do—
would—do—the—same.'

Sir Tristram fell back on his pillow, and the
medical attendant came quickly over, and Tristram
sank beside the bed on his knees.

An hour later Lady Cornelia was borne from the
room a widow, and the great London doctor went
back to town.

Tristram stayed at Garlands until after the funeral. When Sir Tristram's will was read it was found that the codicil had altered the disposal of his property. The brewery was not offered to Tristram; it descended with the landed estates to Cecil, and Dene was no longer a great heiress. There was only one line in the will in which the name of the Baronet's eldest son occurred :

'I leave to my son Tristram one million of money.'

Tristram came back to the East End the day after the funeral. He had to talk to the little Sister about that million. His views had altered lately ; at least, they had been modified. He had learnt what great things money can do. He had re-read that command to the young Ruler, and he had thought over the parable of the Unjust Steward. He saw things now in a different light. He was not so sure, after all, that it was not a question of stewardship.

He could decide nothing until he saw the little

Sister. He had expected her to be full of sympathy, when he went back after that trying time; to greet him with a face, if not sad, yet reflecting his own sorrow.

The little Sister was not sad or sympathetic by any means; there was not a vestige of sorrow on her bright face. He had never seen her face so bright before; it was brimming over with happiness.

'Oh, have you heard?' she said softly, not shyly.

'Heard what?' he asked, in a tone of surprise. He had not been back at the mission an hour; he had not had time to hear anything.

'Percival has come back,' she said softly, with the tears swimming in her eyes. 'He has come back; he has found out that he had made a mistake!'

'And you?' Tristram gasped. He could only gasp; she had quite taken away his breath.

'I? Oh, I have forgiven him, of course! What else could I do?'

What else could she do?

CHAPTER XXVIII.

'I can but trust that good shall fall
At last—far off—at last, to all,
And every winter change to spring.'

WHAT more is there to tell?

The home is not given up, and the mission is still doing a great work. It is extending its usefulness every day. The little Sister is the little Sister no longer. She is the wife of the hard-working curate of an East End parish. She has married an excellent man. The experiment turned out well after all, which is more than most experiments in educating lovers generally do turn out.

Mary Gascoigne—or Sister Mary, rather—has

• taken her place at the home, and she and her rejected lover are thrown a good deal together. They have both suffered a good deal since that sad day when he found Mary reading in the library at Bredwardine, and they have both made mistakes. Their experience has not been unlike ; and the eyes of both have been opened.

Cecil has succeeded to the brewery and the title ; he is Sir Cecil Lushington now, and was returned unopposed the other day in his father's place for the county. Dene is still at Garlands with her mother. Lady Cornelia wants a great deal of comforting and sympathy, and Dene's work is quite cut out. She is always weeping and wringing her hands, like Lady Bredwardine, not for the husband she has lost, but for the Duke who rode away—and for Mary's folly.

The convalescent home prospers. It has been of unspeakable benefit to hundreds of little sick children. It has brought back health and vigour to little weak bodies, and joy and gladness into dull lives. It has done, and is doing, a great work. Who shall measure its benefits? Mary Gascoigne did not stop with the children. She remembered that there were hundreds of gently-nurtured women who were pining in great cities for rest and change, and she has thrown open her beautiful house for a home of rest for Christian workers.

The once empty, desolate rooms are empty and desolate no longer. They are filled all the year round with a goodly company. Here the tired worker enjoys—oh, how she enjoys!—sweet rest and refreshment, and noble, devoted lives are strengthened and built up again for future effort.

The beautiful old house, with its priceless treasures of a bygone age, is a Palace of Delight to weary workers, whose lives are spent amid sad scenes and squalid surroundings. It is doing more good now than it had ever done since it was first built. The voice of the weeper is heard no more; at least, it is hushed. Nervous women, suffering from overstrain, whose nerves have been unstrung, hear—or fancy they hear, which is much the same —a footstep at sunset in the long, low, many-windowed room, which Lady Bredwardine used to pace in the days of her loss and sorrow.

She has passed beyond the reach of loss, and where there is no more weeping. She has found all that she lost ; there is nothing to call her back from her happy place.

Tristram's work is not yet done. It will never be done while a hundred and twenty thousand lives are sacrificed every year in the United Kingdom from the effects of intemperance alone, and a hundred and twenty thousand homes made desolate.

He is not so confident now as he was a year ago about his methods ; but his enthusiasm has by no means abated. He began by attempting to do too much, and in too great a hurry. His intense sympathy and desire to regenerate the world carried him away. He had to learn that the subtle adversary with whom he had to deal often obtains his end by means of the very weapons that are used against him. He had yet to learn that as great danger results from driving too fast as from driving too slow. He is still learning the humbling lesson that it is God who works, not man, and that he who runs before the pillar and the cloud will assuredly be bewildered.

And about that million of money. Tristram has not definitely settled yet whether to accept it or not. There are so many arguments to consider on both sides. He has to give each a fair hearing. He has to decide whether it could be better employed. He will not soon forget how the possession of that rejected million nearly wrecked his young sister's happiness. Channels for its wise and useful distribution are ever opening and widening before his eyes; and he has not forgotten Mrs. Lowry Lomax's scathing rebuke, ' Sickness and suffering have no creed.'

There are arguments for and against the employment of the Mammon of unrighteousness in the work of the Lord. Perhaps Mary Gascoigne will help him to decide. Meanwhile, it still remains an open question.

THE END.

BILLING AND SONS, PRINTERS, GUILDFORD.

𝔄 𝔏ist of 𝔅ooks 𝔓ublished by
CHATTO & WINDUS
214, Piccadilly, London, W.

ABOUT.—THE FELLAH: An Egyptian Novel. By EDMOND ABOUT. Translated by Sir RANDAL ROBERTS. Post 8vo, Illustrated boards, 2s.

ADAMS (W. DAVENPORT), WORKS BY.
A DICTIONARY OF THE DRAMA. Being a comprehensive Guide to the Plays Playwrights, Players, and Playhouses of the United Kingdom and America Crown 8vo half-bound, 12s. 6d. [*Preparing.*
QUIPS AND QUIDDITIES. Selected by W. D. ADAMS. Post 8vo, cloth limp, 2s. 6d.

AGONY COLUMN (THE) OF "THE TIMES," from 1800 to 1870. Edited, with an Introduction, by ALICE CLAY. Post 8vo, cloth limp, 2s. 6d.

AIDE (HAMILTON), WORKS BY. Post 8vo, illustrated boards, 2s. each.
CARR OF CARRLYON. | CONFIDENCES.

ALBERT.—BROOKE FINCHLEY'S DAUGHTER. By MARY ALBERT. Post 8vo, picture boards, 2s.; cloth limp, 2s. 6d.

ALDEN.—A LOST SOUL. By W. L. ALDEN. Fcap. 8vo, cl. bds., 1s. 6d.

ALEXANDER (MRS.), NOVELS BY. Post 8vo, illustrated boards, 2s. each.
MAID, WIFE, OR WIDOW? | VALERIE'S FATE.

ALLEN (F. M.).—GREEN AS GRASS. By F. M. ALLEN, Author of "Through Green Glasses." Frontispiece by J. SMYTH. Cr. 8vo, cloth ex., 3s. 6d.

ALLEN (GRANT), WORKS BY. Crown 8vo, cloth extra, 6s. each.
THE EVOLUTIONIST AT LARGE. | COLIN CLOUT'S CALENDAR.
Crown 8vo, cloth extra, 3s. 6d. each; post 8vo, illustrated boards, 2s. each.

PHILISTIA.	IN ALL SHADES.	DUMARESQ'S DAUGHTER.
BABYLON.	THE DEVIL'S DIE.	THE DUCHESS OF
STRANGE STORIES.	THIS MORTAL COIL.	POWYSLAND.
BECKONING HAND.	THE TENTS OF SHEM.	BLOOD ROYAL.
FOR MAIMIE'S SAKE.	THE GREAT TABOO.	

Crown 8vo, cloth extra, 3s. 6d. each.
IVAN GREET'S MASTERPIECE, &c. With a Frontispiece by STANLEY L. WOOD.
THE SCALLYWAG. With a Frontispiece.
DR. PALLISER'S PATIENT. Fcap. 8vo, cloth extra, 1s. 6d.

ARCHITECTURAL STYLES, A HANDBOOK OF. By A. ROSENGARTEN. Translated by W. COLLETT-SANDARS. With 639 Illusts. Cr. 8vo, cl. ex., 7s. 6d.

ART (THE) OF AMUSING: A Collection of Graceful Arts, Games, Tricks, Puzzles, and Charades. By FRANK BELLEW. 300 Illusts. Cr. 8vo, cl. ex., 4s. 6d.

ARNOLD (EDWIN LESTER), WORKS BY.
THE WONDERFUL ADVENTURES OF PHRA THE PHŒNICIAN. With 12 Illusts. by H. M. PAGET. Crown 8vo, cloth extra, 3s. 6d.; post 8vo, illust. boards, 2s.
THE CONSTABLE OF ST. NICHOLAS. With a Frontispiece by STANLEY WOOD. Crown 8vo, cloth, 3s. 6d.
BIRD LIFE IN ENGLAND. Crown 8vo, cloth extra, 6s.

ARTEMUS WARD'S WORKS. With Portrait and Facsimile. Crown 8vo, cloth extra, 7s. 6d.—Also a POPULAR EDITION, post 8vo, picture boards, 2s.
THE GENIAL SHOWMAN: Life and Adventures of ARTEMUS WARD. By EDWARD P. HINGSTON. With a Frontispiece. Crown 8vo, cloth extra, 3s. 6d.

ASHTON (JOHN), WORKS BY. Crown 8vo, cloth extra, 7s. 6d. each.
HISTORY OF THE CHAP-BOOKS OF THE 18th CENTURY. With 334 Illusts.
SOCIAL LIFE IN THE REIGN OF QUEEN ANNE. With 85 Illustrations.
HUMOUR, WIT, AND SATIRE OF SEVENTEENTH CENTURY. With 82 Illusts.
ENGLISH CARICATURE AND SATIRE ON NAPOLEON THE FIRST. 115 Illusts.
MODERN STREET BALLADS. With 57 Illustrations.

BACTERIA, YEAST FUNGI, AND ALLIED SPECIES, A SYNOPSIS
OF. By W. B. GROVE, B.A With 87 Illustrations, Crown 8vo, cloth extra, 3s. 6d.

BARDSLEY (REV. C. W.), WORKS BY.
ENGLISH SURNAMES: Their Sources and Significations. Cr. 8vo, cloth, 7s. 6d.
CURIOSITIES OF PURITAN NOMENCLATURE. Crown 8vo, cloth extra, 6s.

BARING GOULD (S., Author of "John Herring," &c.), NOVELS BY.
Crown 8vo, cloth extra, 3s. 6d. each; post 8vo, illustrated boards, 2s. each.
RED SPIDER. | EVE.

BARR (ROBERT: LUKE SHARP), STORIES BY. Cr. 8vo, cl., 3s. 6d. ea.
IN A STEAMER CHAIR. With Frontispiece and Vignette by DEMAIN HAMMOND.
FROM WHOSE BOURNE, &c. With 47 Illustrations.

BARRETT (FRANK, Author of "Lady Biddy Fane,") NOVELS BY.
Post 8vo, illustrated boards, 2s. each; cloth, 2s. 6d. each.
FETTERED FOR LIFE. | A PRODIGAL'S PROGRESS.
THE SIN OF OLGA ZASSOULICH. | JOHN FORD; and HIS HELPMATE.
BETWEEN LIFE AND DEATH. | A RECOILING VENGEANCE.
FOLLY MORRISON. | HONEST DAVIE. | LIEUT. BARNABAS. | FOUND GUILTY.
LITTLE LADY LINTON. | FOR LOVE AND HONOUR.
THE WOMAN OF THE IRON BRACELETS. Three Vols., crown 8vo.

BEACONSFIELD, LORD. By T. P. O'CONNOR, M.P. Cr. 8vo, cloth, 5s.

BEAUCHAMP.—GRANTLEY GRANGE: A Novel. By SHELSLEY
BEAUCHAMP. Post 8vo, illustrated boards, 2s.

BEAUTIFUL PICTURES BY BRITISH ARTISTS: A Gathering from
the Picture Galleries, engraved on Steel. Imperial 4to, cloth extra, gilt edges, 21s.

BECHSTEIN.—AS PRETTY AS SEVEN, and other German Stories.
Collected by LUDWIG BECHSTEIN. With Additional Tales by the Brothers GRIMM,
and 98 Illustrations by RICHTER. Square 8vo, cloth extra, 6s. 6d.; gilt edges, 7s. 6d.

BEERBOHM.—WANDERINGS IN PATAGONIA; or, Life among the
Ostrich Hunters. By JULIUS BEERBOHM. With Illusts. Cr. 8vo, cl. extra, 3s. 6d.

BENNETT (W. C., LL.D.), WORKS BY. Post 8vo, cloth limp, 2s. each.
A BALLAD HISTORY OF ENGLAND. | SONGS FOR SAILORS.

BESANT (WALTER), NOVELS BY.
Cr. 8vo, cl. ex., 3s. 6d. each; post 8vo. illust. bds., 2s. each; cl. limp, 2s. 6d. each.
ALL SORTS AND CONDITIONS OF MEN. With Illustrations by FRED. BARNARD.
THE CAPTAINS' ROOM, &c. With Frontispiece by E. J. WHEELER.
ALL IN A GARDEN FAIR. With 6 Illustrations by HARRY FURNISS.
DOROTHY FORSTER. With Frontispiece by CHARLES GREEN.
UNCLE JACK, and other Stories. | CHILDREN OF GIBEON.
THE WORLD WENT VERY WELL THEN. With 12 Illustrations by A. FORESTIER.
HERR PAULUS: His Rise, his Greatness, and his Fall.
FOR FAITH AND FREEDOM. With Illustrations by A. FORESTIER and F. WADDY.
TO CALL HER MINE, &c. With 9 Illustrations by A. FORESTIER.
THE BELL OF ST. PAUL'S.
THE HOLY ROSE, &c. With Frontispiece by F. BARNARD.
ARMOREL OF LYONESSE: A Romance of To-day. With 12 Illusts. by F. BARNARD.
ST. KATHERINE'S BY THE TOWER. With 12 page Illustrations by C. GREEN.
VERBENA CAMELLIA STEPHANOTIS, &c. | THE IVORY GATE: A Novel.
FIFTY YEARS AGO. With 144 Plates and Woodcuts. Crown 8vo, cloth extra, 5s.
THE EULOGY OF RICHARD JEFFERIES. With Portrait. Cr. 8vo, cl. extra, 6s.
THE ART OF FICTION. Demy 8vo, 1s.
LONDON. With 124 Illustrations. Demy 8vo, cloth extra, 18s.
SIR RICHARD WHITTINGTON. Frontispiece. Crown 8vo, Irish Linen, 3s. 6d.
GASPARD DE COLIGNY. With a Portrait. Crown 8vo, Irish linen, 3s. 6d.
THE REBEL QUEEN: A Novel. Three Vols., crown 8vo.
WALTER BESANT: A Study. By JOHN UNDERHILL. With Photograph Portraits.
Crown 8vo, Irish linen, 6s.
[Shortly.

BESANT (WALTER) AND JAMES RICE, NOVELS BY.
Cr. 8vo, cl. ex., 3s. 6d. each ; post 8vo, illust. bds., 2s. each; cl. limp, 2s. 6d. each.

READY-MONEY MORTIBOY.	BY CELIA'S ARBOUR.
MY LITTLE GIRL.	THE CHAPLAIN OF THE FLEET.
WITH HARP AND CROWN.	THE SEAMY SIDE.
THIS SON OF VULCAN.	THE CASE OF MR. LUCRAFT, &c.
THE GOLDEN BUTTERFLY.	'TWAS IN TRAFALGAR'S BAY, &c.
THE MONKS OF THELEMA.	THE TEN YEARS' TENANT, &c.

, There is also a LIBRARY EDITION of the above Twelve Volumes, handsomely set in new type, on a large crown 8vo page, and bound in cloth extra, 6s. each.

BEWICK (THOMAS) AND HIS PUPILS. By AUSTIN DOBSON. With
95 Illustrations. Square 8vo, cloth extra, 6s.

BIERCE.—IN THE MIDST OF LIFE : Tales of Soldiers and Civilians,
By AMBROSE BIERCE. Crown 8vo, cloth extra, 6s.; post 8vo, illustrated boards, 2s.

BLACKBURN'S (HENRY) ART HANDBOOKS.
ACADEMY NOTES, separate years, from 1875-1887, 1889-1892, each 1s.
ACADEMY NOTES, 1893. With Illustrations. 1s.
ACADEMY NOTES, 1875-79. Complete in One Vol., with 600 Illusts. Cloth limp, 6s.
ACADEMY NOTES, 1880-84. Complete in One Vol. with 700 Illusts Cloth limp, 6s.
GROSVENOR NOTES, 1877. 6d.
GROSVENOR NOTES, separate years, from 1878 to 1890, each 1s.
GROSVENOR NOTES, Vol. I., 1877-82. With 300 Illusts. Demy 8vo, cloth limp, 6s.
GROSVENOR NOTES, Vol. II., 1883-87. With 300 Illusts. Demy 8vo, cloth limp, 6s.
GROSVENOR NOTES, Vol. III., 1888-90. With 230 Illusts. Demy 8vo, cloth, 3s. 6d.
THE NEW GALLERY, 1888-1892. With numerous Illustrations, each 1s.
THE NEW GALLERY, 1893. With Illustrations. 1s.
THE NEW GALLERY, Vol. I., 1888-1892. With 250 Illusts. Demy 8vo, cloth, 6s.
ENGLISH PICTURES AT THE NATIONAL GALLERY. 114 Illustrations. 1s.
OLD MASTERS AT THE NATIONAL GALLERY. 128 Il'ustrations. 1s. 6d.
ILLUSTRATED CATALOGUE TO THE NATIONAL GALLERY. 242 Illusts. cl., 3s.

THE PARIS SALON, 1893. With Facsimile Sketches. 3s.
THE PARIS SOCIETY OF FINE ARTS, 1893. With Sketches. 3s. 6d.

BLAKE (WILLIAM) : India-proof Etchings from his Works by WILLIAM
BELL SCOTT. With descriptive Text. Folio, half-bound boards, 21s.

BLIND (MATHILDE), Poems by. Crown 8vo, cloth extra, 5s. each.
THE ASCENT OF MAN.
DRAMAS IN MINIATURE. With a Frontispiece by FORD MADOX BROWN.
SONGS AND SONNETS. Fcap. 8vo, vellum and gold.

BOURNE (H. R. FOX), WORKS BY.
ENGLISH MERCHANTS: Memoirs in Illustration of the Progress of British Commerce. With numerous Illustrations. Crown 8vo, cloth extra, 7s. 6d.
ENGLISH NEWSPAPERS: The History of Journalism. Two Vols., demy 8vo, cl., 25s.
THE OTHER SIDE OF THE EMIN PASHA RELIEF EXPEDITION. Cr. 8vo, 6s.

BOWERS.—LEAVES FROM A HUNTING JOURNAL. By GEORGE
BOWERS. Oblong folio, half-bound, 21s.

BOYLE (FREDERICK), WORKS BY. Post 8vo, illustrated boards, 2s. each.
CHRONICLES OF NO-MAN'S LAND. | CAMP NOTES. | SAVAGE LIFE.

BRAND'S OBSERVATIONS ON POPULAR ANTIQUITIES ; chiefly
illustrating the Origin of our Vulgar Customs, Ceremonies, and Superstitions. With the Additions of Sir HENRY ELLIS, and Illustrations. Cr. 8vo, cloth extra, 7s. 6d.

BREWER (REV. DR.), WORKS BY.
THE READER'S HANDBOOK OF ALLUSIONS, REFERENCES, PLOTS, AND STORIES. Fifteenth Thousand. Crown 8vo, cloth extra, 7s. 6d.
AUTHORS AND THEIR WORKS, WITH THE DATES: Being the Appendices to "The Reader's Handbook," separately printed. Crown 8vo, cloth limp, 2s.
A DICTIONARY OF MIRACLES. Crown 8vo, cloth extra, 7s. 6d.

BREWSTER (SIR DAVID), WORKS BY. Post 8vo, cl., ex., 4s. 6d. each.
MORE WORLDS THAN ONE: Creed of Philosopher and Hope of Christian. Plates.
THE MARTYRS OF SCIENCE: GALILEO, TYCHO BRAHE, and KEPLER. With Portraits.
LETTERS ON NATURAL MAGIC. With numerous Illustrations.

BRILLAT-SAVARIN.—GASTRONOMY AS A FINE ART. By BRILLAT-
SAVARIN. Translated by R. E. ANDERSON, M.A. Post 8vo, half-bound, 2s.

BRET HARTE, WORKS BY.

LIBRARY EDITION. In Seven Volumes, crown 8vo, cloth extra, 6s. each.
BRET HARTE'S COLLECTED WORKS. Arranged and Revised by the Author.
    Vol. I. COMPLETE POETICAL AND DRAMATIC WORKS. With Steel Portrait.
    Vol. II. LUCK OF ROARING CAMP—BOHEMIAN PAPERS—AMERICAN LEGENDS.
    Vol. III. TALES OF THE ARGONAUTS—EASTERN SKETCHES.
    Vol. IV. GABRIEL CONROY. | Vol. V. STORIES—CONDENSED NOVELS, &c.
    Vol. VI. TALES OF THE PACIFIC SLOPE.
    Vol. VII. TALES OF THE PACIFIC SLOPE—II. With Portrait by JOHN PETTIE, R.A.

THE SELECT WORKS OF BRET HARTE, in Prose and Poetry With Introductory
    Essay by J. M. BELLEW, Portrait of Author, and 50 Illusts. Cr. 8vo, cl. ex., 7s. 6d.
BRET HARTE'S POETICAL WORKS. Hand-made paper & buckram. Cr.8vo, 4s.6d.
THE QUEEN OF THE PIRATE ISLE. With 28 original Drawings by KATE
    GREENAWAY, reproduced in Colours by EDMUND EVANS. Small 4to, cloth, 5s.

Crown 8vo, cloth extra, 3s. 6d. each.
A WAIF OF THE PLAINS. With 60 Illustrations by STANLEY L. WOOD.
A WARD OF THE GOLDEN GATE. With 59 Illustrations by STANLEY L. Woon.
A SAPPHO OF GREEN SPRINGS, &c. With Two Illustrations by HUME NISBET.
COLONEL STARBOTTLE'S CLIENT, AND SOME OTHER PEOPLE. With a
    Frontispiece by FRED. BARNARD.
SUSY: A Novel. With Frontispiece and Vignette by J. A. CHRISTIE.
SALLY DOWS, &c. With 47 Illustrations by W. D. ALMOND, &c.
A PROTÉGÉE OF JACK HAMLIN'S. With 25 Illustrations by A. S. BOYD, &c.

Post 8vo, illustrated boards, 2s. each.

GABRIEL CONROY.	THE LUCK OF ROARING CAMP, &c.
AN HEIRESS OF RED DOG, &c.	CALIFORNIAN STORIES.

Post 8vo, illustrated boards, 2s. each; cloth limp, 2s. 6d. each.

FLIP.	MARUJA.	A PHYLLIS OF THE SIERRAS.

Fcap. 8vo. picture cover, 1s. each.

THE TWINS OF TABLE MOUNTAIN.	JEFF BRIGGS'S LOVE STORY.
SNOW-BOUND AT EAGLE'S.	

BRYDGES.—UNCLE SAM AT HOME. By HAROLD BRYDGES. Post
8vo, illustrated boards, 2s.; cloth limp, 2s. 6d.

BUCHANAN'S (ROBERT) WORKS. Crown 8vo, cloth extra, 6s. each.
SELECTED POEMS OF ROBERT BUCHANAN. With Frontispiece by T. DALZIEL.
THE EARTHQUAKE; or, Six Days and a Sabbath.
THE CITY OF DREAM: An Epic Poem. With Two Illustrations by P. MACNAB.
THE WANDERING JEW: A Christmas Carol. Second Edition.
THE OUTCAST: A Rhyme for the Time. With 15 Illustrations by RUDOLF BLIND,
    PETER MACNAB, and HUME NISBET. Small demy 8vo, cloth extra, 8s.
ROBERT BUCHANAN'S COMPLETE POETICAL WORKS. With Steel-plate Por-
    trait. Crown 8vo, cloth extra, 7s. 6d.

Crown 8vo, cloth extra, 3s. 6d. each; post 8vo, illustrated boards, 2s. each.

THE SHADOW OF THE SWORD.	LOVE ME FOR EVER. Frontispiece.
A CHILD OF NATURE. Frontispiece.	ANNAN WATER.	FOXGLOVE MANOR.
GOD AND THE MAN. With 11 Illus-	THE NEW ABELARD.
trations by FRED. BARNARD.	MATT: A Story of a Caravan. Front.
THE MARTYRDOM OF MADELINE.	THE MASTER OF THE MINE. Front.
With Frontispiece by A. W. COOPER.	THE HEIR OF LINNE.
WOMAN AND THE MAN. 2 vols., crown 8vo.	

BURTON (CAPTAIN).—THE BOOK OF THE SWORD: Being a
History of the Sword and its Use in all Countries, from the Earliest Times. By
RICHARD F. BURTON. With over 400 Illustrations. Demy 4to, cloth extra, 32s.

BURTON (ROBERT).
THE ANATOMY OF MELANCHOLY: A New Edition, with translations of the
    Classical Extracts. Demy 8vo, cloth extra, 7s. 6d.
MELANCHOLY ANATOMISED Being an Abridgment, for popular use, of BURTON's
    ANATOMY OF MELANCHOLY. Post 8vo, cloth limp, 2s. 6d.

CAINE (T. HALL), NOVELS BY. Crown 8vo, cloth extra, 3s. 6d. each;
post 8vo, illustrated boards, 2s. each; cloth limp, 2s. 6d. each.
SHADOW OF A CRIME. | A SON OF HAGAR. | THE DEEMSTER.

CAMERON (COMMANDER).—THE CRUISE OF THE "BLACK
PRINCE" PRIVATEER. By V. LOVETT CAMERON, R.N. Post 8vo, boards, 2s.

CAMERON (MRS. H. LOVETT), NOVELS BY. Post 8vo, illust. bds., 2s. each.
JULIET'S GUARDIAN. | DECEIVERS EVER.

CARLYLE (THOMAS) ON THE CHOICE OF BOOKS. With Life
by R. H. SHEPHERD, and Three Illustrations. Post 8vo, cloth extra, **1s. 6d.**
CORRESPONDENCE OF THOMAS CARLYLE AND R. W. EMERSON, 1834 to 1872.
Edited by C. E. NORTON. With Portraits. Two Vols., crown 8vo, cloth, **24s.**

CARLYLE (JANE WELSH), LIFE OF. By Mrs. ALEXANDER IRELAND.
With Portrait and Facsimile Letter. Small demy 8vo, cloth extra, **7s. 6d.**

CHAPMAN'S (GEORGE) WORKS. Vol. I contains the Plays complete,
including the doubtful ones. Vol. II., the Poems and Minor Translations, with an
Introductory Essay by ALGERNON CHARLES SWINBURNE. Vol. III., the Translations
of the Iliad and Odyssey. Three Vols., crown 8vo, cloth extra, **6s.** each.

CHATTO AND JACKSON.—A TREATISE ON WOOD ENGRAVING.
By W. A. CHATTO and J. JACKSON. With 450 fine Illusts. Large 4to, hf.-bd., **28s.**

CHAUCER FOR CHILDREN: A Golden Key. By Mrs. H. R. HAWEIS.
With 8 Coloured Plates and 30 Woodcuts. Small 4to, cloth extra, **3s. 6d.**
CHAUCER FOR SCHOOLS. By Mrs. H. R. HAWEIS. Demy 8vo. cloth limp. **2s. 6d.**

CLARE.—FOR THE LOVE OF A LASS: A Tale of Tynedale. By
AUSTIN CLARE. Post 8vo, picture boards, **2s.**; cloth limp, **2s. 6d.**

CLIVE (MRS. ARCHER), NOVELS BY. Post 8vo, illust. boards **2s.** each.
PAUL FERROLL. | WHY PAUL FERROLL KILLED HIS WIFE.

CLODD.—MYTHS AND DREAMS. By EDWARD CLODD, F.R.A.S.
Second Edition, Revised. Crown 8vo, cloth extra, **3s. 6d.**

COBBAN (J. MACLAREN), NOVELS BY.
THE CURE OF SOULS. Post 8vo, illustrated boards, **2s.**
THE RED SULTAN. Crown 8vo, cloth extra, **3s. 6d.**
THE BURDEN OF ISABEL. Three Vols, crown 8vo.

COLEMAN (JOHN), WORKS BY.
PLAYERS AND PLAYWRIGHTS I HAVE KNOWN. Two Vols., 8vo, cloth, **24s.**
CURLY: An Actor's Story. With 21 Illusts. by J. C. DOLLMAN. Cr. 8vo. cl., **1s. 6d.**

COLERIDGE.—THE SEVEN SLEEPERS OF EPHESUS. By M. E.
COLERIDGE. Fcap. 8vo, cloth, **1s. 6d.**

COLLINS (C. ALLSTON).—THE BAR SINISTER. Post 8vo, 2s.

COLLINS (MORTIMER AND FRANCES), NOVELS BY.
Crown 8vo, cloth extra, **3s. 6d.** each; post 8vo, illustrated boards, **2s.** each.
FROM MIDNIGHT TO MIDNIGHT. | BLACKSMITH AND SCHOLAR.
TRANSMIGRATION. | YOU PLAY ME FALSE. | A VILLAGE COMEDY.
Post 8vo, illustrated boards, **2s.** each.
SWEET ANNE PAGE. | FIGHT WITH FORTUNE. | SWEET & TWENTY. | FRANCES.

COLLINS (WILKIE), NOVELS BY.
Cr. 8vo, cl. ex., **3s. 6d.** each; post 8vo, illust. bds., **2s.** each; cl. limp, **2s. 6d.** each.
ANTONINA. With a Frontispiece by Sir JOHN GILBERT, R.A.
BASIL. Illustrated by Sir JOHN GILBERT, R.A., and J. MAHONEY.
HIDE AND SEEK. Illustrated by Sir JOHN GILBERT, R.A., and J. MAHONEY.
AFTER DARK. Illustrations by A. B. HOUGHTON. | THE TWO DESTINIES.
THE DEAD SECRET. With a Frontispiece by Sir JOHN GILBERT, R.A.
QUEEN OF HEARTS. With a Frontispiece by Sir JOHN GILBERT, R.A.
THE WOMAN IN WHITE. With Illusts. by Sir J. GILBERT, R.A., and F. A. FRASER.
NO NAME. With Illustrations by Sir J. E. MILLAIS, R.A., and A. W. COOPER.
MY MISCELLANIES. With a Steel-plate Portrait of WILKIE COLLINS.
ARMADALE. With Illustrations by G. H. THOMAS.
THE MOONSTONE. With Illustrations by G. DU MAURIER and F. A. FRASER.
MAN AND WIFE. With Illustrations by WILLIAM SMALL.
POOR MISS FINCH. Illustrated by G. DU MAURIER and EDWARD HUGHES.
MISS OR MRS.? With Illusts. by S. L. FILDES, R.A., and HENRY WOODS, A.R.A.
THE NEW MAGDALEN. Illustrated by G. DU MAURIER and C. S. REINHARDT.
THE FROZEN DEEP. Illustrated by G. DU MAURIER and J. MAHONEY.
THE LAW AND THE LADY. Illusts. by S. L. FILDES, R.A., and SYDNEY HALL.
THE HAUNTED HOTEL. Illustrated by ARTHUR HOPKINS.
THE FALLEN LEAVES. | HEART AND SCIENCE. | THE EVIL GENIUS.
JEZEBEL'S DAUGHTER. | "I SAY NO." | LITTLE NOVELS.
THE BLACK ROBE. | A ROGUE'S LIFE. | THE LEGACY OF CAIN.
BLIND LOVE. With Preface by WALTER BESANT, and Illusts. by A. FORESTIER.

COLLINS (JOHN CHURTON, M.A.), BOOKS BY.
ILLUSTRATIONS OF TENNYSON. Crown 8vo, cloth extra, **6s.**
JONATHAN SWIFT: A Biographical and Critical Study. Crown 8vo, cloth extra **8s.**

COLMAN'S (GEORGE) HUMOROUS WORKS: " Broad Grins," " My
Nightgown and Slippers," &c. With Life and Frontis. Cr. 8vo. cl. extra, 7s. 6d.

COLQUHOUN.—EVERY INCH A SOLDIER: A Novel. By M. J.
COLQUHOUN. Post 8vo, illustrated boards, 2s.

CONVALESCENT COOKERY: A Family Handbook. By CATHERINE
RYAN. Crown 8vo, 1s.; cloth limp, 1s. 6d.

CONWAY (MONCURE D.), WORKS BY.
DEMONOLOGY AND DEVIL-LORE. 65 Illustrations. Two Vols., 8vo, cloth 28s.
A NECKLACE OF STORIES. 25 Illusts. by W. J. HENNESSY. Sq. 8vo, cloth, 6s.
GEORGE WASHINGTON'S RULES OF CIVILITY. Fcap. 8vo, Jap. vellum, 2s. 6d.

COOK (DUTTON), NOVELS BY.
PAUL FOSTER'S DAUGHTER. Cr. 8vo, cl. ex., 3s. 6d.; post 8vo, illust. boards, 2s.
LEO. Post 8vo, illustrated boards, 2s.

COOPER (EDWARD H.)—GEOFFORY HAMILTON. Cr. 8vo, 3s. 6d.

CORNWALL.—POPULAR ROMANCES OF THE WEST OF ENG-
LAND; or, The Drolls, Traditions, and Superstitions of Old Cornwall. Collected
by ROBERT HUNT, F.R.S. Two Steel-plates by GEO. CRUIKSHANK. Cr. 8vo, cl., 7s. 6d.

COTES.—TWO GIRLS ON A BARGE. By V. CECIL COTES. With
44 Illustrations by F. H. TOWNSEND. Crown 8vo, cloth extra, 3s. 6d.

CRADDOCK.—THE PROPHET OF THE GREAT SMOKY MOUN-
TAINS. By CHARLES EGBERT CRADDOCK. Post 8vo, illust. bds., 2s.; cl. limp, 2s. 6d.

CRELLIN (H. N.)—THE NAZARENES: A Drama. Crown 8vo, 1s.

CRIM.—ADVENTURES OF A FAIR REBEL. By MATT CRIM. With
a Frontispiece. Crown 8vo, cloth extra, 3s. 6d.; post 8vo, illustrated boards, 2s.

CROKER (B.M.), NOVELS BY. Crown 8vo, cloth extra, 3s. 6d. each; post
8vo, illustrated boards, 2s. each; cloth limp, 2s. 6d. each.
PRETTY MISS NEVILLE. | DIANA BARRINGTON.
A BIRD OF PASSAGE. | PROPER PRIDE.
A FAMILY LIKENESS. | "TO LET."

CRUIKSHANK'S COMIC ALMANACK. Complete in TWO SERIES:
The FIRST from 1835 to 1843; the SECOND from 1844 to 1853. A Gathering of
the BEST HUMOUR of THACKERAY, HOOD, MAYHEW, ALBERT SMITH, A'BECKETT,
ROBERT BROUGH, &c. With numerous Steel Engravings and Woodcuts by CRUIK-
SHANK, HINE, LANDELLS, &c. Two Vols., crown 8vo, cloth gilt, 7s. 6d. each.
THE LIFE OF GEORGE CRUIKSHANK. By BLANCHARD JERROLD. With 84
Illustrations and a Bibliography. Crown 8vo, cloth extra, 7s. 6d.

CUMMING (C. F. GORDON), WORKS BY. Demy 8vo, cl. ex., 8s. 6d. each.
IN THE HEBRIDES. With Autotype Facsimile and 23 Illustrations.
IN THE HIMALAYAS AND ON THE INDIAN PLAINS. With 42 Illustrations.
TWO HAPPY YEARS IN CEYLON. With 28 Illustrations.
VIA CORNWALL TO EGYPT. With Photogravure Frontis. Demy 8vo, cl., 7s. 6d.

CUSSANS.—A HANDBOOK OF HERALDRY; with Instructions for
Tracing Pedigrees and Deciphering Ancient MSS., &c. By JOHN E. CUSSANS. With
408 Woodcuts and 2 Coloured Plates. Fourth edition, revised, crown 8vo, cloth, 6s.

CYPLES(W.)—HEARTS of GOLD. Cr. 8vo, cl., 3s. 6d.; post 8vo, bds., 2s.

DANIEL.—MERRIE ENGLAND IN THE OLDEN TIME. By GEORGE
DANIEL. With Illustrations by ROBERT CRUIKSHANK. Crown 8vo, cloth extra, 3s. 6d.

DAUDET.—THE EVANGELIST; or, Port Salvation. By ALPHONSE
DAUDET. Crown 8vo, cloth extra, 3s. 6d.; post 8vo, illustrated boards, 2s.

DAVENANT.—HINTS FOR PARENTS ON THE CHOICE OF A PRO-
FESSION FOR THEIR SONS. By F. DAVENANT, M.A. Post 8vo, 1s.; cl., 1s. 6d.

DAVIES (DR. N. E. YORKE-), WORKS BY. Cr. 8vo, 1s. ea.; cl., 1s. 6d. ea.
ONE THOUSAND MEDICAL MAXIMS AND SURGICAL HINTS.
NURSERY HINTS: A Mother's Guide in Health and Disease.
FOODS FOR THE FAT: A Treatise on Corpulency, and a Dietary for its Cure.
AIDS TO LONG LIFE. Crown 8vo. 2s.; cloth limp, 2s. 6d.

DAVIES' (SIR JOHN) COMPLETE POETICAL WORKS, for the first time Collected and Edited, with Memorial-Introduction and Notes, by the Rev. A. B. GROSART, D.D. Two Vols., crown 8vo. cloth boards, **12s.**

DAWSON.—THE FOUNTAIN OF YOUTH: A Novel of Adventure. By ERASMUS DAWSON, M.B. Edited by PAUL DEVON. With Two Illustrations by HUME NISBET. Crown 8vo, cloth extra, **3s. 6d.**; post 8vo, illustrated boards, **2s.**

DE GUERIN.—THE JOURNAL OF MAURICE DE GUERIN. Edited by G. S. TREBUTIEN. With a Memoir by SAINTE-BEUVE. Translated from the 20th French Edition by JESSIE P. FROTHINGHAM. Fcap, 8vo, half-bound, **2s. 6d.**

DE MAISTRE.—A JOURNEY ROUND MY ROOM. By XAVIER DE MAISTRE. Translated by HENRY ATTWELL. Post 8vo, cloth limp, **2s. 6d.**

DE MILLE.—A CASTLE IN SPAIN. By JAMES DE MILLE. With a Frontispiece. Crown 8vo, cloth extra, **3s. 6d.**; post 8vo, illustrated boards, **2s.**

DERBY (THE).—THE BLUE RIBBON OF THE TURF: A Chronicle of the RACE FOR THE DERBY, from Diomed to Donovan. With Brief Accounts of THE OAKS. By LOUIS HENRY CURZON. Crown 8vo, cloth limp, **2s. 6d.**

DERWENT (LEITH), NOVELS BY. Cr.8vo,cl., **3s.6d.** ea.; post 8vo,bds.,**2s.**ea.
OUR LADY OF TEARS. | CIRCE'S LOVERS.

DICKENS (CHARLES), NOVELS BY. Post 8vo, illustrated boards, **2s.** each.
SKETCHES BY BOZ. | NICHOLAS NICKLEBY.
THE PICKWICK PAPERS. | OLIVER TWIST.
THE SPEECHES OF CHARLES DICKENS, 1841–1870. With a New Bibliography. Edited by RICHARD HERNE SHEPHERD. Crown 8vo, cloth extra, **6s.**—Also a SMALLER EDITION, in the *Mayfair Library*, post 8vo, cloth limp, **2s. 6d.**
ABOUT ENGLAND WITH DICKENS. By ALFRED RIMMER. With 57 Illustrations by C. A. VANDERHOOF, ALFRED RIMMER, and others. Sq. 8vo, cloth extra, **7s. 6d.**

DICTIONARIES.
A DICTIONARY OF MIRACLES: Imitative, Realistic, and Dogmatic. By the Rev. E. C. BREWER, LL.D. Crown 8vo, cloth extra, **7s. 6d.**
THE READER'S HANDBOOK OF ALLUSIONS, REFERENCES, PLOTS, AND STORIES. By the Rev. E. C. BREWER, LL.D. With an ENGLISH BIBLIOGRAPHY. Fifteenth Thousand. Crown 8vo, cloth extra, **7s. 6d.**
AUTHORS AND THEIR WORKS, WITH THE DATES. Cr. 8vo, cloth limp, **2s.**
FAMILIAR SHORT SAYINGS OF GREAT MEN. With Historical and Explanatory Notes. By SAMUEL A. BENT, A.M. Crown 8vo, cloth extra, **7s. 6d.**
SLANG DICTIONARY: Etymological, Historical, and Anecdotal. Cr. 8vo, cl., **6s. 6d.**
WOMEN OF THE DAY: A Biographical Dictionary. By F. HAYS. Cr. 8vo, cl., **5s.**
WORDS, FACTS, AND PHRASES: A Dictionary of Curious, Quaint, and Out-of-the-Way Matters. By ELIEZER EDWARDS. Crown 8vo, cloth extra, **7s. 6d.**

DIDEROT.—THE PARADOX OF ACTING. Translated, with Annotations, from Diderot's " Le Paradoxe sur le Comédien," by WALTER HERRIES POLLOCK. With a Preface by HENRY IRVING. Crown 8vo, parchment, **4s. 6d.**

DOBSON (AUSTIN), WORKS BY.
THOMAS BEWICK & HIS PUPILS. With 95 Illustrations. Square 8vo, cloth. **6s.**
FOUR FRENCHWOMEN. With 4 Portraits. Crown 8vo, buckram, gilt top, **6s.**
EIGHTEENTH CENTURY VIGNETTES. Crown 8vo, buckram, gilt top, **6s.**—A SECOND SERIES, uniform in size and price, is now in preparation.

DOBSON (W. T.)—POETICAL INGENUITIES AND ECCENTRICI-TIES. Post 8vo, cloth limp, **2s. 6d.**

DONOVAN (DICK), DETECTIVE STORIES BY.
Post 8vo, illustrated boards, **2s.** each; cloth limp, **2s. 6d.** each.
THE MAN-HUNTER. | WANTED! | A DETECTIVE'S TRIUMPHS.
CAUGHT AT LAST! | IN THE GRIP OF THE LAW.
TRACKED AND TAKEN. | FROM INFORMATION RECEIVED.
WHO POISONED HETTY DUNCAN? | LINK BY LINK.
SUSPICION AROUSED.
Crown 8vo, cloth extra, **3s. 6d.** each; post 8vo, illustrated boards, **2s.** each; cloth limp, **2s. 6d.** each.
THE MAN FROM MANCHESTER. With 23 Illustrations.
TRACKED TO DOOM. With 6 full-page Illustrations by GORDON BROWNE.

DOYLE (CONAN).—THE FIRM OF GIRDLESTONE. By A. CONAN DOYLE, Author of " Micah Clarke." Crown 8vo, cloth extra, **3s. 6d.**

8 BOOKS PUBLISHED BY

DRAMATISTS, THE OLD. With Vignette Portraits. Cr. 8vo, cl. ex., 6s. per Vol.
BEN JONSON'S WORKS. With Notes Critical and Explanatory, and a Bio-
graphical Memoir by WM. GIFFORD. Edited by Col. CUNNINGHAM. Three Vols.
CHAPMAN'S WORKS. Complete in Three Vols. Vol. I. contains the Plays
complete; Vol. II., Poems and Minor Translations, with an Introductory Essay
by A. C. SWINBURNE; Vol. III., Translations of the Iliad and Odyssey.
MARLOWE'S WORKS. Edited, with Notes, by Col. CUNNINGHAM. One Vol.
MASSINGER'S PLAYS. From GIFFORD's Text. Edit by Col.CUNNINGHAM. OneVol.

DUNCAN (SARA JEANNETTE), WORKS BY.
Crown 8vo, cloth extra, 7s. 6d. each.
A SOCIAL DEPARTURE: How Orthodocia and I Went round the World by Our-
selves. With 111 Illustrations by F. H. TOWNSEND.
AN AMERICAN GIRL IN LONDON. With 80 Illustrations by F. H. TOWNSEND.
THE SIMPLE ADVENTURES OF A MEMSAHIB. Illustrated by F. H. TOWNSEND.
A DAUGHTER OF TO-DAY. Two Vols., crown 8vo. [Shortly.

DYER.—THE FOLK-LORE OF PLANTS. By Rev. T. F. THISELTON
DYER, M.A. Crown 8vo, cloth extra, 6s.

EARLY ENGLISH POETS. Edited, with Introductions and Annota-
tions, by Rev. A. B. GROSART, D.D. Crown 8vo, cloth boards, 6s. per Volume.
FLETCHER'S (GILES) COMPLETE POEMS. One Vol.
DAVIES' (SIR JOHN) COMPLETE POETICAL WORKS. Two Vols.
HERRICK'S (ROBERT) COMPLETE COLLECTED POEMS. Three Vols.
SIDNEY'S (SIR PHILIP) COMPLETE POETICAL WORKS. Three Vols.

EDGCUMBE.—ZEPHYRUS : A Holiday in Brazil and on the River Plate.
By E. R. PEARCE EDGCUMBE. With 41 Illustrations. Crown 8vo, cloth extra, 5s.

EDWARDES (MRS. ANNIE), NOVELS BY:
A POINT OF HONOUR. Post 8vo, illustrated boards, 2s.
ARCHIE LOVELL. Crown 8vo, cloth extra, 3s. 6d.; post 8vo, illust. boards, 2s.

EDWARDS (ELIEZER).—WORDS, FACTS, AND PHRASES: A
Dictionary of Curious, Quaint, and Out-of-the-Way Matters. By ELIEZER EDWARDS.
Crown 8vo, cloth extra, 7s. 6d.

EDWARDS (M. BETHAM-), NOVELS BY.
KITTY. Post 8vo, illustrated boards, 2s.; cloth limp, 2s. 6d.
FELICIA. Post 8vo, illustrated boards, 2s.

EGERTON.—SUSSEX FOLK & SUSSEX WAYS. By Rev. J. C. EGERTON.
With Introduction by Rev. Dr. H. WACE, and 4 Illustrations. Cr. 8vo, cloth ex., 5s.

EGGLESTON (EDWARD).—ROXY : A Novel. Post 8vo, illust. bds., 2s.

ENGLISHMAN'S HOUSE, THE : A Practical Guide to all interested in
Selecting or Building a House; with Estimates of Cost, Quantities, &c. By C. J.
RICHARDSON. With Coloured Frontispiece and 600 Illusts. Crown 8vo, cloth, 7s. 6d.

EWALD (ALEX. CHARLES, F.S.A.), WORKS BY.
THE LIFE AND TIMES OF PRINCE CHARLES STUART, Count of Albany
(THE YOUNG PRETENDER). With a Portrait. Crown 8vo, cloth extra, 7s. 6d.
STORIES FROM THE STATE PAPERS. With an Autotype. Crown 8vo, cloth, 6s.

EYES, OUR : How to Preserve Them from Infancy to Old Age. By
JOHN BROWNING, F.R.A.S. With 70 Illusts. Eighteenth Thousand. Crown 8vo, 1s.

FAMILIAR SHORT SAYINGS OF GREAT MEN. By SAMUEL ARTHUR
BENT, A.M. Fifth Edition, Revised and Enlarged. Crown 8vo, cloth extra, 7s. 6d.

FARADAY (MICHAEL), WORKS BY. Post 8vo, cloth extra, 4s. 6d. each.
THE CHEMICAL HISTORY OF A CANDLE: Lectures delivered before a Juvenile
Audience. Edited by WILLIAM CROOKES, F.C.S. With numerous Illustrations.
ON THE VARIOUS FORCES OF NATURE, AND THEIR RELATIONS TO
EACH OTHER. Edited by WILLIAM CROOKES, F.C.S. With Illustrations.

FARRER (J. ANSON), WORKS BY.
MILITARY MANNERS AND CUSTOMS. Crown 8vo, cloth extra, 6s.
WAR: Three Essays, reprinted from "Military Manners." Cr. 8vo, 1s.; cl., 1s. 6d.

FENN (G. MANVILLE), NOVELS BY.
THE NEW MISTRESS. Cr. 8vo, cloth extra, 3s. 6d.; post 8vo, illust. boards, 2s.
WITNESS TO THE DEED. Crown 8vo, cloth extra. 3s. 6d.
THE TIGER LILY: A Tale of Two Passions. Two Vols.

FIN-BEC.—THE CUPBOARD PAPERS: Observations on the Art of Living and Dining. By FIN-BEC. Post 8vo, cloth limp, 2s. 6d.

FIREWORKS, THE COMPLETE ART OF MAKING; or, The Pyrotechnist's Treasury. By THOMAS KENTISH. With 267 Illustrations. Cr. 8vo, cl., 5s.

FITZGERALD (PERCY, M.A., F.S.A.), WORKS BY.
THE WORLD BEHIND THE SCENES. Crown 8vo, cloth extra, 3s. 6d.
LITTLE ESSAYS: Passages from Letters of CHARLES LAMB. Post 8vo, cl., 2s. 6d.
A DAY'S TOUR: Journey through France and Belgium. With Sketches. Cr. 4to, 1s.
FATAL ZERO. Crown 8vo, cloth extra, 3s. 6d.; post 8vo, illustrated boards, 2s.
Post 8vo, illustrated boards, 2s. each.
BELLA DONNA. | LADY OF BRANTOME. | THE SECOND MRS. TILLOTSON.
POLLY. | NEVER FORGOTTEN. | SEVENTY-FIVE BROOKE STREET.
LIFE OF JAMES BOSWELL (of Auchinleck). With an Account of his Sayings, Doings, and Writings; and Four Portraits. Two Vols., demy 8vo, cloth, 21s.
THE SAVOY OPERA. With numerous Illustrations and a Portrait. Crown 8vo, cloth extra, 6s. [Shortly.

FLAMMARION (CAMILLE), WORKS BY.
POPULAR ASTRONOMY: A General Description of the Heavens. By CAMILLE FLAMMARION. Translated by J. ELLARD GORE, F.R.A.S. With nearly 300 Illustrations. Medium 8vo, cloth extra, 16s. [Preparing.
URANIA: A Romance. Translated by A. R. STETSON. With 87 Illustrations by DE BIELER, MYRBACH, &c. Crown 8vo, cloth extra, 5s.

FLETCHER'S (GILES, B.D.) COMPLETE POEMS: Christ's Victorie in Heaven, Christ's Victorie on Earth, Christ's Triumph over Death, and Minor Poems. With Notes by Rev. A. B. GROSART, D.D. Crown 8vo, cloth boards, 6s.

FONBLANQUE (ALBANY).—FILTHY LUCRE. Post 8vo, illust. bds., 2s.

FRANCILLON (R. E.), NOVELS BY.
Crown 8vo, cloth extra, 3s. 6d. each; post 8vo, illustrated boards, 2s. each.
ONE BY ONE. | QUEEN COPHETUA. | A REAL QUEEN. | KING OR KNAVE?
Crown 8vo, cloth extra, 3s. 6d. each.
ROPES OF SAND. | A DOG AND HIS SHADOW.
OLYMPIA. Post 8vo, illust. bds., 2s. | ESTHER'S GLOVE. Fcap. 8vo, pict. cover, 1s.
ROMANCES OF THE LAW. Post 8vo, illustrated boards, 2s.

FREDERIC (HAROLD), NOVELS BY. Post 8vo, illust. bds., 2s. each.
SETH'S BROTHER'S WIFE. | THE LAWTON GIRL.

FRENCH LITERATURE, A HISTORY OF. By HENRY VAN LAUN. Three Vols., demy 8vo, cloth boards, 7s. 6d. each.

FRERE.—PANDURANG HARI; or, Memoirs of a Hindoo. With Preface by Sir BARTLE FRERE. Crown 8vo, cloth, 3s. 6d.; post 8vo, illust. bds., 2s.

FRISWELL (HAIN).—ONE OF TWO: A Novel. Post 8vo, illust. bds., 2s.

FROST (THOMAS), WORKS BY. Crown 8vo, cloth extra, 3s. 6d. each.
CIRCUS LIFE AND CIRCUS CELEBRITIES. | LIVES OF THE CONJURERS.
THE OLD SHOWMEN AND THE OLD LONDON FAIRS.

FRY'S (HERBERT) ROYAL GUIDE TO THE LONDON CHARITIES. Showing their Name, Date of Foundation, Objects, Income, Officials, &c. Edited by JOHN LANE. Published Annually. Crown 8vo, cloth, 1s. 6d.

GARDENING BOOKS. Post 8vo, 1s. each; cloth limp, 1s. 6d. each.
A YEAR'S WORK IN GARDEN AND GREENHOUSE. By GEORGE GLENNY.
HOUSEHOLD HORTICULTURE. By TOM and JANE JERROLD. Illustrated.
THE GARDEN THAT PAID THE RENT. By TOM JERROLD.
OUR KITCHEN GARDEN. By TOM JERROLD. Crown 8vo, cloth, 1s. 6d.
MY GARDEN WILD. By FRANC'S G. HEATH. Crown 8vo, cloth extra, 6s.

GARRETT.—THE CAPEL GIRLS: A Novel. By EDWARD GARRETT. Crown 8vo, cloth extra, 3s. 6d.; post 8vo, illustrated boards, 2s.

GAULOT.—THE RED SHIRTS: A Story of the Revolution. By PAUL GAULOT. Translated by J. A. J. DE VILLIERS. Crown 8vo, cloth, 3s. 6d. [Shortly.

GENTLEMAN'S MAGAZINE, THE. 1s. Monthly. In addition to Articles upon subjects in Literature, Science, and Art, "TABLE TALK" by SYLVANUS URBAN, and "PAGES ON PLAYS" by JUSTIN H. McCARTHY, appear monthly.
. Bound Volumes for recent years kept in stock. 8s. 6d. each. Cases for binding, 2s.

GENTLEMAN'S ANNUAL, THE. Published Annually in November. 1s.

GERMAN POPULAR STORIES. Collected by the Brothers GRIMM
and Translated by EDGAR TAYLOR. With Introduction by JOHN RUSKIN, and 22 Steel
Plates after GEORGE CRUIKSHANK. Square 8vo, cloth, 6s. 6d.; gilt edges, 7s. 6d.

GIBBON (CHARLES), NOVELS BY.
Crown 8vo, cloth extra, 3s. 6d. each; post 8vo, illustrated boards, 2s. each.

ROBIN GRAY. | LOVING A DREAM. | THE GOLDEN SHAFT.
THE FLOWER OF THE FOREST. | OF HIGH DEGREE.

Post 8vo, illustrated boards, 2s. each.

THE DEAD HEART. | IN LOVE AND WAR.
FOR LACK OF GOLD. | A HEART'S PROBLEM.
WHAT WILL THE WORLD SAY? | BY MEAD AND STREAM.
FOR THE KING. | A HARD KNOT. | THE BRAES OF YARROW.
QUEEN OF THE MEADOW. | FANCY FREE. | IN HONOUR BOUND.
IN PASTURES GREEN. | HEART'S DELIGHT. | BLOOD-MONEY.

GIBNEY (SOMERVILLE).—SENTENCED! Cr. 8vo, 1s. ; cl., 1s. 6d.

GILBERT (WILLIAM), NOVELS BY. Post 8vo, illustrated boards, 2s. each.
DR. AUSTIN'S GUESTS. | JAMES DUKE, COSTERMONGER.
THE WIZARD OF THE MOUNTAIN. |

GILBERT (W. S.), ORIGINAL PLAYS BY. Two Series, 2s. 6d. each.
The FIRST SERIES contains: The Wicked World—Pygmalion and Galatea—
Charity—The Princess—The Palace of Truth—Trial by Jury.
The SECOND SERIES: Broken Hearts—Engaged—Sweethearts—Gretchen—Dan'l
Druce—Tom Cobb—H.M.S. " Pinafore "—The Sorcerer—Pirates of Penzance.

EIGHT ORIGINAL COMIC OPERAS written by W. S. GILBERT. Containing:
The Sorcerer—H.M.S. "Pinafore"—Pirates of Penzance—Iolanthe—Patience—
Princess Ida—The Mikado—Trial by Jury. Demy 8vo, cloth limp, 2s. 6d.
THE "GILBERT AND SULLIVAN" BIRTHDAY BOOK: Quotations for Every
Day in the Year, Selected from Plays by W. S. GILBERT set to Music by Sir A.
SULLIVAN. Compiled by ALEX. WATSON. Royal 16mo, Jap. leather, 2s. 6d.

GLANVILLE (ERNEST), NOVELS BY.
Crown 8vo, cloth extra, 3s. 6d. each; post 8vo, illustrated boards, 2s. each.
THE LOST HEIRESS: A Tale of Love, Battle, and Adventure. With 2 Illusts.
THE FOSSICKER: A Romance of Mashonaland. With 2 Illusts. by HUME NISBET.
A FAIR COLONIST. With a Frontispiece. Cr. 8vo, cl. extra, 3s. 6d.

GLENNY.—A YEAR'S WORK IN GARDEN AND GREENHOUSE:
Practical Advice to Amateur Gardeners as to the Management of the Flower, Fruit,
and Frame Garden. By GEORGE GLENNY. Post 8vo, 1s.; cloth limp, 1s. 6d.

GODWIN.—LIVES OF THE NECROMANCERS. By WILLIAM GOD-
WIN. Post 8vo, cloth limp, 2s.

GOLDEN TREASURY OF THOUGHT, THE: An Encyclopædia of
QUOTATIONS. Edited by THEODORE TAYLOR. Crown 8vo, cloth gilt, 7s. 6d.

GOODMAN.—THE FATE OF HERBERT WAYNE. By E. J. GOOD-
MAN, Author of "Too Curious." Crown 8vo, cloth, 3s. 6d.

GOWING.—FIVE THOUSAND MILES IN A SLEDGE: A Midwinter
Journey Across Siberia. By LIONEL F. GOWING. With 30 Illustrations by C. J.
UREN, and a Map by E. WELLER. Large crown 8vo, cloth extra, 8s.

GRAHAM.—THE PROFESSOR'S WIFE: A Story   By LEONARD
GRAHAM. Fcap. 8vo, picture cover, 1s.

GREEKS AND ROMANS, THE LIFE OF THE, described from
Antique Monuments. By ERNST GUHL and W. KONER. Edited by Dr. F. HUEFFER.
With 545 Illustrations. Large crown 8vo, cloth extra, 7s. 6d.

GREENWOOD (JAMES), WORKS BY. Cr. 8vo. cloth extra, 3s. 6d. each.
THE WILDS OF LONDON. | LOW-LIFE DEEPS.

GREVILLE (HENRY), NOVELS BY:
NIKANOR. Translated by ELIZA E. CHASE. With 8 Illustrations. Crown 8vo,
cloth extra, 6s.; post 8vo, illustrated boards, 2s.
A NOBLE WOMAN. Crown 8vo, cloth extra, 5s.; post 8vo, illustrated boards, 2s.

GRIFFITH.—CORINTHIA MARAZION: A Novel. By CECIL GRIF-
FITH, Crown 8vo, cloth extra, 3s. 6d.; post 8vo, illustrated boards, 2s.

GRUNDY.—THE DAYS OF HIS VANITY: A Passage in the Life of
a Young Man. By SYDNEY GRUNDY. Crown 8vo, cloth extra, 3s. 6d.

HABBERTON (JOHN, Author of "Helen's Babies"), NOVELS BY.
Post 8vo, illustrated boards **2s.** each; cloth limp, **2s. 6d.** each.
BRUETON'S BAYOU. | COUNTRY LUCK.

HAIR, THE : Its Treatment in Health, Weakness, and Disease. Translated from the German of Dr. J. Pincus. Crown 8vo, **1s.**; cloth, **1s. 6d.**

HAKE (DR. THOMAS GORDON), POEMS BY. Cr. 8vo, cl. ex., **6s.** each.
NEW SYMBOLS. | LEGENDS OF THE MORROW. | THE SERPENT PLAY.
MAIDEN ECSTASY. Small 4to, cloth extra, **8s.**

HALL.—SKETCHES OF IRISH CHARACTER. By Mrs. S. C. Hall.
With numerous Illustrations on Steel and Wood by Maclise, Gilbert, Harvey, and George Cruikshank. Medium 8vo, cloth extra, **7s. 6d.**

HALLIDAY (ANDR.).—EVERY-DAY PAPERS. Post 8vo, bds., **2s.**

HANDWRITING, THE PHILOSOPHY OF. With over 100 Facsimiles and Explanatory Text. By Don Felix de Salamanca. Post 8vo, cloth limp, **2s. 6d.**

HANKY-PANKY : Easy Tricks, White Magic, Sleight of Hand, &c.
Edited by W. H. Cremer. With 200 Illustrations. Crown 8vo, cloth extra, **4s. 6d.**

HARDY (LADY DUFFUS).—PAUL WYNTER'S SACRIFICE. 2s.

HARDY (THOMAS).—UNDER THE GREENWOOD TREE. By Thomas Hardy, Author of "Tess." With Portrait and 15 Illustrations. Crown 8vo, cloth extra, **3s. 6d.**; post 8vo, illustrated boards, **2s.**; cloth limp, **2s. 6d.**

HARPER (CHARLES G.), WORKS BY. Demy 8vo, cloth extra, **16s.** each.
THE BRIGHTON ROAD. With Photogravure Frontispiece and 90 Illustrations.
FROM PADDINGTON TO PENZANCE: The Record of a Summer Tramp. 105 Illusts.

HARWOOD.—THE TENTH EARL. By J. Berwick Harwood. Post 8vo, illustrated boards, **2s.**

HAWEIS (MRS. H. R.), WORKS BY. Square 8vo, cloth extra, **6s.** each.
THE ART OF BEAUTY. With Coloured Frontispiece and 91 Illustrations.
THE ART OF DECORATION. With Coloured Frontispiece and 74 Illustrations.
THE ART OF DRESS. With 32 Illustrations. Post 8vo, **1s.**; cloth, **1s. 6d.**
CHAUCER FOR SCHOOLS. Demy 8vo, cloth limp, **2s. 6d.**
CHAUCER FOR CHILDREN. 38 Illusts. (8 Coloured). Sm. 4to, cl. extra, **3s. 6d.**

HAWEIS (Rev. H. R., M. A.).—AMERICAN HUMORISTS : Washington Irving, Oliver Wendell Holmes, James Russell Lowell, Artemus Ward, Mark Twain, and Bret Harte. Third Edition. Crown 8vo, cloth extra, **6s.**

HAWLEY SMART.—WITHOUT LOVE OR LICENCE: A Novel. By Hawley Smart. Crown 8vo, cloth extra, **3s. 6d.**; post 8vo, illustrated boards, **2s.**

HAWTHORNE. —OUR OLD HOME. By Nathaniel Hawthorne.
Annotated with Passages from the Author's Note-book, and Illustrated with 31 Photogravures. Two Vols., crown 8vo, buckram, gilt top, **15s.**

HAWTHORNE (JULIAN), NOVELS BY.
Crown 8vo, cloth extra, **3s. 6d.** each; post 8vo, illustrated boards, **2s.** each.
GARTH. | ELLICE QUENTIN. | BEATRIX RANDOLPH. | DUST.
SEBASTIAN STROME. | | DAVID POINDEXTER.
FORTUNE'S FOOL. | | THE SPECTRE OF THE CAMERA.

Post 8vo, illustrated boards, **2s.** each.
MISS CADOGNA. | LOVE—OR A NAME.
MRS. GAINSBOROUGH'S DIAMONDS. Fcap. 8vo. illustrated cover, **1s.**

HEATH.—MY GARDEN WILD, AND WHAT I GREW THERE.
By Francis George Heath. Crown 8vo, cloth extra, gilt edges, **6s.**

HELPS (SIR ARTHUR), WORKS BY. Post 8vo, cloth limp, **2s. 6d.** each.
ANIMALS AND THEIR MASTERS. | SOCIAL PRESSURE.
IVAN DE BIRON: A Novel. Cr. 8vo, cl. extra, **3s. 6d.**; post 8vo, illust. bds., **2s.**

HENDERSON.—AGATHA PAGE : A Novel. By Isaac Henderson.
Crown 8vo, cloth extra, **3s. 6d.**

HENTY.—RUJUB, THE JUGGLER. By G. A. Henty. With 8 Illustrations by Stanley L. Wood. Crown 8vo, cloth extra, gilt edges, **5s.**

HERMAN.—A LEADING LADY. By Henry Herman, joint-Author of "The Bishops' Bible." Post 8vo, illustrated boards, **2s.**; cloth extra, **2s. 6d.**

HERRICK'S (ROBERT) HESPERIDES, NOBLE NUMBERS, AND COMPLETE COLLECTED POEMS. With Memorial-Introduction and Notes by the Rev. A. B. GROSART, D.D.; Steel Portrait, &c. Three Vols., crown 8vo, cl. bds., 18s.

HERTZKA.—FREELAND: A Social Anticipation. By Dr. THEODOR HERTZKA. Translated by ARTHUR RANSOM. Crown 8vo, cloth extra, 6s.

HESSE-WARTEGG.—TUNIS: The Land and the People. By Chevalier ERNST VON HESSE-WARTEGG. With 22 Illustrations. Cr. 8vo, cloth extra, 3s. 6d.

HILL (HEADON).—ZAMBRA THE DETECTIVE. By HEADON HILL. Post 8vo, illustrated boards, 2s.; cloth, 2s. 6d.

HILL (JOHN, M.A.), WORKS BY.
TREASON-FELONY. Post 8vo, 2s. | THE COMMON ANCESTOR. Three Vols.

HINDLEY (CHARLES), WORKS BY.
TAVERN ANECDOTES AND SAYINGS: Including Reminiscences connected with Coffee Houses, Clubs, &c. With Illustrations. Crown 8vo, cloth, 3s. 6d.
THE LIFE AND ADVENTURES OF A CHEAP JACK. Cr. 8vo. cloth ex., 3s. 6d.

HOEY.—THE LOVER'S CREED. By Mrs. CASHEL HOEY. Post 8vo, 2s.

HOLLINGSHEAD (JOHN).—NIAGARA SPRAY. Crown 8vo, 1s.

HOLMES.—THE SCIENCE OF VOICE PRODUCTION AND VOICE PRESERVATION. By GORDON HOLMES, M.D. Crown 8vo, 1s.; cloth, 1s. 6d.

HOLMES (OLIVER WENDELL), WORKS BY.
THE AUTOCRAT OF THE BREAKFAST-TABLE. Illustrated by J. GORDON THOMSON. Post 8vo, cloth limp 2s. 6d.—Another Edition, post 8vo, cloth, 2s.
THE AUTOCRAT OF THE BREAKFAST-TABLE and THE PROFESSOR AT THE BREAKFAST-TABLE. In One Vol. Post 8vo, half-bound, 2s.

HOOD'S (THOMAS) CHOICE WORKS, in Prose and Verse. With Life of the Author, Portrait, and 200 Illustrations. Crown 8vo, cloth extra, 7s. 6d.
HOOD'S WHIMS AND ODDITIES. With 85 Illusts. Post 8vo, half-bound, 2s.

HOOD (TOM).—FROM NOWHERE TO THE NORTH POLE: A Noah's Arkæological Narrative. By TOM HOOD. With 25 Illustrations by W. BRUNTON and E. C. BARNES. Square 8vo, cloth extra, gilt edges, 6s.

HOOK'S (THEODORE) CHOICE HUMOROUS WORKS; including his Ludicrous Adventures, Bons Mots, Puns, and Hoaxes. With Life of the Author, Portraits, Facsimiles, and Illustrations. Crown 8vo, cloth extra, 7s. 6d.

HOOPER.—THE HOUSE OF RABY: A Novel. By Mrs. GEORGE HOOPER. Post 8vo, illustrated boards, 2s.

HOPKINS.—"'TWIXT LOVE AND DUTY:" A Novel. By TIGHE HOPKINS. Post 8vo, illustrated boards, 2s.

HORNE.—ORION: An Epic Poem. By RICHARD HENGIST HORNE. With Photographic Portrait by SUMMERS. Tenth Edition. Cr. 8vo, cloth extra, 7s.

HUNGERFORD (MRS.), Author of "Molly Bawn," NOVELS BY. Post 8vo, illustrated boards, 2s. each; cloth limp, 2s. 6d. each.
A MAIDEN ALL FORLORN. | IN DURANCE VILE. | A MENTAL STRUGGLE.
MARVEL. | A MODERN CIRCE.
LADY VERNER'S FLIGHT. Crown 8vo, cloth extra, 3s. 6d.
THE RED-HOUSE MYSTERY. Two Vols., crown 8vo.

HUNT.—ESSAYS BY LEIGH HUNT: A TALE FOR A CHIMNEY CORNER, &c. Edited by EDMUND OLLIER. Post 8vo, printed on laid paper and half-bd., 2s.

HUNT (MRS. ALFRED), NOVELS BY.
Crown 8vo, cloth extra, 3s. 6d. each; post 8vo, illustrated boards, 2s. each.
THE LEADEN CASKET. | SELF-CONDEMNED. | THAT OTHER PERSON.
THORNICROFT'S MODEL. Post 8vo, illustrated boards, 2s.
MRS. JULIET. Crown 8vo, cloth extra, 3s. 6d.

HUTCHISON.—HINTS ON COLT-BREAKING. By W. M. HUTCHISON. With 25 Illustrations. Crown 8vo, cloth extra, 3s. 6d.

HYDROPHOBIA: An Account of M. PASTEUR'S System; Technique of his Method, and Statistics. By RENAUD SUZOR, M.B. Crown 8vo, cloth extra, 6s.

IDLER (THE): A Monthly Magazine. Edited by JEROME K. JEROME and ROBERT E. BARR. Profusely Illustrated. Sixpence Monthly. The first FOUR VOLUMES are now ready, cloth extra, 5s. each; Cases for Binding, 1s. 6d.

INGELOW (JEAN).—FATED TO BE FREE. Post 8vo, illustrated bds., 2s.

INDOOR PAUPERS. By One of Them. Crown 8vo, 1s.; cloth, 1s. 6d.

INNKEEPER'S HANDBOOK (THE) AND LICENSED VICTUALLER'S MANUAL. By J. Trevor-Davies. Crown 8vo, 1s.; cloth, 1s. 6d.

IRISH WIT AND HUMOUR, SONGS OF. Collected and Edited by A. Perceval Graves. Post 8vo, cloth limp, 2s. 6d.

JAMES.—A ROMANCE OF THE QUEEN'S HOUNDS. By Charles James. Post 8vo, picture cover, 1s.; cloth limp, 1s. 6d.

JAMESON.—MY DEAD SELF. By William Jameson. Post 8vo, illustrated boards, 2s.; cloth, 2s. 6d.

JANVIER.—PRACTICAL KERAMICS FOR STUDENTS. By Catherine A. Janvier. Crown 8vo, cloth extra, 6s.

JAPP.—DRAMATIC PICTURES, SONNETS, &c. By A. H. Japp, LL.D. Crown 8vo, cloth extra, 5s.

JAY (HARRIETT), NOVELS BY. Post 8vo, illustrated boards, 2s. each.
THE DARK COLLEEN. | THE QUEEN OF CONNAUGHT.

JEFFERIES (RICHARD), WORKS BY. Post 8vo, cloth limp, 2s. 6d. each.
NATURE NEAR LONDON. | THE LIFE OF THE FIELDS. | THE OPEN AIR.
** Also the Hand-made Paper Edition, crown 8vo, buckram, gilt top, 6s. each.

THE EULOGY OF RICHARD JEFFERIES. By Walter Besant. Second Edition. With a Photograph Portrait. Crown 8vo, cloth extra, 6s.

JENNINGS (H. J.), WORKS BY.
CURIOSITIES OF CRITICISM. Post 8vo, cloth limp, 2s. 6d.
LORD TENNYSON: A Biographical Sketch. With a Photograph. Cr. 8vo, cl., 6s.

JEROME.—STAGELAND. By Jerome K. Jerome. With 64 Illustrations by J. Bernard Partridge. Square 8vo, picture cover, 1s.; cloth limp, 2s.

JERROLD.—THE BARBER'S CHAIR; & THE HEDGEHOG LETTERS. By Douglas Jerrold. Post 8vo, printed on laid paper and half-bound, 2s.

JERROLD (TOM), WORKS BY. Post 8vo, 1s. each; cloth limp, 1s. 6d. each.
THE GARDEN THAT PAID THE RENT.
HOUSEHOLD HORTICULTURE: A Gossip about Flowers. Illustrated.
OUR KITCHEN GARDEN: The Plants, and How we Cook Them. Cr. 8vo, cl., 1s. 6d.

JESSE.—SCENES AND OCCUPATIONS OF A COUNTRY LIFE. By Edward Jesse. Post 8vo, cloth limp, 2s.

JONES (WILLIAM, F.S.A.), WORKS BY. Cr. 8vo, cl. extra, 7s. 6d. each.
FINGER-RING LORE: Historical, Legendary, and Anecdotal. With nearly 300 Illustrations. Second Edition, Revised and Enlarged.
CREDULITIES, PAST AND PRESENT. Including the Sea and Seamen, Miners, Talismans, Word and Letter Divination, Exorcising and Blessing of Animals, Birds, Eggs, Luck, &c. With an Etched Frontispiece.
CROWNS AND CORONATIONS: A History of Regalia. With 100 Illustrations.

JONSON'S (BEN) WORKS. With Notes Critical and Explanatory, and a Biographical Memoir by William Gifford. Edited by Colonel Cunningham. Three Vols., crown 8vo, cloth extra, 6s. each.

JOSEPHUS, THE COMPLETE WORKS OF. Translated by Whiston. Containing "The Antiquities of the Jews" and "The Wars of the Jews." With 52 Illustrations and Maps. Two Vols., demy 8vo, half-bound, 12s. 6d.

KEMPT.—PENCIL AND PALETTE: Chapters on Art and Artists. By Robert Kempt. Post 8vo, cloth limp, 2s. 6d.

KERSHAW. — COLONIAL FACTS AND FICTIONS: Humorous Sketches. By Mark Kershaw. Post 8vo, illustrated boards, 2s.; cloth, 2s. 6d.

KEYSER. — CUT BY THE MESS: A Novel. By Arthur Keyser. Crown 8vo, picture cover, 1s.; cloth limp, 1s. 6d.

KING (R. ASHE), NOVELS BY. Cr. 8vo, cl., 3s. 6d. ea.; post 8vo, bds., 2s. ea.
A DRAWN GAME. | "THE WEARING OF THE GREEN."

Post 8vo, illustrated boards, 2s. each.
PASSION'S SLAVE. | BELL BARRY.

KNIGHT.—THE PATIENT'S VADE MECUM: How to Get Most
Benefit from Medical Advice. By WILLIAM KNIGHT, M.R.C.S., and EDWARD
KNIGHT, L.R.C.P. Crown 8vo, 1s.; cloth limp, 1s. 6d.

KNIGHTS (THE) OF THE LION: A Romance of the Thirteenth Century.
Edited. with an Introduction, by the MARQUESS of LORNE, K.T. Cr. 8vo. cl. ex. 6s.

LAMB'S (CHARLES) COMPLETE WORKS, in Prose and Verse,
including "Poetry for Children" and "Prince Dorus." Edited, with Notes and
Introduction, by R. H. SHEPHERD. With Two Portraits and Facsimile of a page
of the "Essay on Roast Pig." Crown 8vo, half-bound, 7s. 6d.
THE ESSAYS OF ELIA. Post 8vo, printed on laid paper and half-bound, 2s.
LITTLE ESSAYS: Sketches and Characters by CHARLES LAMB, selected from his
Letters by PERCY FITZGERALD. Post 8vo, cloth limp, 2s. 6d.
THE DRAMATIC ESSAYS OF CHARLES LAMB. With Introduction and Notes
by BRANDER MATTHEWS, and Steel-plate Portrait. Fcap. 8vo, hf.-bd., 2s. 6d.

LANDOR.—CITATION AND EXAMINATION OF WILLIAM SHAKS-
PEARE, &c., before Sir THOMAS LUCY, touching Deer-stealing, 19th September, 1582.
To which is added, A CONFERENCE OF MASTER EDMUND SPENSER with the
Earl of Essex, touching the State of Ireland, 1595. By WALTER SAVAGE LANDOR.
Fcap. 8vo, half-Roxburghe, 2s. 6d.

LANE.—THE THOUSAND AND ONE NIGHTS, commonly called in
England THE ARABIAN NIGHTS' ENTERTAINMENTS. Translated from the
Arabic, with Notes, by EDWARD WILLIAM LANE. Illustrated by many hundred
Engravings from Designs by HARVEY. Edited by EDWARD STANLEY POOLE. With a
Preface by STANLEY LANE-POOLE. Three Vols., demy 8vo, cloth extra, 7s. 6d. each.

LARWOOD (JACOB), WORKS BY.
THE STORY OF THE LONDON PARKS. With Illusts. Cr. 8vo, cl. extra, 3s. 6d.
ANECDOTES OF THE CLERGY: The Antiquities, Humours, and Eccentricities of
the Cloth. Post 8vo, printed on laid paper and half-bound, 2s.
                    Post 8vo, cloth limp, 2s. 6d. each.
FORENSIC ANECDOTES. | THEATRICAL ANECDOTES.

LEHMANN.—HARRY FLUDYER AT CAMBRIDGE. By R. C. LEH
MANN. Post 8vo, 1s.; cloth, 1s. 6d.

LEIGH (HENRY S.), WORKS BY.
CAROLS OF COCKAYNE. Printed on hand-made paper, bound in buckram, 5s.
JEUX D'ESPRIT. Edited by HENRY S. LEIGH. Post 8vo, cloth limp, 2s. 6d.

LEYS (JOHN).—THE LINDSAYS: A Romance. Post 8vo, illust. bds., 2s.

LIFE IN LONDON; or, The History of JERRY HAWTHORN and COR-
INTHIAN TOM. With CRUIKSHANK's Coloured Illustrations. Crown 8vo, cloth extra,
7s. 6d.   [New Edition preparing.

LINTON (E. LYNN), WORKS BY. Post 8vo, cloth limp, 2s. 6d. each.
WITCH STORIES. | OURSELVES: ESSAYS ON WOMEN.
Crown 8vo, cloth extra, 3s. 6d. each; post 8vo, illustrated boards, 2s. each.
PATRICIA KEMBALL. | IONE.   UNDER WHICH LORD?
ATONEMENT OF LEAM DUNDAS.   "MY LOVE!" | SOWING THE WIND.
THE WORLD WELL LOST.   PASTON CAREW, Millionaire & Miser.
                Post 8vo, illustrated boards, 2s. each.
THE REBEL OF THE FAMILY. | WITH A SILKEN THREAD.
THE ONE TOO MANY. Three Vols., crown 8vo.
FREESHOOTING: Extracts from Works of Mrs. L. LINTON. Post 8vo, cl., 2s. 6d.

LONGFELLOW'S POETICAL WORKS. With numerous Illustrations
on Steel and Wood. Crown 8vo, cloth extra, 7s. 6d.

LUCY.—GIDEON FLEYCE: A Novel. By HENRY W. LUCY. Crown
8vo, cloth extra, 3s. 6d.: post 8vo, illustrated boards, 2s.

MACALPINE (AVERY), NOVELS BY.
TERESA ITASCA. Crown 8vo, cloth extra, 1s.
BROKEN WINGS. With 6 Illusts. by W. J. HENNESSY. Crown 8vo, cloth extra, 6s.

MACCOLL (HUGH), NOVELS BY.
MR. STRANGER'S SEALED PACKET. Post 8vo, illustrated boards, 2s.
EDNOR WHITLOCK. Crown 8vo, cloth extra, 6s.

MACDONELL.—QUAKER COUSINS: A Novel. By AGNES MACDONELL.
Crown 8vo, cloth extra, 3s. 6d.; post 8vo. illustrated boards, 2s.

McCARTHY (JUSTIN, M.P.), WORKS BY.

A HISTORY OF OUR OWN TIMES, from the Accession of Queen Victoria to the General Election of 1880. Four Vols. demy 8vo, cloth extra, **12s.** each.—Also a POPULAR EDITION, in Four Vols., crown 8vo, cloth extra, **6s.** each.—And a JUBILEE EDITION, with an Appendix of Events to the end of 1886, in Two Vols., large crown 8vo, cloth extra, **7s. 6d.** each.

A SHORT HISTORY OF OUR OWN TIMES. One Vol., crown 8vo, cloth extra, **6s.** —Also a CHEAP POPULAR EDITION, post 8vo, cloth limp, **2s. 6d.**

A HISTORY OF THE FOUR GEORGES. Four Vols. demy 8vo, cloth extra, **12s.** each.   [Vols. I. & II. *ready.*

Cr. 8vo, cl. extra, **3s. 6d.** each; post 8vo, illust. bds., **2s.** each; cl. limp, **2s. 6d.** each.

THE WATERDALE NEIGHBOURS.	MISS MISANTHROPE.
MY ENEMY'S DAUGHTER.	DONNA QUIXOTE.
A FAIR SAXON.	THE COMET OF A SEASON.
LINLEY ROCHFORD.	MAID OF ATHENS.
DEAR LADY DISDAIN.	CAMIOLA: A Girl with a Fortune.

THE DICTATOR. Crown 8vo, cloth extra, **3s. 6d.**

RED DIAMONDS. Three Vols., crown 8vo.

"THE RIGHT HONOURABLE." By JUSTIN McCARTHY, M.P., and Mrs. CAMPBELL-PRAED. Fourth Edition. Crown 8vo, cloth extra. **6s.**

McCARTHY (JUSTIN H.), WORKS BY.

THE FRENCH REVOLUTION. Four Vols., 8vo, **12s.** each.   [Vols. I. & II. *ready.*

AN OUTLINE OF THE HISTORY OF IRELAND. Crown 8vo, **1s.**; cloth, **1s. 6d.**

IRELAND SINCE THE UNION: Irish History, 1798-1886. Crown 8vo, cloth, **6s.**

HAFIZ IN LONDON: Poems. Small 8vo, gold cloth, **3s. 6d.**

HARLEQUINADE: Poems. Small 4to, Japanese vellum, **8s.**

OUR SENSATION NOVEL. Crown 8vo, picture cover, **1s.**; cloth limp, **1s. 6d.**

DOOM! An Atlantic Episode. Crown 8vo, picture cover, **1s.**

DOLLY: A Sketch. Crown 8vo, picture cover, **1s.**; cloth limp, **1s. 6d.**

LILY LASS: A Romance. Crown 8vo, picture cover, **1s.**; cloth limp, **1s. 6d.**

THE THOUSAND AND ONE DAYS: Persian Tales. With 2 Photogravures by STANLEY L. WOOD. Two Vols., crown 8vo, half-bound, **12s.**

MACDONALD (GEORGE, LL.D.), WORKS BY.

WORKS OF FANCY AND IMAGINATION. Ten Vols., cl. extra, gilt edges, in cloth case, **21s.** Or the Vols. may be had separately, in grolier cl., at **2s. 6d.** each.

Vol.   I. WITHIN AND WITHOUT.—THE HIDDEN LIFE.

„   II. THE DISCIPLE.—THE GOSPEL WOMEN.—BOOK OF SONNETS.—ORGAN SONGS.

„   III. VIOLIN SONGS.—SONGS OF THE DAYS AND NIGHTS.—A BOOK OF DREAMS.—ROADSIDE POEMS.—POEMS FOR CHILDREN.

„   IV. PARABLES.—BALLADS.—SCOTCH SONGS.

„ V. & VI. PHANTASTES: A Faerie Romance. | Vol. VII. THE PORTENT.

„ VIII. THE LIGHT PRINCESS.—THE GIANT'S HEART.—SHADOWS.

„ IX. CROSS PURPOSES.—THE GOLDEN KEY.—THE CARASOYN.—LITTLE DAYLIGHT.

„   X. THE CRUEL PAINTER.—THE WOW O' RIVVEN.—THE CASTLE.—THE BROKEN SWORDS.—THE GRAY WOLF.—UNCLE CORNELIUS.

POETICAL WORKS OF GEORGE MACDONALD. Collected and arranged by the Author. 2 Vols., crown 8vo, buckram, **12s.**

A THREEFOLD CORD. Edited by GEORGE MACDONALD. Post 8vo, cloth, **5s.**

HEATHER AND SNOW: A Novel. Crown 8vo, cloth extra, **3s. 6d.**

MACGREGOR. — PASTIMES AND PLAYERS: Notes on Popular Games. By ROBERT MACGREGOR. Post 8vo, cloth limp, **2s. 6d.**

MACKAY.—INTERLUDES AND UNDERTONES; or, Music at Twilight.
By CHARLES MACKAY, LL.D. Crown 8vo, cloth extra, **6s.**

MACLISE PORTRAIT GALLERY (THE) OF ILLUSTRIOUS LITER-
ARY CHARACTERS: 85 PORTRAITS; with Memoirs — Biographical, Critical, Bibliographical, and Anecdotal—illustrative of the Literature of the former half of the Present Century, by WILLIAM BATES, B.A. Crown 8vo, cloth extra, **7s. 6d.**

MACQUOID (MRS.), WORKS BY. Square 8vo, cloth extra, **7s. 6d.** each.

IN THE ARDENNES. With 50 Illustrations by THOMAS R. MACQUOID

PICTURES AND LEGENDS FROM NORMANDY AND BRITTANY. With 34 Illustrations by THOMAS R. MACQUOID.

THROUGH NORMANDY. With 92 Illustrations by T. R. MACQUOID, and a Map.

THROUGH BRITTANY. With 35 Illustrations by T. R. MACQUOID, and a Map.

ABOUT YORKSHIRE. With 67 Illustrations by T. R. MACQUOID.

Post 8vo, illustrated boards, **2s.** each.

THE EVIL EYE, and other Stories. | **LOST ROSE.**

MAGIC LANTERN, THE, and its Management: including full Practical Directions. By T. C. HEPWORTH. 10 Illustrations. Cr. 8vo, 1s.; cloth, 1s. 6d.

MAGICIAN'S OWN BOOK, THE: Performances with Cups and Balls, Eggs, Hats, Handkerchiefs, &c. All from actual Experience. Edited by W. H. CREMER. With 200 Illustrations. Crown 8vo, cloth extra, 4s. 6d.

MAGNA CHARTA: An Exact Facsimile of the Original in the British Museum, 3 feet by 2 feet, with Arms and Seals emblazoned in Gold and Colours, 5s.

MALLOCK (W. H.), WORKS BY.
THE NEW REPUBLIC. Post 8vo, picture cover, 2s.; cloth limp, 2s. 6d.
THE NEW PAUL & VIRGINIA: Positivism on an Island. Post 8vo, cloth, 2s. 6d.
POEMS. Small 4to, parchment, 8s.
IS LIFE WORTH LIVING? Crown 8vo, cloth extra, 6s.
A ROMANCE OF THE NINETEENTH CENTURY. Crown 8vo, cloth, 6s.; post 8vo, illustrated boards, 2s.

MALLORY'S (SIR THOMAS) MORT D'ARTHUR: The Stories of King Arthur and of the Knights of the Round Table. (A Selection.) Edited by B. MONTGOMERIE RANKING. Post 8vo, cloth limp, 2s.

MARK TWAIN, WORKS BY. Crown 8vo, cloth extra, 7s. 6d. each.
THE CHOICE WORKS OF MARK TWAIN. Revised and Corrected throughout by the Author. With Life, Portrait, and numerous Illustrations.
ROUGHING IT, and INNOCENTS AT HOME. With 200 Illusts. by F. A. FRASER.
MARK TWAIN'S LIBRARY OF HUMOUR. With 197 Illustrations.
Crown 8vo, cloth extra (illustrated), 7s. 6d. each; post 8vo, illust. boards, 2s. each.
THE INNOCENTS ABROAD; or, New Pilgrim's Progress. With 234 Illustrations. (The Two-Shilling Edition is entitled MARK TWAIN'S PLEASURE TRIP.)
THE GILDED AGE. By MARK TWAIN and C. D. WARNER. With 212 Illustrations.
THE ADVENTURES OF TOM SAWYER. With 111 Illustrations.
A TRAMP ABROAD. With 314 Illustrations.
THE PRINCE AND THE PAUPER. With 190 Illustrations.
LIFE ON THE MISSISSIPPI. With 300 Illustrations.
ADVENTURES OF HUCKLEBERRY FINN. With 174 Illusts. by E. W. KEMBLE.
A YANKEE AT THE COURT OF KING ARTHUR. With 220 Illusts. by BEARD.
MARK TWAIN'S SKETCHES. Post 8vo, illustrated boards, 2s.
THE STOLEN WHITE ELEPHANT, &c. Cr. 8vo, cl., 6s.; post 8vo, illust. bds., 2s.
Crown 8vo, cloth extra, 3s. 6d. each.
THE AMERICAN CLAIMANT. With 81 Illustrations by HAL HURST, &c.
THE £1,000,000 BANK-NOTE, and other New Stories.

MARLOWE'S WORKS. Including his Translations. Edited, with Notes and Introductions, by Col. CUNNINGHAM. Crown 8vo, cloth extra, 6s.

MARRYAT (FLORENCE), NOVELS BY. Post 8vo, illust. boards, 2s. each.
A HARVEST OF WILD OATS. | FIGHTING THE AIR.
OPEN! SESAME! | WRITTEN IN FIRE.

MASSINGER'S PLAYS. From the Text of WILLIAM GIFFORD. Edited by Col. CUNNINGHAM. Crown 8vo, cloth extra, 6s.

MASTERMAN.—HALF-A-DOZEN DAUGHTERS: A Novel. By J. MASTERMAN. Post 8vo, illustrated boards, 2s.

MATTHEWS.—A SECRET OF THE SEA, &c. By BRANDER MATTHEWS. Post 8vo, illustrated boards, 2s.; cloth limp, 2s. 6d.

MAYHEW.—LONDON CHARACTERS AND THE HUMOROUS SIDE OF LONDON LIFE. By HENRY MAYHEW. With Illusts. Crown 8vo, cloth, 3s. 6d.

MENKEN.—INFELICIA: Poems by ADAH ISAACS MENKEN. With Illustrations by F. E. LUMMIS and F. O. C. DARLEY. Small 4to, cloth extra, 7s. 6d.

MERRICK.—THE MAN WHO WAS GOOD. By LEONARD MERRICK, Author of "Violet Moses," &c. Post 8vo, illustrated boards, 2s.

MEXICAN MUSTANG (ON A), through Texas to the Rio Grande. By A. E. SWEET and J. ARMOY KNOX. With 265 Illusts. Cr. 8vo, cloth extra, 7s. 6d.

MIDDLEMASS (JEAN), NOVELS BY. Post 8vo, illust. boards, 2s. each.
TOUCH AND GO. | MR. DORILLION.

MILLER.—PHYSIOLOGY FOR THE YOUNG; or, The House of Life. By Mrs. F. FENWICK MILLER. With Illustrations. Post 8vo, cloth limp, 2s. 6d.

MILTON (J. L.), WORKS BY. Post 8vo, 1s. each; cloth, 1s. 6d. each.
THE HYGIENE OF THE SKIN. With Directions for Diet, Soaps, Baths, &c.
THE BATH IN DISEASES OF THE SKIN.
THE LAWS OF LIFE, AND THEIR RELATION TO DISEASES OF THE SKIN.
THE SUCCESSFUL TREATMENT OF LEPROSY. Demy 8vo, 1s.

MINTO (WM.)—WAS SHE GOOD OR BAD? Cr. 8vo, 1s.; cloth, 1s. 6d.

MITFORD (BERTRAM), NOVELS BY. Crown 8vo, cloth extra, 3s. 6d. each.
THE GUN-RUNNER: A Romance of Zululand. With Frontispiece by S. L. WOOD.
THE LUCK OF GERARD RIDGELEY. With a Frontispiece by STANLEY L. WOOD.
THE KING'S ASSEGAI. With Six full-page Illustrations.

MOLESWORTH (MRS.), NOVELS BY.
HATHERCOURT RECTORY. Post 8vo, illustrated boards, 2s.
THAT GIRL IN BLACK. Crown 8vo, cloth, 1s. 6d.

MOORE (THOMAS), WORKS BY.
THE EPICUREAN; and ALCIPHRON. Post 8vo, half-bound, 2s.
PROSE AND VERSE. With Suppressed Passages from the MEMOIRS OF LORD
BYRON. Edited by R. H. SHEPHERD. With Portrait. Cr. 8vo, cl. ex., 7s. 6d.

MUDDOCK (J. E.), STORIES BY.
STORIES WEIRD AND WONDERFUL. Post 8vo, illust. boards, 2s.; cloth, 2s. 6d.
THE DEAD MAN'S SECRET; or, The Valley of Gold. With Frontispiece by
F. BARNARD. Crown 8vo. cloth extra, 5s.; post 8vo, illustrated boards, 2s.
FROM THE BOSOM OF THE DEEP. Post 8vo, illustrated boards, 2s.
MAID MARIAN AND ROBIN HOOD: A Romance of Old Sherwood Forest. With
12 Illustrations by STANLEY L. WOOD. Crown 8vo, cloth extra, 5s.

MURRAY (D. CHRISTIE), NOVELS BY.
Crown 8vo, cloth extra, 3s. 6d. each; post 8vo, illustrated boards. 2s. each.

A LIFE'S ATONEMENT.	WAY OF THE WORLD	BY THE GATE OF THE SEA.
JOSEPH'S COAT.	A MODEL FATHER.	A BIT OF HUMAN NATURE.
COALS OF FIRE.	OLD BLAZER'S HERO.	FIRST PERSON SINGULAR.
VAL STRANGE.	HEARTS.	CYNIC FORTUNE.	BOB MARTIN'S LITTLE

TIME'S REVENGES. Crown 8vo, cloth extra, 3s. 6d.	[GIRL.
A WASTED CRIME. Two Vols., crown 8vo.
IN DIREST PERIL. Three Vols., crown 8vo.
THE MAKING OF A NOVELIST: An Experiment in Autobiography. With a
Collotype Portrait and Vignette. Crown 8vo, Irish linen, 6s.

MURRAY (D. CHRISTIE) & HENRY HERMAN, WORKS BY.
Crown 8vo, cloth extra, 3s. 6d. each; post 8vo, illustrated boards, 2s. each.
ONE TRAVELLER RETURNS. | PAUL JONES'S ALIAS. | THE BISHOPS' BIBLE.

MURRAY (HENRY), NOVELS BY. Post 8vo, illust. bds., 2s. ea.; cl., 2s. 6d. ea.
A GAME OF BLUFF. | A SONG OF SIXPENCE.

NEWBOLT.—TAKEN FROM THE ENEMY. By HENRY NEWBOLT.
Fcap. 8vo, cloth boards, 1s. 6d.

NISBET (HUME), BOOKS BY.
"BAIL UP!" Crown 8vo, cloth extra, 3s. 6d.; post 8vo, illustrated boards, 2s.
DR. BERNARD ST. VINCENT. Post 8vo, illustrated boards, 2s.
LESSONS IN ART. With 21 Illustrations. Crown 8vo, cloth extra, 2s. 6d.
WHERE ART BEGINS. With 27 Illusts. Square 8vo, cloth extra, 7s. 6d.

NORRIS.—ST. ANN'S: A Novel. By W. E. NORRIS. Two Vols. [Shortly.

O'HANLON (ALICE), NOVELS BY. Post 8vo, illustrated boards, 2s. each.
THE UNFORESEEN. | CHANCE? OR FATE?

OHNET (GEORGES), NOVELS BY. Post 8vo, illustrated boards, 2s. each.
DOCTOR RAMEAU. | A LAST LOVE.
A WEIRD GIFT. Crown 8vo, cloth, 3s. 6d., post 8vo, picture boards, 2s.

OLIPHANT (MRS.), NOVELS BY. Post 8vo, illustrated boards, 2s. each.
THE PRIMROSE PATH. | WHITELADIES.
THE GREATEST HEIRESS IN ENGLAND.

O'REILLY (HARRINGTON).—LIFE AMONG THE AMERICAN IN-
DIANS: Fifty Years on the Trail. 100 Illusts. by P. FRENZENY. Crown 8vo, 3s. 6d.

O'REILLY (MRS.).—PHŒBE'S FORTUNES. Post 8vo, illust. bds., 2s.

OUIDA, NOVELS BY. Cr. 8vo, cl., **3s. 6d.** each; post 8vo, illust. bds., **2s.** each.

HELD IN BONDAGE.	FOLLE-FARINE.	MOTHS.	PIPISTRELLO.
TRICOTRIN.	A DOG OF FLANDERS.	A VILLAGE COMMUNE.
STRATHMORE.	PASCAREL.	SIGNA.	IN MAREMMA.
CHANDOS.	TWO LITTLE WOODEN	BIMBI.	SYRLIN.
CECIL CASTLEMAINE'S	SHOES.	WANDA.
GAGE.	IN A WINTER CITY.	FRESCOES.	OTHMAR.
UNDER TWO FLAGS.	ARIADNE.	PRINCESS NAPRAXINE.
PUCK.	IDALIA.	FRIENDSHIP.	GUILDEROY.	RUFFINO.

Square 8vo, cloth extra, **5s.** each.
BIMBI. With Nine Illustrations by EDMUND H. GARRETT.
A DOG OF FLANDERS, &c. With Six Illustrations by EDMUND H. GARRETT.
SANTA BARBARA, &c. Square 8vo, cloth, **6s.**; crown 8vo, cloth, **3s. 6d.**; post 8vo, illustrated boards, **2s.**
TWO OFFENDERS. Square 8vo, cloth extra, **6s.**
WISDOM, WIT, AND PATHOS, selected from the Works of OUIDA by F. SYDNEY MORRIS. Post 8vo, cloth extra, **5s.** CHEAP EDITION, illustrated boards, **2s.**

PAGE (H. A.), WORKS BY.
THOREAU : His Life and Aims. With Portrait. Post 8vo, cloth limp, **2s. 6d.**
ANIMAL ANECDOTES. Arranged on a New Principle. Crown 8vo, cloth extra, **5s.**

PARLIAMENTARY ELECTIONS AND ELECTIONEERING, A HIS-
TORY OF, from the Stuarts to Queen Victoria. By JOSEPH GREGO. A New Edition, with 93 Illustrations. Demy 8vo, cloth extra, **7s. 6d.**

PASCAL'S PROVINCIAL LETTERS. A New Translation, with Historical Introduction and Notes by T. M'CRIE, D.D. Post 8vo, cloth limp, **2s.**

PAUL.—GENTLE AND SIMPLE. By MARGARET A. PAUL. With Frontis-
piece by HELEN PATERSON. Crown 8vo, cloth, **3s. 6d.**; post 8vo, illust. boards, **2s.**

PAYN (JAMES), NOVELS BY.
Crown 8vo, cloth extra, **3s. 6d.** each; post 8vo, illustrated boards, **2s.** each.

LOST SIR MASSINGBERD.	A GRAPE FROM A THORN.
WALTER'S WORD.	FROM EXILE.
LESS BLACK THAN WE'RE	THE CANON'S WARD.
PAINTED.	THE TALK OF THE TOWN.
BY PROXY.	FOR CASH ONLY.	HOLIDAY TASKS.
HIGH SPIRITS.	GLOW-WORM TALES.
UNDER ONE ROOF.	THE MYSTERY OF MIRBRIDGE.
A CONFIDENTIAL AGENT.	THE WORD AND THE WILL.

Post 8vo, illustrated boards, **2s.** each.

HUMOROUS STORIES.	FOUND DEAD.
THE FOSTER BROTHERS.	GWENDOLINE'S HARVEST.
THE FAMILY SCAPEGRACE.	A MARINE RESIDENCE.
MARRIED BENEATH HIM.	MIRK ABBEY.	SOME PRIVATE VIEWS.
BENTINCK'S TUTOR.	NOT WOOED, BUT WON.
A PERFECT TREASURE.	TWO HUNDRED POUNDS REWARD.
A COUNTY FAMILY.	THE BEST OF HUSBANDS.
LIKE FATHER, LIKE SON.	HALVES.	THE BURNT MILLION.
A WOMAN'S VENGEANCE.	FALLEN FORTUNES.
CARLYON'S YEAR.	CECIL'S TRYST.	WHAT HE COST HER.
MURPHY'S MASTER.	KIT: A MEMORY.
AT HER MERCY.	A PRINCE OF THE BLOOD.
THE CLYFFARDS OF CLYFFE.	SUNNY STORIES.

Crown 8vo, cloth extra, **3s. 6d.** each.
A TRYING PATIENT, &c. With a Frontispiece by STANLEY L. WOOD.
IN PERIL AND PRIVATION : Stories of MARINE ADVENTURE. With 17 Illusts.
NOTES FROM THE "NEWS." Crown 8vo, portrait cover, **1s.**; cloth, **1s. 6d.**

PENNELL (H. CHOLMONDELEY), WORKS BY. Post 8vo, cl., **2s. 6d.** each.
PUCK ON PEGASUS. With Illustrations.
PEGASUS RE-SADDLED. With Ten full-page Illustrations by G. DU MAURIER.
THE MUSES OF MAYFAIR. Vers de Société, Selected by H. C. PENNELL.

PHELPS (E. STUART), WORKS BY. Post 8vo **1s.** each; cloth **1s. 6d.** each.
BEYOND THE GATES. | OLD MAID'S PARADISE. | BURGLARS IN PARADISE.
JACK THE FISHERMAN. Illustrated by C. W. REED. Cr. 8vo, **1s.**; cloth, **1s. 6d.**

PIRKIS (C. L.), NOVELS BY.
TROOPING WITH CROWS. Fcap. 8vo, picture cover, **1s.**
LADY LOVELACE. Post 8vo, illustrated boards, **2s.**

PLANCHE (J. R.), WORKS BY.
THE PURSUIVANT OF ARMS. With Six Plates, and 209 Illusts. Cr. 8vo, cl. 7s. 6d.
SONGS AND POEMS, 1819-1879. Introduction by Mrs. MACKARNESS. Cr. 8vo, cl., 6s.

PLUTARCH'S LIVES OF ILLUSTRIOUS MEN. With Notes and Life
of Plutarch by J. and WM. LANGHORNE. Portraits. Two Vols., demy 8vo, 10s. 6d.

POE'S (EDGAR ALLAN) CHOICE WORKS, in Prose and Poetry. Intro-
duction by CHAS. BAUDELAIRE, Portrait, and Facsimiles. Cr. 8vo, cloth, 7s. 6d.
THE MYSTERY OF MARIE ROGET, &c. Post 8vo, illustrated boards, 2s.

POPE'S POETICAL WORKS. Post 8vo, cloth limp, 2s.

PRAED (MRS. CAMPBELL), NOVELS BY. Post 8vo, illust. bds., 2s. ea.
THE ROMANCE OF A STATION. | **THE SOUL OF COUNTESS ADRIAN.**
OUTLAW AND LAWMAKER. Three Vols., crown 8vo.

PRICE (E. C.), NOVELS BY.
Crown 8vo, cloth extra, 3s. 6d. each; post 8vo, illustrated boards, 2s. each.
VALENTINA. | **THE FOREIGNERS.** | **MRS. LANCASTER'S RIVAL.**
GERALD. Post 8vo, illustrated boards, 2s.

PRINCESS OLGA.—RADNA; or, The Great Conspiracy of 1881. By
the Princess OLGA. Crown 8vo, cloth extra, 6s.

PROCTOR (RICHARD A., B.A.), WORKS BY.
FLOWERS OF THE SKY. With 55 Illusts. Small crown 8vo, cloth extra, 3s. 6d.
EASY STAR LESSONS. With Star Maps for Every Night in the Year. Cr. 8vo, 6s.
FAMILIAR SCIENCE STUDIES. Crown 8vo, cloth extra, 6s.
SATURN AND ITS SYSTEM. With 13 Steel Plates. Demy 8vo, cloth ex., 10s. 6d.
MYSTERIES OF TIME AND SPACE. With Illustrations. Cr. 8vo, cloth extra, 6s.
THE UNIVERSE OF SUNS. With numerous Illustrations. Cr. 8vo, cloth ex., 6s.
WAGES AND WANTS OF SCIENCE WORKERS. Crown 8vo, 1s. 6d.

PRYCE.—MISS MAXWELL'S AFFECTIONS. By RICHARD PRYCE.
Frontispiece by HAL LUDLOW. Cr. 8vo, cl., 3s. 6d. ; post 8vo, illust. boards., 2s.

RAMBOSSON.—POPULAR ASTRONOMY. By J. RAMBOSSON, Laureate
of the Institute of France. With numerous Illusts. Crown 8vo, cloth extra, 7s. 6d.

RANDOLPH.—AUNT ABIGAIL DYKES: A Novel. By Lt.-Colonel
GEORGE RANDOLPH, U.S.A. Crown 8vo, cloth extra, 7s. 6d.

READE (CHARLES), NOVELS BY.
Crown 8vo, cloth extra, illustrated, 3s. 6d. each; post 8vo, illust. bds., 2s. each.
PEG WOFFINGTON. Illustrated by S. L. FILDES, R.A.—Also a POCKET EDITION,
set in New Type, in Elzevir style, fcap. 8vo, half-leather, 2s. 6d.—And a Cheap
POPULAR EDITION of PEG WOFFINGTON and CHRISTIE JOHNSTONE, the two
Stories in One Volume, medium 8vo, 6d. ; cloth, 1s.
CHRISTIE JOHNSTONE. Illustrated by WILLIAM SMALL.—Also a POCKET EDITION,
set in New Type, in Elzevir style, fcap. 8vo, half-leather, 2s. 6d.
IT IS NEVER TOO LATE TO MEND. Illustrated by G. J. PINWELL.—Also a Cheap
POPULAR EDITION, medium 8vo, portrait cover, 6d. ; cloth, 1s.
COURSE OF TRUE LOVE NEVER DID RUN SMOOTH. Illust. HELEN PATERSON.
THE AUTOBIOGRAPHY OF A THIEF, &c. Illustrated by MATT STRETCH.
LOVE ME LITTLE, LOVE ME LONG. Illustrated by M. ELLEN EDWARDS.
THE DOUBLE MARRIAGE. Illusts. by Sir JOHN GILBERT, R.A., and C. KEENE.
THE CLOISTER AND THE HEARTH. Illustrated by CHARLES KEENE.—Also a
CHEAP POPULAR EDITION, medium 8vo, 6d. ; cloth, 1s.
HARD CASH. Illustrated by F. W. LAWSON.
GRIFFITH GAUNT. Illustrated by S. L. FILDES, R.A., and WILLIAM SMALL.
FOUL PLAY. Illustrated by GEORGE DU MAURIER.
PUT YOURSELF IN HIS PLACE. Illustrated by ROBERT BARNES.
A TERRIBLE TEMPTATION. Illustrated by EDWARD HUGHES and A. W. COOPER.
A SIMPLETON. Illustrated by KATE CRAUFURD.
THE WANDERING HEIR. Illust. by H. PATERSON, S. L. FILDES, C. GREEN, &c.
A WOMAN-HATER. Illustrated by THOMAS COULDERY.
SINGLEHEART AND DOUBLEFACE. Illustrated by P. MACNAB.
GOOD STORIES OF MEN AND OTHER ANIMALS. Illust. by E. A. ABBEY, &c.
THE JILT, and other Stories. Illustrated by JOSEPH NASH.
A PERILOUS SECRET. Illustrated by FRED. BARNARD.
READIANA. With a Steel-plate Portrait of CHARLES READE.
BIBLE CHARACTERS: Studies of David, Paul, &c. Fcap. 8vo, leatherette, 1s.
THE CLOISTER AND THE HEARTH. With an Introduction by WALTER BESANT.
Elzevir Edition. 4 vols., post 8vo, each with Front., cl. ex., gilt top, 14s. the set.
SELECTIONS FROM THE WORKS OF CHARLES READE. Cr. 8vo, buckram 6s.

RIDDELL (MRS. J. H.), NOVELS BY.
Crown 8vo, cloth extra, **3s. 6d.** each; post 8vo, illustrated boards, **2s.** each.
THE PRINCE OF WALES'S GARDEN PARTY. | WEIRD STORIES.
Post 8vo, illustrated boards, **2s.** each.
THE UNINHABITED HOUSE. | HER MOTHER'S DARLING.
MYSTERY IN PALACE GARDENS. | THE NUN'S CURSE.
FAIRY WATER. | IDLE TALES.

RIMMER (ALFRED), WORKS BY. Square 8vo, cloth gilt, **7s. 6d.** each.
OUR OLD COUNTRY TOWNS. With 55 Illustrations.
RAMBLES ROUND ETON AND HARROW. With 50 Illustrations.
ABOUT ENGLAND WITH DICKENS. With 58 Illusts. by C. A. VANDERHOOF, &c.

RIVES.—BARBARA DERING. By AMÉLIE RIVES, Author of " The
Quick or the Dead?" Crown 8vo, cloth extra, **3s. 6d.**; post 8vo, illust. bds., **2s.**

ROBINSON CRUSOE. By DANIEL DEFOE. (MAJOR'S EDITION.) With
37 Illustrations by GEORGE CRUIKSHANK. Post 8vo, half-bound, **2s.**

ROBINSON (F. W.), NOVELS BY.
WOMEN ARE STRANGE. Post 8vo, illustrated boards, **2s.**
THE HANDS OF JUSTICE. Cr. 8vo, cloth ex., **3s. 6d.**; post 8vo, illust. bds., **2s.**

ROBINSON (PHIL), WORKS BY. Crown 8vo, cloth extra, **6s.** each.
THE POETS' BIRDS. | THE POETS' BEASTS.
THE POETS AND NATURE: REPTILES, FISHES, AND INSECTS.

ROCHEFOUCAULD'S MAXIMS AND MORAL REFLECTIONS. With
Notes, and an Introductory Essay by SAINTE-BEUVE. Post 8vo, cloth limp, **2s.**

ROLL OF BATTLE ABBEY, THE : A List of the Principal Warriors
who came from Normandy with William the Conqueror, and Settled in this Country,
A.D. 1066-7. With Arms emblazoned in Gold and Colours. Handsomely printed, **5s.**

ROWLEY (HON. HUGH), WORKS BY. Post 8vo, cloth, **2s. 6d.** each.
PUNIANA: RIDDLES AND JOKES. With numerous Illustrations.
MORE PUNIANA. Profusely Illustrated.

RUNCIMAN (JAMES), STORIES BY. Post 8vo, bds., **2s.** ea.; cl., **2s. 6d.** ea.
SKIPPERS AND SHELLBACKS. | GRACE BALMAIGN'S SWEETHEART.
SCHOOLS AND SCHOLARS.

RUSSELL (W. CLARK), BOOKS AND NOVELS BY :
Cr. 8vo, cloth extra, **6s.** each; post 8vo, illust. boards, **2s.** each; cloth limp, **2s. 6d.** ea.
ROUND THE GALLEY-FIRE. | A BOOK FOR THE HAMMOCK.
IN THE MIDDLE WATCH. | MYSTERY OF THE "OCEAN STAR."
A VOYAGE TO THE CAPE. | THE ROMANCE OF JENNY HARLOWE.
Cr. 8vo, cl. extra, **3s. 6d.** ea.; post 8vo, illust. boards, **2s.** ea.; cloth limp, **2s. 6d.** ea.
AN OCEAN TRAGEDY. | MY SHIPMATE LOUISE.
          ALONE ON A WIDE WIDE SEA.
ON THE FO'K'SLE HEAD. Post 8vo, illust. boards, **2s.**; cloth limp, **2s. 6d.**

SAINT AUBYN (ALAN), NOVELS BY.
Crown 8vo, cloth extra, **3s. 6d.** each; post 8vo, illust. boards, **2s.** each.
A FELLOW OF TRINITY. Note by OLIVER WENDELL HOLMES and Frontispiece.
THE JUNIOR DEAN. | THE MASTER OF ST. BENEDICT'S.
Fcap. 8vo, cloth boards, **1s. 6d.** each.
THE OLD MAID'S SWEETHEART. | MODEST LITTLE SARA.
TO HIS OWN MASTER. Three Vols., crown 8vo.

SALA (G. A.).—GASLIGHT AND DAYLIGHT. Post 8vo, boards, 2s.

SANSON.—SEVEN GENERATIONS OF EXECUTIONERS : Memoirs
of the Sanson Family (1688 to 1847). Crown 8vo, cloth extra, **3s. 6d.**

SAUNDERS (JOHN), NOVELS BY.
Crown 8vo, cloth extra, **3s. 6d.** each; post 8vo, illustrated boards, **2s.** each.
GUY WATERMAN. | THE LION IN THE PATH. | THE TWO DREAMERS.
BOUND TO THE WHEEL. Crown 8vo, cloth extra, **3s. 6d.**

SAUNDERS (KATHARINE), NOVELS BY.
Crown 8vo, cloth extra, **3s. 6d.** each; post 8vo, illustrated boards, **2s.** each.
MARGARET AND ELIZABETH. | HEART SALVAGE.
THE HIGH MILLS. | SEBASTIAN.
JOAN MERRYWEATHER. Post 8vo, illustrated boards, **2s.**
GIDEON'S ROCK. Crown 8vo, cloth extra, **3s. 6d.**

SCOTLAND YARD, Past and Present: Experiences of 37 Years. By Ex-Chief-Inspector CAVANAGH. Post 8vo, illustrated boards, **2s.**; cloth, **2s. 6d.**

SECRET OUT, THE: One Thousand Tricks with Cards; with Entertaining Experiments in Drawing-room or "White Magic." By W. H. CREMER. With 300 Illustrations. Crown 8vo, cloth extra, **4s. 6d.**

SEGUIN (L. G.), WORKS BY.
THE COUNTRY OF THE PASSION PLAY (OBERAMMERGAU) and the Highlands of Bavaria. With Map and 37 Illustrations. Crown 8vo, cloth extra, **3s. 6d.**
WALKS IN ALGIERS. With 2 Maps and 16 Illusts. Crown 8vo, cloth extra, **6s.**

SENIOR (WM.).—BY STREAM AND SEA. Post 8vo, cloth, **2s. 6d.**

SHAKESPEARE FOR CHILDREN: LAMB'S TALES FROM SHAKE-
SPEARE. With Illusts., coloured and plain, by J. MOYR SMITH. Cr. 4to, **3s. 6d.**

SHARP.—CHILDREN OF TO-MORROW: A Novel. By WILLIAM SHARP. Crown 8vo, cloth extra, **6s.**

SHELLEY.—THE COMPLETE WORKS IN VERSE AND PROSE OF
PERCY BYSSHE SHELLEY. Edited, Prefaced, and Annotated by R. HERNE SHEPHERD. Five Vols., crown 8vo, cloth boards, **3s. 6d.** each.
POETICAL WORKS, in Three Vols.:
Vol. I. Introduction by the Editor; Posthumous Fragments of Margaret Nicholson; Shelley's Correspondence with Stockdale; The Wandering Jew; Queen Mab, with the Notes; Alastor, and other Poems; Rosalind and Helen; Prometheus Unbound; Adonais, &c.
Vol. II. Laon and Cythna; The Cenci; Julian and Maddalo; Swellfoot the Tyrant; The Witch of Atlas; Epipsychidion; Hellas.
Vol. III. Posthumous Poems; The Masque of Anarchy; and other Pieces.
PROSE WORKS, in Two Vols.:
Vol. I. The Two Romances of Zastrozzi and St. Irvyne; the Dublin and Marlow Pamphlets; A Refutation of Deism; Letters to Leigh Hunt, and some Minor Writings and Fragments.
Vol. II. The Essays; Letters from Abroad; Translations and Fragments, Edited by Mrs. SHELLEY. With a Bibliography of Shelley, and an Index of the Prose Works.

SHERARD (R. H.).—ROGUES: A Novel. Crown 8vo, **1s.**; cloth, **1s. 6d.**

SHERIDAN (GENERAL). — PERSONAL MEMOIRS OF GENERAL
P. H. SHERIDAN. With Portraits and Facsimiles. Two Vols., demy 8vo, cloth, **24s.**

SHERIDAN'S (RICHARD BRINSLEY) COMPLETE WORKS. With Life and Anecdotes. Including his Dramatic Writings, his Works in Prose and Poetry, Translations, Speeches and Jokes. 10 Illusts. Cr. 8vo, hf.-bound, **7s. 6d.**
THE RIVALS, THE SCHOOL FOR SCANDAL, and other Plays. Post 8vo, printed on laid paper and half-bound, **2s.**
SHERIDAN'S COMEDIES: THE RIVALS and THE SCHOOL FOR SCANDAL. Edited, with an Introduction and Notes to each Play, and a Biographical Sketch, by BRANDER MATTHEWS. With Illustrations. Demy 8vo, half-parchment, **12s. 6d.**

SIDNEY'S (SIR PHILIP) COMPLETE POETICAL WORKS, including all those in "Arcadia." With Portrait, Memorial-Introduction, Notes, &c. by the Rev. A. B. GROSART, D.D. Three Vols., crown 8vo, cloth boards, **18s.**

SIGNBOARDS: Their History. With Anecdotes of Famous Taverns and Remarkable Characters. By JACOB LARWOOD and JOHN CAMDEN HOTTEN. With Coloured Frontispiece and 94 Illustrations. Crown 8vo, cloth extra, **7s. 6d.**

SIMS (GEORGE R.), WORKS BY.
Post 8vo, illustrated boards, **2s.** each; cloth limp, **2s. 6d.** each.
ROGUES AND VAGABONDS. | MARY JANE MARRIED.
THE RING O' BELLS. | TALES OF TO-DAY.
MARY JANE'S MEMOIRS. | DRAMAS OF LIFE. With 60 Illustrations.
TINKLETOP'S CRIME. With a Frontispiece by MAURICE GREIFFENHAGEN.
ZEPH: A Circus Story, &c. | MY TWO WIVES.
Crown 8vo, picture cover, **1s.** each; cloth, **1s. 6d.** each.
HOW THE POOR LIVE; and HORRIBLE LONDON.
THE DAGONET RECITER AND READER: being Readings and Recitations in Prose and Verse, selected from his own Works by GEORGE R. SIMS.
THE CASE OF GEORGE CANDLEMAS. | DAGONET DITTIES.

SISTER DORA: A Biography. By MARGARET LONSDALE. With Four Illustrations. Demy 8vo, picture cover, **4d.**; cloth, **6d.**

SKETCHLEY.—A MATCH IN THE DARK. By ARTHUR SKETCHLEY. Post 8vo, illustrated boards, **2s.**

SLANG DICTIONARY (THE): Etymological, Historical, and Anecdotal. Crown 8vo, cloth extra, 6s. 6d.

SMITH (J. MOYR), WORKS BY.
THE PRINCE OF ARGOLIS. With 130 Illusts. Post 8vo, cloth extra, 3s. 6d.
TALES OF OLD THULE. With numerous Illustrations. Crown 8vo, cloth gilt, 6s.
THE WOOING OF THE WATER WITCH. Illustrated. Post 8vo, cloth, 6s.

SOCIETY IN LONDON. By A FOREIGN RESIDENT. Crown 8vo, 1s.; cloth, 1s. 6d.

SOCIETY IN PARIS: The Upper Ten Thousand. A Series of Letters from Count PAUL VASILI to a Young French Diplomat. Crown 8vo, cloth, 6s.

SOMERSET.—SONGS OF ADIEU. By Lord HENRY SOMERSET. Small 4to, Japanese vellum, 6s.

SPALDING.—ELIZABETHAN DEMONOLOGY: An Essay on the Belief in the Existence of Devils. By T. A. SPALDING, LL.B. Crown 8vo, cloth extra, 5s.

SPEIGHT (T. W.), NOVELS BY.
Post 8vo, illustrated boards, 2s. each.

THE MYSTERIES OF HERON DYKE.	THE GOLDEN HOOP.
BY DEVIOUS WAYS, &c.	BACK TO LIFE.
HOODWINKED; and THE SANDY-	THE LOUDWATER TRAGEDY.
CROFT MYSTERY.	BURGO'S ROMANCE.

Post 8vo, cloth limp, 1s. 6d. each.

A BARREN TITLE.	WIFE OR NO WIFE?

THE SANDYCROFT MYSTERY. Crown 8vo, picture cover, 1s.

SPENSER FOR CHILDREN. By M. H. TOWRY. With Illustrations by WALTER J. MORGAN. Crown 4to, cloth extra, 3s. 6d.

STARRY HEAVENS (THE): A POETICAL BIRTHDAY BOOK. Royal 16mo, cloth extra, 2s. 6d.

STAUNTON.—THE LAWS AND PRACTICE OF CHESS. With an Analysis of the Openings. By HOWARD STAUNTON. Edited by ROBERT B. WORMALD. Crown 8vo, cloth extra, 5s.

STEDMAN (E. C.), WORKS BY.
VICTORIAN POETS. Thirteenth Edition. Crown 8vo. cloth extra, 9s.
THE POETS OF AMERICA. Crown 8vo, cloth extra, 9s.

STERNDALE.—THE AFGHAN KNIFE: A Novel. By ROBERT ARMITAGE STERNDALE. Cr. 8vo, cloth extra, 3s. 6d.; post 8vo, illust. boards, 2s.

STEVENSON (R. LOUIS), WORKS BY. Post 8vo, cl. limp, 2s. 6d. each.
TRAVELS WITH A DONKEY. Seventh Edit. With a Frontis. by WALTER CRANE.
AN INLAND VOYAGE. Fourth Edition. With a Frontispiece by WALTER CRANE.

Crown 8vo, buckram, gilt top, 6s. each.
FAMILIAR STUDIES OF MEN AND BOOKS. Sixth Edition.
THE MERRY MEN. Third Edition. | UNDERWOODS: Poems. Fifth Edition.
MEMORIES AND PORTRAITS. Third Edition.
VIRGINIBUS PUERISQUE, and other Papers. Seventh Edition. | BALLADS.
ACROSS THE PLAINS, with other Memories and Essays.

NEW ARABIAN NIGHTS. Eleventh Edition. Crown 8vo, buckram, gilt top, 6s.; post 8vo, illustrated boards, 2s.
THE SUICIDE CLUB; and THE RAJAH'S DIAMOND. (From NEW ARABIAN NIGHTS.) With Six Illustrations by J. BERNARD PARTRIDGE. Crown 8vo, cloth extra, 5s. [Shortly.
PRINCE OTTO. Sixth Edition. Post 8vo, illustrated boards, 2s.
FATHER DAMIEN: An Open Letter to the Rev. Dr. Hyde. Second Edition. Crown 8vo, hand-made and brown paper, 1s.

STODDARD.—SUMMER CRUISING IN THE SOUTH SEAS. By C. WARREN STODDARD. Illustrated by WALLIS MACKAY. Cr. 8vo, cl. extra, 3s. 6d.

STORIES FROM FOREIGN NOVELISTS. With Notices by HELEN and ALICE ZIMMERN. Crown 8vo, cloth extra, 3s. 6d.; post 8vo, illustrated boards, 2s.

STRANGE MANUSCRIPT (A) FOUND IN A COPPER CYLINDER. With 19 Illustrations by GILBERT GAUL. Crown 8vo, cloth extra, 5s.; post 8vo, illustrated boards, 2s.

STRANGE SECRETS. Told by CONAN DOYLE, PERCY FITZGERALD, FLORENCE MARRYAT, &c. Post 8vo, illustrated boards, 2s.

STRUTT'S SPORTS AND PASTIMES OF THE PEOPLE OF

ENGLAND; including the Rural and Domestic Recreations, May Games, Mummeries, Shows, &c., from the Earliest Period to the Present Time. Edited by WILLIAM HONE. With 140 Illustrations. Crown 8vo, cloth extra, **7s. 6d.**

SWIFT'S (DEAN) CHOICE WORKS, in Prose and Verse. With Memoir,

Portrait, and Facsimiles of the Maps in "Gulliver's Travels." Cr. 8vo, cl., **7s. 6d.**
GULLIVER'S TRAVELS, and A TALE OF A TUB. Post 8vo, half-bound, **2s.**
JONATHAN SWIFT: A Study. By J. CHURTON COLLINS. Crown 8vo, cloth extra, **8s.**

SWINBURNE (ALGERNON C.), WORKS BY.

SELECTIONS FROM POETICAL WORKS OF A. C. SWINBURNE. Fcap. 8vo, 6s.	ERECHTHEUS : A Tragedy. Crown 8vo, 6s.
ATALANTA IN CALYDON. Crown 8vo, 6s.	A NOTE ON CHARLOTTE BRONTE. Cr. 8vo, 6s.
CHASTELARD : A Tragedy. Crown 8vo, 7s.	SONGS OF THE SPRINGTIDES. Crown 8vo, 6s.
POEMS AND BALLADS. FIRST SERIES. Crown 8vo or fcap. 8vo, 9s.	STUDIES IN SONG. Crown 8vo, 7s.
POEMS AND BALLADS. SECOND SERIES. Crown 8vo or fcap. 8vo, 9s.	MARY STUART: A Tragedy. Crown 8vo, 8s.
POEMS & BALLADS. THIRD SERIES. Cr. 8vo, 7s.	TRISTRAM OF LYONESSE. Crown 8vo, 9s.
SONGS BEFORE SUNRISE. Crown 8vo. 10s. 6d.	A CENTURY OF ROUNDELS. Small 4to, 8s.
BOTHWELL : A Tragedy. Crown 8vo, 12s. 6d.	A MIDSUMMER HOLIDAY. Crown 8vo, 7s.
SONGS OF TWO NATIONS. Crown 8vo, 6s.	MARINO FALIERO: A Tragedy. Crown 8vo, 6s.
GEORGE CHAPMAN. (See Vol. II. of G. CHAPMAN'S Works.) Crown 8vo, 6s.	A STUDY OF VICTOR HUGO. Crown 8vo, 6s.
ESSAYS AND STUDIES. Crown 8vo, 12s.	M'SCELLANIES. Crown 8vo, 12s.
	LOCRINE : A Tragedy. Crown 8vo, 6s.
	A STUDY OF BEN JONSON. Crown 8vo, 7s.
	THE SISTERS : A Tragedy. Crown 8vo, 6s.
	ASTROPHEL, &c. Crown 8vo, 7s. [Shortly.

SYNTAX'S (DR.) THREE TOURS : In Search of the Picturesque, in

Search of Consolation, and in Search of a Wife. With ROWLANDSON's Coloured Illustrations, and Life of the Author by J. C. HOTTEN. Crown 8vo, cloth extra, **7s. 6d.**

TAINE'S HISTORY OF ENGLISH LITERATURE. Translated by

HENRY VAN LAUN. Four Vols., small demy 8vo, cl. bds., **30s.**—POPULAR EDITION, Two Vols., large crown 8vo, cloth extra, **15s.**

TAYLOR'S (BAYARD) DIVERSIONS OF THE ECHO CLUB : Bur-

lesques of Modern Writers. Post 8vo, cloth limp, **2s.**

TAYLOR (DR. J. E., F.L.S.), WORKS BY. Crown 8vo, cloth, 5s. each.

THE SAGACITY AND MORALITY OF PLANTS : A Sketch of the Life and Conduct of the Vegetable Kingdom. With a Coloured Frontispiece and 100 Illustrations.
OUR COMMON BRITISH FOSSILS, and Where to Find Them. 331 Illustrations.
THE PLAYTIME NATURALIST. With 366 Illustrations.

TAYLOR'S (TOM) HISTORICAL DRAMAS. Containing "Clancarty,"

"Jeanne Darc," "'Twixt Axe and Crown," "The Fool's Revenge," "Arkwright's Wife," "Anne Boleyn," "Plot and Passion." Crown 8vo, cloth extra, **7s. 6d.**
* The Plays may also be had separately, at **1s.** each.

TENNYSON (LORD): A Biographical Sketch. By H. J. JENNINGS.

With a Photograph-Portrait. Crown 8vo, cloth extra, **6s.**—Cheap Edition, post 8vo, portrait cover, **1s.**; cloth, **1s. 6d.**

THACKERAYANA : Notes and Anecdotes. Illustrated by Hundreds of

Sketches by WILLIAM MAKEPEACE THACKERAY. Crown 8vo, cloth extra, **7s. 6d.**

THAMES.—A NEW PICTORIAL HISTORY OF THE THAMES.

By A. S. KRAUSSE. With 340 Illustrations Post 8vo, **1s.**; cloth, **1s. 6d.**

THIERS.—HISTORY OF THE CONSULATE & EMPIRE OF FRANCE

UNDER NAPOLEON. By A. THIERS. Translated by D. FORBES CAMPBELL and JOHN STEBBING. New Edition, reset in a specially-cast type, with 36 Steel Plates. 12 vols., demy 8vo, cl. ex., 12s. each. (Monthly Volumes. beginning September, 1893.)

THOMAS (BERTHA), NOVELS BY. Cr. 8vo, cl., 3s. 6d. ea.; post 8vo, 2s. ea.

THE VIOLIN-PLAYER.	PROUD MAISIE.
CRESSIDA. Post 8vo, illustrated boards, **2s.**	

THOMSON'S SEASONS, and CASTLE OF INDOLENCE. With Intro-

duction by ALLAN CUNNINGHAM, and 48 Illustrations. Post 8vo, half-bound, **2s.**

THORNBURY (WALTER), WORKS BY.

THE LIFE AND CORRESPONDENCE OF J. M. W. TURNER. With Illustrations in Colours. Crown 8vo, cloth extra, **7s. 6d.**

Post 8vo, illustrated boards, **2s.** each.
OLD STORIES RE-TOLD.	TALES FOR THE MARINES.

TIMBS (JOHN), WORKS BY. Crown 8vo, cloth extra, **7s. 6d.** each.
THE HISTORY OF CLUBS AND CLUB LIFE IN LONDON: Anecdotes of its
Famous Coffee-houses, Hostelries, and Taverns. With 42 Illustrations.
ENGLISH ECCENTRICS AND ECCENTRICITIES: Stories of Delusions, Impos-
tures, Sporting Scenes, Eccentric Artists, Theatrical Folk, &c. 48 Illustrations.

TROLLOPE (ANTHONY), NOVELS BY.
Crown 8vo, cloth extra, 3s. 6d. each; post 8vo, illustrated boards, 2s. each.
THE WAY WE LIVE NOW. | MR. SCARBOROUGH'S FAMILY.
FRAU FROHMANN. | MARION FAY. | THE LAND-LEAGUERS.
Post 8vo, illustrated boards, 2s. each.
KEPT IN THE DARK. | AMERICAN SENATOR.
GOLDEN LION OF GRANPERE. | JOHN CALDIGATE.

TROLLOPE (FRANCES E.), NOVELS BY.
Crown 8vo, cloth extra, 3s. 6d. each; post 8vo, illustrated boards, 2s. each.
LIKE SHIPS UPON THE SEA. | MABEL'S PROGRESS. | ANNE FURNESS.

TROLLOPE (T. A.).—DIAMOND CUT DIAMOND. Post 8vo, illust. bds., 2s.

TROWBRIDGE.—FARNELL'S FOLLY: A Novel. By J. T. TROW-
BRIDGE. Post 8vo, illustrated boards, 2s.

TYTLER (C. C. FRASER-).—MISTRESS JUDITH: A Novel. By
C. C. FRASER-TYTLER. Crown 8vo, cloth extra, 3s. 6d.; post 8vo, illust. boards, 2s.

TYTLER (SARAH), NOVELS BY.
Crown 8vo, cloth extra, 3s. 6d. each; post 8vo, illustrated boards, 2s. each.
THE BRIDE'S PASS. | BURIED DIAMONDS.
LADY BELL. | THE BLACKHALL GHOSTS.
Post 8vo, illustrated boards, 2s. each.
WHAT SHE CAME THROUGH. | BEAUTY AND THE BEAST.
CITOYENNE JACQUELINE | DISAPPEARED. | NOBLESSE OBLIGE.
SAINT MUNGO'S CITY. | THE HUGUENOT FAMILY.

UNDERHILL.—WALTER BESANT: A Study. By JOHN UNDERHILL.
With Portraits. Crown 8vo, Irish linen, 6s.   [Shortly.

UPWARD.—THE QUEEN AGAINST OWEN. By ALLEN UPWARD.
With a Frontispiece. Crown 8vo, cloth extra, 3s. 6d.

VASHTI AND ESTHER. By the Writer of "Belle's" Letters in The
World. Two Vols., crown 8vo.

VILLARI.—A DOUBLE BOND. By LINDA VILLARI. Fcap. 8vo, 1s.

WALFORD (EDWARD, M.A.), WORKS BY.
WALFORD'S COUNTY FAMILIES OF THE UNITED KINGDOM (1894). Containing the Descent,
Birth, Marriage, Education, &c., of 12,000 Heads of Families, their Heirs, Offices, Addresses,
Clubs, &c. Royal 8vo, cloth gilt, 50s.
WALFORD'S WINDSOR PEERAGE, BARONETAGE, AND KNIGHTAGE (1894). Crown 8vo, cloth
extra, 12s. 6d.
WALFORD'S SHILLING PEERAGE (1894). Containing a List of the House of Lords, Scotch and
Irish Peers, &c. 32mo, cloth, 1s.
WALFORD'S SHILLING BARONETAGE (1894). Containing a List of the Baronets of the United
Kingdom, Biographical Notices Addresses, &c. 32mo, cloth, 1s.
WALFORD'S SHILLING KNIGHTAGE (1894). Containing a List of the Knights of the United
Kingdom, Biographical Notices, Addresses, &c. 32mo, cloth, 1s.
WALFORD'S SHILLING HOUSE OF COMMONS (1894). Containing a List of all the Members of the
New Parliament, their Addresses, Clubs, &c. 32mo, cloth, 1s.
WALFORD'S COMPLETE PEERAGE, BARONETAGE, KNIGHTAGE, AND HOUSE OF COMMONS
(1894). Royal 32mo, cloth, gilt edges, 5s.
TALES OF OUR GREAT FAMILIES. Crown 8vo, cloth extra, 3s. 6d.

WALT WHITMAN, POEMS BY. Edited, with Introduction, by
WILLIAM M. ROSSETTI. With Portrait. Cr. 8vo, hand-made paper and buckram, 6s.

WALTON AND COTTON'S COMPLETE ANGLER; or, The Con-
templative Man's Recreation, by IZAAK WALTON; and Instructions how to Angle for a
Trout or Grayling in a clear Stream, by CHARLES COTTON. With Memoirs and Notes
by Sir HARRIS NICOLAS, and 61 Illustrations. Crown 8vo, cloth antique, 7s. 6d.

WARD (HERBERT), WORKS BY.
FIVE YEARS WITH THE CONGO CANNIBALS. With 92 Illustrations by the
Author, VICTOR PERARD, and W. B. DAVIS. Third ed. Roy. 8vo, cloth ex., 14s.
MY LIFE WITH STANLEY'S REAR GUARD. With a Map by F. S. WELLER,
F.R.G.S. Post 8vo, 1s.; cloth, 1s. 6d.

WARNER.—A ROUNDABOUT JOURNEY. By CHARLES DUDLEY
WARNER. Crown 8vo, cloth extra, 6s.

WARRANT TO EXECUTE CHARLES I. A Facsimile, with the 59
Signatures and Seals. Printed on paper 22 in. by 14 in. **2s.**
WARRANT TO EXECUTE MARY QUEEN OF SCOTS. A Facsimile, including
Queen Elizabeth's Signature and the Great Seal. **2s.**

WASSERMANN (LILLIAS), NOVELS BY.
THE DAFFODILS. Crown 8vo, **1s.**; cloth, **1s. 6d.**
THE MARQUIS OF CARABAS. By AARON WATSON and LILLIAS WASSERMANN.
Post 8vo, illustrated boards, **2s.**

WEATHER, HOW TO FORETELL THE, WITH POCKET SPEC-
TROSCOPE. By F. W. CORY. With 10 Illustrations. Cr. 8vo, **1s.**; cloth, **1s. 6d.**

WESTALL (William).—TRUST-MONEY. Post 8vo, illust. bds., **2s.**

WHIST.—HOW TO PLAY SOLO WHIST. By ABRAHAM S. WILKS
and CHARLES F. PARDON. New Edition. Post 8vo, cloth limp, **2s.**

WHITE.—THE NATURAL HISTORY OF SELBORNE. By GILBERT
WHITE, M.A. Post 8vo, printed on laid paper and half-bound, **2s.**

WILLIAMS (W. MATTIEU, F.R.A.S.), WORKS BY.
SCIENCE IN SHORT CHAPTERS. Crown 8vo, cloth extra, **7s. 6d.**
A SIMPLE TREATISE ON HEAT. With Illusts. Cr. 8vo, cloth limp, **2s. 6d.**
THE CHEMISTRY OF COOKERY. Crown 8vo, cloth extra, **6s.**
THE CHEMISTRY OF IRON AND STEEL MAKING. Crown 8vo, cloth extra, **9s.**
A VINDICATION OF PHRENOLOGY. With over 40 Illustrations. Demy 8vo,
cloth extra, **12s. 6d.** [*Shortly.*

WILLIAMSON (MRS. F. H.).—A CHILD WIDOW. Post 8vo, bds., **2s.**

WILSON (DR. ANDREW, F.R.S.E.), WORKS BY.
CHAPTERS ON EVOLUTION. With 259 Illustrations. Cr. 8vo, cloth extra, **7s. 6d.**
LEAVES FROM A NATURALIST'S NOTE-BOOK. Post 8vo, cloth limp, **2s. 6d.**
LEISURE-TIME STUDIES. With Illustrations. Crown 8vo, cloth extra, **6s.**
STUDIES IN LIFE AND SENSE. With numerous Illusts. Cr. 8vo, cl. ex., **6s.**
COMMON ACCIDENTS: HOW TO TREAT THEM. Illusts. Cr. 8vo, **1s.**; cl., **1s.6d.**
GLIMPSES OF NATURE. With 35 Illustrations. Crown 8vo, cloth extra, **3s. 6d.**

WINTER (J. S.), STORIES BY. Post 8vo, illustrated boards, **2s.** each;
cloth limp, **2s. 6d.** each.
CAVALRY LIFE. | REGIMENTAL LEGENDS.
A SOLDIER'S CHILDREN. With 34 Illustrations by E. G. THOMSON and E. STUART
HARDY. Crown 8vo, cloth extra, **3s. 6d.**

WISSMANN.—MY SECOND JOURNEY THROUGH EQUATORIAL
AFRICA. By HERMANN VON WISSMANN. With 92 Illusts. Demy 8vo, **16s.**

WOOD.—SABINA : A Novel. By Lady WOOD. Post 8vo, boards, **2s.**

WOOD (H. F.), DETECTIVE STORIES BY. Post 8vo, boards, **2s.** each.
PASSENGER FROM SCOTLAND YARD. | ENGLISHMAN OF THE RUE CAIN.

WOOLLEY.—RACHEL ARMSTRONG ; or, Love and Theology. By
CELIA PARKER WOOLLEY. Post 8vo, illustrated boards, **2s.**; cloth, **2s. 6d.**

WRIGHT (THOMAS), WORKS BY. Crown 8vo, cloth extra, **7s. 6d.** each.
CARICATURE HISTORY OF THE GEORGES. With 400 Caricatures, Squibs, &c.
HISTORY OF CARICATURE AND OF THE GROTESQUE IN ART, LITERA-
TURE, SCULPTURE, AND PAINTING. Illustrated by F. W. FAIRHOLT, F.S.A.

WYNMAN.—MY FLIRTATIONS. By MARGARET WYNMAN. With 13
Illustrations by J. BERNARD PARTRIDGE. Crown 8vo, cloth extra, **3s. 6d.**

YATES (EDMUND), NOVELS BY. Post 8vo, illustrated boards, **2s.** each.
LAND AT LAST. | THE FORLORN HOPE. | CASTAWAY.

ZOLA (EMILE), NOVELS BY. Crown 8vo, cloth extra, **3s. 6d.** each.
THE DOWNFALL. Translated by E. A. VIZETELLY. Fourth Edition, Revised.
THE DREAM. Translated by ELIZA CHASE. With 8 Illustrations by JEANNIOT.
DOCTOR PASCAL. Translated by E. A. VIZETELLY. With Portrait of the Author.
MONEY. Translated by ERNEST A. VIZETELLY.
EMILE ZOLA : A Biography. By R. H. SHERARD. With Portraits, Illustrations.
and Facsimile Letter. Demy 8vo, cloth extra, **12s.**

LISTS OF BOOKS CLASSIFIED IN SERIES.

₊ *For fuller cataloguing, see alphabetical arrangement, pp.* 1–25.

THE MAYFAIR LIBRARY. Post 8vo, cloth limp, 2s. 6d. per Volume.

A Journey Round My Room. By XAVIER DE MAISTRE.
Quips and Quiddities. By W. D. ADAMS.
The Agony Column of "The Times."
Melancholy Anatomised: Abridgment of "Burton's Anatomy of Melancholy."
The Speeches of Charles Dickens.
Poetical Ingenuities. By W. T. DODSON.
The Cupboard Papers. By FIN-BEC.
W. S. Gilbert's Plays. FIRST SERIES.
W. S. Gilbert's Plays. SECOND SERIES.
Songs of Irish Wit and Humour.
Animals and Masters. By Sir A. HELPS.
Social Pressure. By Sir A. HELPS.
Curiosities of Criticism. H. J. JENNINGS.
Holmes's Autocrat of Breakfast-Table.
Pencil and Palette. By R. KEMPT.
Little Essays: from LAMB's Letters.

Forensic Anecdotes. By JACOB LARWOOD.
Theatrical Anecdotes. JACOB LARWOOD.
Jeux d'Esprit. Edited by HENRY S. LEIGH.
Witch Stories. By E. LYNN LINTON.
Ourselves. By E. LYNN LINTON.
Pastimes & Players. By R. MACGREGOR.
New Paul and Virginia. W. H. MALLOCK.
New Republic. By W. H. MALLOCK.
Puck on Pegasus. By H. C. PENNELL.
Pegasus Re-Saddled. By H. C. PENNELL.
Muses of Mayfair. Ed. H. C. PENNELL.
Thoreau: His Life & Aims. By H. A. PAGE.
Puniana. By Hon. HUGH ROWLEY.
More Puniana. By Hon. HUGH ROWLEY.
The Philosophy of Handwriting.
By Stream and Sea. By WM. SENIOR.
Leaves from a Naturalist's Note-Book.
   By Dr. ANDREW WILSON.

THE GOLDEN LIBRARY. Post 8vo, cloth limp, 2s. per Volume.

Bayard Taylor's Diversions of the Echo Club.
Bennett's Ballad History of England.
Bennett's Songs for Sailors.
Godwin's Lives of the Necromancers.
Pope's Poetical Works.
Holmes's Autocrat of Breakfast Table.

Jesse's Scenes of Country Life.
Leigh Hunt's Tale for a Chimney Corner.
Mallory's Mort d'Arthur: Selections.
Pascal's Provincial Letters.
Rochefoucauld's Maxims & Reflections.

THE WANDERER'S LIBRARY. Crown 8vo, cloth extra, 3s. 6d. each.

Wanderings in Patagonia. By JULIUS BEERBOHM. Illustrated.
Camp Notes. By FREDERICK BOYLE.
Savage Life. By FREDERICK BOYLE.
Merrie England in the Olden Time. By G. DANIEL. Illustrated by CRUIKSHANK.
Circus Life. By THOMAS FROST.
Lives of the Conjurers. THOMAS FROST.
The Old Showmen and the Old London Fairs. By THOMAS FROST.
Low-Life Deeps. By JAMES GREENWOOD.

Wilds of London. JAMES GREENWOOD.
Tunis. Chev. HESSE-WARTEGG. 22 Illusts.
Life and Adventures of a Cheap Jack.
World Behind the Scenes. P. FITZGERALD.
Tavern Anecdotes and Sayings.
The Genial Showman. By E. P. HINGSTON.
Story of London Parks. JACOB LARWOOD.
London Characters. By HENRY MAYHEW.
Seven Generations of Executioners.
Summer Cruising in the South Seas.
   By C. WARREN STODDARD. Illustrated.

POPULAR SHILLING BOOKS.

Harry Fludyer at Cambridge.
Jeff Briggs's Love Story. BRET HARTE.
Twins of Table Mountain. BRET HARTE.
Snow-bound at Eagle's. By BRET HARTE.
A Day's Tour. By PERCY FITZGERALD.
Esther's Glove. By R. E. FRANCILLON.
Sentenced! By SOMERVILLE GIBNEY.
The Professor's Wife. By L. GRAHAM.
Mrs. Gainsborough's Diamonds. By JULIAN HAWTHORNE.
Niagara Spray. By J. HOLLINGSHEAD.
A Romance of the Queen's Hounds. By CHARLES JAMES.
Garden that Paid Rent. TOM JERROLD.
Cut by the Mess. By ARTHUR KEYSER.
Teresa Itasca. By A. MACALPINE.
Our Sensation Novel. J. H. McCARTHY.
Doom! By JUSTIN H. McCARTHY.
Dolly. By JUSTIN H. McCARTHY.

Lily Lass. JUSTIN H. McCARTHY.
Was She Good or Bad? By W. MINTO.
Notes from the "News." By JAS. PAYN.
Beyond the Gates. By E. S. PHELPS.
Old Maid's Paradise. By E. S. PHELPS.
Burglars in Paradise. By E. S. PHELPS.
Jack the Fisherman. By E. S. PHELPS.
Trooping with Crows. By C. L. PIRKIS.
Bible Characters. By CHARLES READE.
Rogues. By R. H. SHERARD.
The Dagonet Reciter. By G. R. SIMS.
How the Poor Live. By G. R. SIMS.
Case of George Candlemas. G. R. SIMS.
Sandycroft Mystery. T. W. SPEIGHT.
Hoodwinked. By T. W. SPEIGHT.
Father Damien. By R. L. STEVENSON.
A Double Bond. By LINDA VILLARI.
My Life with Stanley's Rear Guard. By HERBERT WARD.

HANDY NOVELS. Fcap. 8vo, cloth boards, 1s. 6d. each.

The Old Maid's Sweetheart. A. ST. AUBYN
Modest Little Sara. ALAN ST. AUBYN
Seven Sleepers of Ephesus. M. E. COLERIDGE.

Taken from the Enemy. H. NEWBOLT.
A Lost Soul. By W. L. ALDEN.
Dr. Palliser's Patient. GRANT ALLEN.

MY LIBRARY. Printed on laid paper, post 8vo, half-Roxburghe, **2s. 6d.** each.

Four Frenchwomen. By Austin Dobson. | Christie Johnstone. By Charles Reade.
Citation and Examination of William | With a Photogravure Frontispiece.
Shakspeare. By W. S. Landor. | Peg Woffington. By Charles Reade.
The Journal of Maurice de Guerin. | The Dramatic Essays of Charles Lamb.

THE POCKET LIBRARY. Post 8vo, printed on laid paper and hf.-bd., **2s.** each.

The Essays of Elia. By Charles Lamb. | White's Natural History of Selborne.
Robinson Crusoe. Edited by John Major, | Gulliver's Travels, and **The Tale of a**
  With 37 Illusts. by George Cruikshank, | **Tub.** By Dean Swift.
Whims and Oddities. By Thomas Hood. | The Rivals, School for Scandal, and other
  With 85 Illustrations. | Plays by Richard Brinsley Sheridan.
The Barber's Chair, and **The Hedgehog** | Anecdotes of the Clergy. J. Larwood.
  Letters. By Douglas Jerrold | Thomson's Seasons. Illustrated.
Gastronomy. By Brillat-Savarin. | The Autocrat of the Breakfast-Table
The Epicurean, &c. By Thomas Moore. | and **The Professor at the Breakfast-**
Leigh Hunt's Essays. Ed. E. Ollier. | Table. By Oliver Wendell Holmes.

THE PICCADILLY NOVELS.

Library Editions of Novels, many Illustrated, crown 8vo, cloth extra, **3s. 6d.** each.

By F. M. ALLEN.
Green as Grass.

By GRANT ALLEN.
Philistia. | The Tents of Shem.
Babylon. | For Maimie's Sake.
Strange Stories. | The Devil's Die.
Beckoning Hand. | This Mortal Coil.
In all Shades. | The Great Taboo.
Dumaresq's Daughter. | Blood Royal.
The Duchess of Powysland.
Ivan Greet's Masterpiece.

By EDWIN L. ARNOLD.
Phra the Phœnician.
The Constable of St. Nicholas.

By ALAN ST. AUBYN.
A Fellow of Trinity. | The Junior Dean.
The Master of St. Benedict's.

By Rev. S. BARING GOULD.
Red Spider. | Eve.

By ROBERT BARR.
In Steamer Chair | From Whose Bourne

By W. BESANT & J. RICE.
My Little Girl. | By Celia's Arbour.
Case of Mr. Lucraft. | Monks of Thelema.
This Son of Vulcan. | The Seamy Side.
Golden Butterfly. | Ten Years' Tenant.
Ready-Money Mortiboy.
With Harp and Crown.
'Twas in Trafalgar's Bay.
The Chaplain of the Fleet.

By WALTER BESANT.
All Sorts and Conditions of Men.
The Captains' Room. | Herr Paulus.
All in a Garden Fair | The Ivory Gate.
The World Went Very Well Then.
For Faith and Freedom.
Dorothy Forster. | The Holy Rose.
Uncle Jack. | Armorel of Lyon-
Children of Gibeon. | esse.
Bell of St. Paul's. | St. Katherine's by
To Call Her Mine. | the Tower.
Verbena Camellia Stephanotis.

By ROBERT BUCHANAN.
The Shadow of the Sword. | Matt.
A Child of Nature. | Heir of Linne.
The Martyrdom of Madeline.
God and the Man. | The New Abelard.
Love Me for Ever. | Foxglove Manor.
Annan Water. | Master of the Mine.

By HALL CAINE.
The Shadow of a Crime.
A Son of Hagar. | The Deemster.

By MACLAREN COBBAN.
The Red Sultan.

MORT. & FRANCES COLLINS.
Transmigration. | Blacksmith & Scholar.
From Midnight to Midnight.
Village Comedy. | You Play Me False.

By WILKIE COLLINS.
Armadale. | The Frozen Deep.
After Dark. | The Two Destinies.
No Name. | Law and the Lady.
Antonina. | Basil. | Haunted Hotel.
Hide and Seek. | The Fallen Leaves.
The Dead Secret. | Jezebel's Daughter.
Queen of Hearts. | The Black Robe.
My Miscellanies. | Heart and Science.
Woman in White. | "I Say No."
The Moonstone. | Little Novels.
Man and Wife. | The Evil Genius.
Poor Miss Finch. | The Legacy of Cain
Miss or Mrs? | A Rogue's Life.
New Magdalen. | Blind Love.

By DUTTON COOK.
Paul Foster's Daughter.

By EDWARD H. COOPER.
Geoffory Hamilton.

By V. CECIL COTES.
Two Girls on a Barge.

By MATT CRIM.
Adventures of a Fair Rebel.

By B. M. CROKER.
Diana Barrington. | Pretty Miss Neville.
Proper Pride. | A Bird of Passage.
A Family Likeness. | "To Let."

By WILLIAM CYPLES.
Hearts of Gold.

By ALPHONSE DAUDET.
The Evangelist; or, Port Salvation.

By ERASMUS DAWSON.
The Fountain of Youth.

By JAMES DE MILLE.
A Castle in Spain.

By J. LEITH DERWENT.
Our Lady of Tears. | Circe's Lovers.

By DICK DONOVAN.
Tracked to Doom.
Man from Manchester.

By A. CONAN DOYLE.
The Firm of Girdlestone.

By Mrs. ANNIE EDWARDES.
Archie Lovell.

By G. MANVILLE FENN.
The New Mistress. | Witness to the Deed.

THE PICCADILLY (3/6) NOVELS—*continued*.

By PERCY FITZGERALD.
Fatal Zero.

By R. E. FRANCILLON.
Queen Cophetua. | A Real Queen.
One by One. | King or Knave.
Dog & his Shadow. | Ropes of Sand.

Pref. by Sir BARTLE FRERE.
Pandurang Hari.

ED. GARRETT.—The Capel Girls.

By PAUL GAULOT.
The Red Shirts.

By CHARLES GIBBON.
Robin Gray. | The Golden Shaft.
Loving a Dream. | Of High Degree.
The Flower of the Forest.

By E. GLANVILLE.
The Lost Heiress. | The Fossicker.
A Fair Colonist.

By E. J. GOODMAN.
The Fate of Herbert Wayne.

By CECIL GRIFFITH.
Corinthia Marazion.

By SYDNEY GRUNDY.
The Days of his Vanity.

By THOMAS HARDY
Under the Greenwood Tree.

By BRET HARTE.
A Waif of the Plains. | Sally Dows.
A Ward of the Golden Gate.
A Sappho of Green Springs.
Colonel Starbottle's Client. | Susy.
A Protégée of Jack Hamlin's.

By JULIAN HAWTHORNE.
Garth. | Dust.
Ellice Quentin. | Fortune's Fool.
Sebastian Strome. | Beatrix Randolph.
David Poindexter's Disappearance.
The Spectre of the Camera.

By Sir A. HELPS.—Ivan de Biron.

By ISAAC HENDERSON.
Agatha Page.

By Mrs. HUNGERFORD.
Lady Verner's Flight.

By Mrs. ALFRED HUNT.
The Leaden Casket. | Self-Condemned.
That Other Person. | Mrs. Juliet.

By R. ASHE KING.
A Drawn Game.
"The Wearing of the Green."

By E. LYNN LINTON.
Patricia Kemball. | Ione.
Under which Lord? | Paston Carew.
"My Love!" | Sowing the Wind!
The Atonement of Leam Dundas.
The World Well Lost.

By HENRY W. LUCY.
Gideon Fleyce.

By JUSTIN McCARTHY.
A Fair Saxon. | Donna Quixote.
Linley Rochford. | Maid of Athens.
Miss Misanthrope. | Camiola.
The Waterdale Neighbours.
My Enemy's Daughter.
Dear Lady Disdain. | The Dictator.
The Comet of a Season.

By GEORGE MACDONALD.
Heather and Snow.

By AGNES MACDONELL.
Quaker Cousins.

By BERTRAM MITFORD.
The Gun-Runner. | The King's Assegai.
The Luck of Gerard Ridgeley.

THE PICCADILLY (3/6) NOVELS—*continued*.

By D. CHRISTIE MURRAY.
Life's Atonement. | Val Strange.
Joseph's Coat. | Hearts.
Coals of Fire. | A Model Father.
Old Blazer's Hero. | Time's Revenges.
By the Gate of the Sea.
A Bit of Human Nature.
First Person Singular. | Cynic Fortune.
The Way of the World.
Bob Martin's Little Girl.

By MURRAY & HERMAN.
The Bishops' Bible. | Paul Jones's Alias.
One Traveller Returns.

By HUME NISBET.
"Bail Up!"

By GEORGES OHNET.
A Weird Gift.

By OUIDA.
Held in Bondage. | Two Little Wooden
Strathmore. | Shoes.
Chandos. | In a Winter City.
Under Two Flags. | Ariadne.
Idalia. | Friendship.
CecilCastlemaine's | Moths. | Ruffino.
Gage. | Pipistrello.
Tricotrin. | Puck. | A Village Commune
Folle Farine. | Bimbi. | Wanda.
A Dog of Flanders. | Frescoes. | Othmar.
Pascarel. | Signa. | In Maremma.
Princess Naprax- | Syrlin. | Guilderoy.
ine. | Santa Barbara.

By MARGARET A. PAUL.
Gentle and Simple.

By JAMES PAYN.
Lost Sir Massingberd.
Less Black than We're Painted.
A Confidential Agent.
A Grape from a Thorn.
In Peril and Privation.
The Mystery of Mirbridge
The Canon's Ward.
Walter's Word. | Holiday Tasks.
By Proxy. | For Cash Only.
High Spirits. | The Burnt Million.
Under One Roof. | The Word and the
From Exile. | Will.
Glow-worm Tales. | Sunny Stories.
Talk of the Town. | A Trying Patient.

By E. C. PRICE.
Valentina. | The Foreigners.
Mrs. Lancaster's Rival.

By RICHARD PRYCE.
Miss Maxwell's Affections.

By CHARLES READE.
It is Never Too Late to Mend.
The Double Marriage.
Love Me Little, Love Me Long.
The Cloister and the Hearth.
The Course of True Love.
The Autobiography of a Thief.
Put Yourself in his Place.
A Terrible Temptation. | The Jilt.
Singleheart and Doubleface.
Good Stories of Men and other Animals.
Hard Cash. | Wandering Heir.
Peg Woffington. | A Woman-Hater.
ChristieJohnstone. | A Simpleton.
Griffith Gaunt. | Readiana.
Foul Play. | A Perilous Secret.

By Mrs. J. H. RIDDELL.
The Prince of Wales's Garden Party.
Weird Stories.

THE PICCADILLY (3/6) NOVELS—*continued.*
By AMELIE RIVES.
Barbara Dering.
By F. W. ROBINSON.
The Hands of Justice.
By W. CLARK RUSSELL.
Ocean Tragedy. | My Shipmate Louise.
Alone on a Wide Wide Sea.
By JOHN SAUNDERS.
Guy Waterman. | Two Dreamers.
Bound to Wheel. | Lion in the Path.
By KATHARINE SAUNDERS.
Margaret and Elizabeth.
Gideon's Rock. | Heart Salvage.
The High Mills. | Sebastian.
By HAWLEY SMART.
Without Love or Licence.
By R. A. STERNDALE.
The Afghan Knife.
By BERTHA THOMAS.
Proud Maisie. | The Violin-player.
By FRANCES E. TROLLOPE.
Like Ships upon the Sea.
Anne Furness. | Mabel's Progress.

THE PICCADILLY (3/6) NOVELS—*continued.*
By IVAN TURGENIEFF, &c.
Stories from Foreign Novelists.
By ANTHONY TROLLOPE.
Frau Frohmann. | Land-Leaguers.
Marion Fay. | The Way We Live Now.
Mr. Scarborough's Family.
By C. C. FRASER-TYTLER.
Mistress Judith.
By SARAH TYTLER.
The Bride's Pass. | Lady Bell.
Buried Diamonds. | Blackhall Ghosts.
By MARK TWAIN.
The American Claimant.
The £1,000,000 Bank-note.
By ALLEN UPWARD.
The Queen Against Owen.
By J. S. WINTER.
A Soldier's Children.
By MARGARET WYNMAN.
My Flirtations.
By E. ZOLA.
The Downfall. | Dr. Pascal.
The Dream. | Money.

CHEAP EDITIONS OF POPULAR NOVELS.

Post 8vo, illustrated boards, **2s.** each.

By ARTEMUS WARD.
Artemus Ward Complete.
By EDMOND ABOUT.
The Fellah.
By HAMILTON AIDE.
Carr of Carrlyon. | Confidences.
By MARY ALBERT.
Brooke Finchley's Daughter.
By Mrs. ALEXANDER.
Maid, Wife, or Widow? | Valerie' Fate.
By GRANT ALLEN.
Strange Stories. | The Devil's Die.
Philistia. | This Mortal Coil.
Babylon. | In all Shades.
The Beckoning Hand. | Blood Royal.
For Maimie's Sake. | Tents of Shem.
Great Taboo. | Dumaresq's Daughter.
The Duchess of Powysland.
By E. LESTER ARNOLD.
Phra the Phœnician.
By ALAN ST. AUBYN.
A Fellow of Trinity. | The Junior Dean.
The Master of St. Benedict's.
By Rev. S. BARING GOULD.
Red Spider. | Eve.
By FRANK BARRETT.
Fettered for Life. | Little Lady Linton.
Between Life and Death.
The Sin of Olga Zassoulich.
Folly Morrison. | Honest Davie.
Lieut. Barnabas. A Prodigal's Progress.
Found Guilty. | A Recoiling Vengeance.
For Love and Honour.
John Ford; and His Helpmate.
By W. BESANT & J. RICE.
This Son of Vulcan. | By Celia's Arbour.
My Little Girl. | Monks of Thelema.
Case of Mr. Lucraft. | The Seamy Side.
Golden Butterfly. | Ten Years' Tenant.
Ready-Money Mortiboy.
With Harp and Crown.
'Twas in Trafalgar's Bay.
The Chaplain of the Fleet.

By WALTER BESANT.
Dorothy Forster. | Uncle Jack.
Children of Gibeon. | Herr Paulus.
All Sorts and Conditions of Men.
The Captains' Room.
All in a Garden Fair.
The World Went Very Well Then.
For Faith and Freedom.
To Call Her Mine.
The Bell of St. Paul's. | The Holy Rose.
Armorel of Lyonesse. | The Ivory Gate.
St. Katherine's by the Tower.
Verbena Camellia Stephanotis.
By SHELSLEY BEAUCHAMP.
Grantley Grange.
By AMBROSE BIERCE.
In the Midst of Life.
By FREDERICK BOYLE.
Camp Notes. | Savage Life.
Chronicles of No-man's Land.
By BRET HARTE.
Californian Stories. | Gabriel Conroy.
An Heiress of Red Dog. | Flip.
The Luck of Roaring Camp. | Maruja.
A Phyllis of the Sierras.
By HAROLD BRYDGES.
Uncle Sam at Home.
By ROBERT BUCHANAN.
The Shadow of the | The Martyrdom of
Sword. | Madeline.
A Child of Nature. | Annan Water.
God and the Man. | The New Abelard.
Love Me for Ever. | Matt.
Foxglove Manor. | The Heir of Linne.
The Master of the Mine.
By HALL CAINE.
The Shadow of a Crime.
A Son of Hagar. | The Deemster.
By Commander CAMERON.
The Cruise of the "Black Prince."
By Mrs. LOVETT CAMERON.
Deceivers Ever. | Juliet's Guardian.

TWO-SHILLING NOVELS—*continued.*

By AUSTIN CLARE.
For the Love of a Lass.
By Mrs. ARCHER CLIVE.
Paul Ferroll.
Why Paul Ferroll Killed his Wife.
By MACLAREN COBBAN.
The Cure of Souls.
By C. ALLSTON COLLINS.
The Bar Sinister.
MORT. & FRANCES COLLINS.
Sweet Anne Page. | Transmigration.
From Midnight to Midnight.
Fight with Fortune. | Village Comedy.
Sweet and Twenty. | You Play me False.
Blacksmith and Scholar. | Frances.
By WILKIE COLLINS.
Armadale. | My Miscellanies.
After Dark. | Woman in White.
No Name. | The Moonstone.
Antonina. | Basil. | Man and Wife.
Hide and Seek. | Poor Miss Finch.
The Dead Secret. | The Fallen Leaves.
Queen of Hearts. | Jezebel's Daughter
Miss or Mrs? | The Black Robe.
New Magdalen. | Heart and Science.
The Frozen Deep. | "I Say No."
Law and the Lady. | The Evil Genius.
The Two Destinies. | Little Novels.
Haunted Hotel. | Legacy of Cain.
A Rogue's Life. | Blind Love.
By M. J. COLQUHOUN.
Every Inch a Soldier.
By DUTTON COOK.
Leo. | Paul Foster's Daughter.
By C. EGBERT CRADDOCK.
Prophet of the Great Smoky Mountains.
By MATT CRIM.
Adventures of a Fair Rebel.
By B. M. CROKER.
Pretty Miss Neville. | Bird of Passage.
Diana Barrington. | Proper Pride.
"To Let." | A Family Likeness.
By W. CYPLES.—Hearts of Gold.
By ALPHONSE DAUDET.
The Evangelist; or, Port Salvation.
By ERASMUS DAWSON.
The Fountain of Youth.
By JAMES DE MILLE.
A Castle in Spain.
By J. LEITH DERWENT.
Our Lady of Tears. | Circe's Lovers.
By CHARLES DICKENS.
Sketches by Boz. | Oliver Twist.
Pickwick Papers. | Nicholas Nickleby.
By DICK DONOVAN.
The Man-Hunter. | Caught at Last!
Tracked and Taken. | Wanted!
Who Poisoned Hetty Duncan?
The Man from Manchester.
A Detective's Triumphs.
In the Grip of the Law.
From Information Received.
Tracked to Doom. | Link by Link.
Suspicion Aroused.
By Mrs. ANNIE EDWARDES.
A Point of Honour. | Archie Lovell.
By M. BETHAM-EDWARDS.
Felicia. | Kitty.
By EDW. EGGLESTON.—Roxy.
By G. MANVILLE FENN.
The New Mistress.

TWO-SHILLING NOVELS—*continued.*

By PERCY FITZGERALD.
Bella Donna. | Polly.
Never Forgotten. | Fatal Zero.
The Second Mrs. Tillotson.
Seventy-five Brooke Street.
The Lady of Brantome.
By P. FITZGERALD and others.
Strange Secrets.
ALBANY DE FONBLANQUE.
Filthy Lucre.
By R. E. FRANCILLON.
Olympia. | Queen Cophetua.
One by One. | King or Knave?
A Real Queen. | Romances of Law.
By HAROLD FREDERIC.
Seth's Brother's Wife. | Lawton Girl.
Pref. by Sir BARTLE FRERE.
Pandurang Hari.
HAIN FRISWELL.—One of Two.
By EDWARD GARRETT.
The Capel Girls.
By GILBERT GAUL.
A Strange Manuscript.
By CHARLES GIBBON.
Robin Gray. | In Honour Bound.
Fancy Free. | Flower of Forest.
For Lack of Gold. | Braes of Yarrow.
What will the | The Golden Shaft.
World Say? | Of High Degree.
In Love and War. | Mead and Stream.
For the King. | Loving a Dream.
In Pastures Green. | A Hard Knot.
Queen of Meadow. | Heart's Delight.
A Heart's Problem. | Blood-Money.
The Dead Heart.
By WILLIAM GILBERT.
Dr. Austin's Guests. | James Duke.
The Wizard of the Mountain.
By ERNEST GLANVILLE.
The Lost Heiress. | The Fossicker.
By HENRY GREVILLE.
A Noble Woman. | Nikanor.
By CECIL GRIFFITH.
Corinthia Marazion.
By JOHN HABBERTON.
Brueton's Bayou. | Country Luck.
By ANDREW HALLIDAY.
Every-Day Papers.
By Lady DUFFUS HARDY.
Paul Wynter's Sacrifice.
By THOMAS HARDY.
Under the Greenwood Tree.
By J. BERWICK HARWOOD.
The Tenth Earl.
By JULIAN HAWTHORNE.
Garth. | Sebastian Strome.
Ellice Quentin. | Dust.
Fortune's Fool. | Beatrix Randolph.
Miss Cadogna. | Love—or a Name.
David Poindexter's Disappearance.
The Spectre of the Camera.
By Sir ARTHUR HELPS.
Ivan de Biron.
By HENRY HERMAN.
A Leading Lady.
By HEADON HILL.
Zambra the Detective.
By JOHN HILL.—Treason-Felony.
By Mrs. CASHEL HOEY.
The Lover's Creed.

Two-Shilling Novels—*continued.*

By Mrs. GEORGE HOOPER.
The House of Raby.

By TIGHE HOPKINS.
'Twixt Love and Duty.

By Mrs. HUNGERFORD.
A Maiden all Forlorn.
In Durance Vile. | A Mental Struggle.
Marvel. | A Modern Circe.

By Mrs. ALFRED HUNT.
Thornicroft's Model. | Self-Condemned.
That Other Person. | Leaden Casket.

By JEAN INGELOW.
Fated to be Free.

WM. JAMESON.—My Dead Self.

By HARRIETT JAY.
Dark Colleen. | Queen of Connaught.

By MARK KERSHAW.
Colonial Facts and Fictions.

By R. ASHE KING.
A Drawn Game. | Passion's Slave.
"The Wearing of the Green."
Bell Barry.

By JOHN LEYS.—The Lindsays.

By E. LYNN LINTON.
Patricia Kemball. | Paston Carew.
World Well Lost. | "My Love!"
Under which Lord? | Ione.
The Atonement of Leam Dundas.
With a Silken Thread.
The Rebel of the Family.
Sowing the Wind.

By HENRY W. LUCY.
Gideon Fleyce.

By JUSTIN McCARTHY.
A Fair Saxon. | Donna Quixote.
Linley Rochford. | Maid of Athens.
Miss Misanthrope. | Camiola.
Dear Lady Disdain.
The Waterdale Neighbours.
My Enemy's Daughter.
The Comet of a Season.

By HUGH MACCOLL.
Mr. Stranger's Sealed Packet.

By AGNES MACDONELL.
Quaker Cousins.

KATHARINE S. MACQUOID.
The Evil Eye. | Lost Rose.

By W. H. MALLOCK.
The New Republic.
A Romance of the Nineteenth Century.

By FLORENCE MARRYAT.
Open! Sesame! | Fighting the Air.
A Harvest of Wild Oats.
Written in Fire.

By J. MASTERMAN.
Half-a-dozen Daughters.

By BRANDER MATTHEWS.
A Secret of the Sea.

By LEONARD MERRICK.
The Man who was Good.

By JEAN MIDDLEMASS.
Touch and Go. | Mr. Dorillion.

By Mrs. MOLESWORTH.
Hathercourt Rectory.

By J. E. MUDDOCK.
Stories Weird and Wonderful.
The Dead Man's Secret.
From the Bosom of the Deep.

By MURRAY and HERMAN.
One Traveller Returns. | The Bishops' Bible.
Paul Jones's Alias.

Two-Shilling Novels—*continued.*

By D. CHRISTIE MURRAY.
A Model Father. | Old Blazer's Hero.
Joseph's Coat. | Hearts.
Coals of Fire. | Way of the World.
Val Strange. | Cynic Fortune.
A Life's Atonement.
By the Gate of the Sea.
A Bit of Human Nature.
First Person Singular.
Bob Martin's Little Girl.

By HENRY MURRAY.
A Game of Bluff. | A Song of Sixpence.

By HUME NISBET.
"Bail Up!" | Dr. Bernard St. Vincent.

By ALICE O'HANLON.
The Unforeseen. | Chance? or Fate?

By GEORGES OHNET.
Dr. Rameau. | Last Love. | Weird Gift.

By Mrs. OLIPHANT.
Whiteladies. | The Primrose Path.
The Greatest Heiress in England.

By Mrs. ROBERT O'REILLY.
Phœbe's Fortunes.

By OUIDA.
Held in Bondage. | Two Little Wooden
Strathmore. | Shoes.
Chandos. | Idalia. | Friendship.
Under Two Flags. | Moths. | Bimbi.
CecilCastlemaine's | Pipistrello. [mune.
Gage. | A Village Com-
Tricotrin. | Puck. | Wanda. | Othmar.
Folle Farine. | Frescoes.
A Dog of Flanders. | In Maremma.
Pascarel. | Guilderoy.
Signa. [ine. | Ruffino. | Syrlin.
Princess Naprax- | Santa Barbara.
In a Winter City. | Ouida's Wisdom,
Ariadne. | Wit, and Pathos.

MARGARET AGNES PAUL.
Gentle and Simple.

By JAMES PAYN.
Bentinck's Tutor. | By Proxy.
Murphy's Master. | Under One Roof.
A County Family. | High Spirits.
At Her Mercy. | Carlyon's Year.
Cecil's Tryst. | From Exile.
Clyffards of Clyffe. | For Cash Only.
Foster Brothers. | Kit.
Found Dead. | The Canon's Ward
Best of Husbands. | Talk of the Town.
Walter's Word. | Holiday Tasks.
Halves. | A Perfect Treasure.
Fallen Fortunes. | What He Cost Her.
Humorous Stories. | Confidential Agent.
£200 Reward. | Glow-worm Tales.
Marine Residence. | The Burnt Million.
Mirk Abbey. | Sunny Stories.
Lost Sir Massingberd.
A Woman's Vengeance.
The Family Scapegrace.
Gwendoline's Harvest.
Like Father, Like Son.
Married Beneath Him.
Not Wooed, but Won.
Less Black than We're Painted.
Some Private Views.
A Grape from a Thorn.
The Mystery of Mirbridge.
The Word and the Will.
A Prince of the Blood.

Two-Shilling Novels—*continued.*

By C. L. PIRKIS.
Lady Lovelace.

By EDGAR A. POE.
The Mystery of Marie Roget.

By Mrs. CAMPBELL PRAED.
The Romance of a Station.
The Soul of Countess Adrian.

By E. C. PRICE.
Valentina. | The Foreigners.
Mrs. Lancaster's Rival. | Gerald.

By RICHARD PRYCE.
Miss Maxwell's Affections.

By CHARLES READE.
It is Never Too Late to Mend.
Christie Johnstone. | Double Marriage.
Put Yourself in His Place.
Love Me Little, Love Me Long.
The Cloister and the Hearth.
The Course of True Love. | The Jilt.
Autobiography of a Thief.
A Terrible Temptation. | Foul Play.
The Wandering Heir. | Hard Cash.
Singleheart and Doubleface.
Good Stories of Men and other Animals.
Peg Woffington. | A Simpleton.
Griffith Gaunt. | Readiana.
A Perilous Secret. | A Woman-Hater.

By Mrs. J. H. RIDDELL.
Weird Stories. | Fairy Water.
Her Mother's Darling.
Prince of Wales's Garden Party.
The Uninhabited House.
The Mystery in Palace Gardens.
The Nun's Curse. | Idle Tales.

By AMELIE RIVES.
Barbara Dering.

By F. W. ROBINSON.
Women are Strange.
The Hands of Justice.

By JAMES RUNCIMAN.
Skippers and Shellbacks.
Grace Balmaign's Sweetheart.
Schools and Scholars.

By W. CLARK RUSSELL.
Round the Galley Fire.
On the Fo'k'sle Head.
In the Middle Watch.
A Voyage to the Cape.
A Book for the Hammock.
The Mystery of the "Ocean Star."
The Romance of Jenny Harlowe.
An Ocean Tragedy.
My Shipmate Louise.
Alone on a Wide Wide Sea.

GEORGE AUGUSTUS SALA.
Gaslight and Daylight.

By JOHN SAUNDERS.
Guy Waterman. | Two Dreamers.
The Lion in the Path.

By KATHARINE SAUNDERS.
Joan Merryweather. | Heart Salvage.
The High Mills. | Sebastian.
Margaret and Elizabeth.

By GEORGE R. SIMS.
Rogues and Vagabonds.
The Ring o' Bells.
Mary Jane's Memoirs.
Mary Jane Married.
Tales of To-day. | Dramas of Life.
Tinkletop's Crime.
Zeph. | My Two Wives.

Two-Shilling Novels—*continued.*

By ARTHUR SKETCHLEY.
A Match in the Dark.

By HAWLEY SMART.
Without Love or Licence.

By T. W. SPEIGHT.
The Mysteries of Heron Dyke.
The Golden Hoop. | By Devious Ways.
Hoodwinked, &c. | Back to Life.
The Loudwater Tragedy.
Burgo's Romance.

By R. A. STERNDALE.
The Afghan Knife.

By R. LOUIS STEVENSON.
New Arabian Nights. | Prince Otto.

By BERTHA THOMAS.
Cressida. | Proud Maisie. | Violin-player.

By WALTER THORNBURY.
Tales for Marines. | Old Stories Re-told.

T. ADOLPHUS TROLLOPE.
Diamond Cut Diamond.

By F. ELEANOR TROLLOPE.
Like Ships upon the Sea.
Anne Furness. | Mabel's Progress.

By ANTHONY TROLLOPE.
Frau Frohmann. | Kept in the Dark.
Marion Fay. | John Caldigate.
Way We Live Now. | Land-Leaguers.
The American Senator.
Mr. Scarborough's Family.
The Golden Lion of Granpere.

By J. T. TROWBRIDGE.
Farnell's Folly.

By IVAN TURGENIEFF, &c.
Stories from Foreign Novelists.

By MARK TWAIN.
A Pleasure Trip on the Continent.
The Gilded Age. | Huckleberry Finn.
Mark Twain's Sketches.
Tom Sawyer. | A Tramp Abroad.
The Stolen White Elephant.
Life on the Mississippi.
The Prince and the Pauper.
A Yankee at the Court of King Arthur.

By C. C. FRASER-TYTLER.
Mistress Judith.

By SARAH TYTLER.
The Bride's Pass. | Noblesse Oblige.
Buried Diamonds. | Disappeared.
Saint Mungo's City. | Huguenot Family.
Lady Bell. | Blackhall Ghosts.
What She Came Through.
Beauty and the Beast.
Citoyenne Jaqueline.

By AARON WATSON and LILLIAS WASSERMANN.
The Marquis of Carabas.

By WILLIAM WESTALL.
Trust-Money.

By Mrs. F. H. WILLIAMSON.
A Child Widow.

By J. S. WINTER.
Cavalry Life. | Regimental Legends.

By H. F. WOOD.
The Passenger from Scotland Yard.
The Englishman of the Rue Cain.

By Lady WOOD.—Sabina.

CELIA PARKER WOOLLEY.
Rachel Armstrong; or, Love & Theology

By EDMUND YATES.
The Forlorn Hope. | Land at Last.
Castaway.

OGDEN, SMALE AND CO, LIMITED, PRINTERS, GREAT SAFFRON HILL, E.C.

www.ingramcontent.com/pod-product-compliance
Lightning Source LLC
Chambersburg PA
CBHW020102030726
47498CB00006B/1916